ONE LIFE FOR ANOTHER

GREG LAIRD

ACKNOWLEDGMENTS

To Brian Harvey and Jeff Laird Jr., the two most important men in my life. Your love, encouragement and guidance made me the man I am today. I never could have written this book without you. I miss you both everyday.

I would also like to thank Joe Hight for convincing me to do one "last" edit. What I had before was a puzzle with two pieces missing, he advised me to search for them before sharing it with the world.

And a special thank you to our Creator without whom none of this would be happening.

PROLOGUE

August 9, 2008

Ashley Pinkerton screamed as her assailant rushed towards her with a butcher knife in hand. The first strike easily plunged deep through her breast, breaking two ribs before puncturing her right lung. She fell backwards. When her head contacted the floor she immediately raised her arms in self-defense. The barrage of attacks that came thereafter felt like the days upon days that one endures after being dumped by the one who told you that you were his soulmate, his forever. Her breathing slowed. She lowered her arms.

As I lay here on my living room floor. I am in awe of the mechanism of the human anatomy. The first time the knife pierced my chest was a pain more intense than I thought possible, but now, after 38 more cuts, slices and stabs, I feel nothing. I am at peace. As I take my last breath, my biggest fear is not my life passing. My biggest fear is…

CHAPTER 1

The young attorney sat at his desk, running a hand through his thick curly hair as he stared at the files scattered in front of him. He grabbed the Bohannon divorce file from under his half empty coffee cup and looked over the list detailing which specific items his client wanted from her marital residence: the blue couch in the living room, the small pearl mirror in the bathroom, the ten-inch purple vibrator. He grinned, shook his head and thought: The things people fight over.

The buzzing intercom jarred him from his musings. "Hey, big shot!, United States Judge Michael W. Henry's office on line one," said Carol, the receptionist and assistant he was economically forced to have working for him.

He reached for the phone, straightened out his back, took a deep breath, and said as calmly and articulately as he could muster, "This is Steve Hanson, Your Honor."

"Hi, Steve, this is Gail with Judge Henry's office." He relaxed into his chair. "I will patch you through to His Honor in just a second. But tell me, real quick, how have you been?"

"Doing well, Gail, and what about you?"

"I'm good, although we still miss you around here. I know it has only been a little over four months, but it's felt like forever. Even the judge said he was glad this case came up because it gave him an excuse to give you a call. I'm going to put you on hold while I get His Honor on the phone."

Steve was just getting into the piano version of U2's "One" when the line picked up.

"Steve, Judge Henry here. How is your practice going?"

"Very well, Your Honor. I'm doing mostly divorces, misdemeanors, and small claims right now. It is not all that glamorous, but it pays the bills, and it is actually kind of fun most days. I honestly feel like I am helping people through their toughest times, which makes up for the fact that most of them usually can't afford to pay me much."

"That's true; anyone who loves practicing law at the street level does it more for the sense of helping others than the fees charged. But it is also the best way to become a great trial lawyer. Those cases give you the courtroom experience you need to be able to handle the bigger cases later in your career."

"Yes, Your Honor." Steve smiled. "I remember you saying that to many young lawyers at different events during the two years I worked for you."

"I'm glad you are finding your way in the world of being a solo practitioner. However, that is not the purpose of my call. I just received a new capital habeas appeal file on my docket, and I was wondering if you would accept an appointment to represent the appellant in this matter, one Scottie Wayne Pinkerton. The case originated in Rogers County, Oklahoma."

"Yes, I would be honored to help sir," said Steve, deferentially.

"Glad to hear it. I will sign this order, and as soon as we hang up, Gail will get it filed in the clerk's office and email you a copy. After the appointment is official, you'll need to contact Sam Parker, the attorney who represented Mr. Pinkerton on his state court appeals. She will provide you the boxes containing everything that has been gathered over the last seven years for Mr. Pinkerton's defense. From there, you are on your own. I expect you not to let me down on this case. I know you will give him the quality representation our constitution confers upon all the individuals facing our nation's harshest punishment. Good luck with your law practice, I'm glad to hear you are enjoying it, goodbye."

Steve barely got out, "Thank you, Your Honor. Goodbye," before the line clicked dead on the other end. After Steve hung up the phone, his stomach tightened. I am actually going to be representing someone on death row, he thought. A convicted murderer whose life or death will now be determined by the quality of my representation.

A wave of anxiety swept over him. He thought about the challenges that now faced him. He would have to go to death row and meet Scottie in person. He would have to write a 100–120-page brief on Scottie's behalf. Someday, he would have to argue in front of a three-judge panel at the United States Tenth Circuit Court of Appeals in Denver, Colorado and, one day, possibly argue his case in front of the nine justices who made up the United States Supreme Court.

If he were unsuccessful at all levels of the appeal, he would have to spend Scottie's last twenty-four hours with him. He would watch the prison officials escort Scottie, someone he would have known for years by that point, into the execution chamber. Watch the prison guards strap his client to a gurney as the nurse stuck a needle into Scottie's arm. Watch the tubes deliver the statutory doses of the government-approved pharmaceuticals created to end a man's life in a manner that was theoretically not cruel or unusual. And then sit in the viewing room and watch his friend die, knowing he had failed him. Steve wondered how he would handle that. He made an oath to himself to never have to find out.

Carol, a sixty-two-year-old redhead from rural Oklahoma

with a voice and attitude reminiscent of Flo from Alice, opened the door to his office, startling Steve out of his grim daydream. "What did that highfalutin' federal judge want with a little baby lawyer like you?" Carol quipped.

"He was calling to appoint me to represent Scottie Pinkerton, a death row inmate, on his federal capital punishment habeas appeal- you probably don't know but that is the last appeal death row inmates get before they are executed."

"Shiiiiit, you barely know how to draw up a legally binding divorce decree, let alone find the clerk's office at the courthouse. Why in the hell would any federal judge appoint you to such a muy importante' case?"

"Before I got an office here, I spent two years working as a law clerk on death penalty cases at the federal courthouse. I did nothing but that type of work every day. I worked side-by-side with all three federal judges in the Northern District of Oklahoma Courthouse." Steve's back straightened and chest involuntarily swelled as he listed off the details of his previous work with growing confidence, "So, although I have only handled divorces for two months, I dealt exclusively with death penalty jurisprudence for two years and I know it inside and out."

"That's nice, but don't they usually appoint attorneys who have been doin' this shit for several years to those cases?"

"Yes. But all three presiding judges at the federal court decided my work experience there qualified me for appointments. And now one of them has appointed me to be the only thing standing between Scottie Pinkerton and death." He smiled proudly as he said this last sentence, thinking of all the times Carol had made him feel ignorant and unqualified over the last 134 days.

She turned without another word and brusquely walked out of the room.

Ever since Steve started practicing at the office, she had treated him like a moron. In the beginning, she did know more than he did about divorce procedure and other simple tasks, like how to file a pleading at the courthouse. Yet even when he gradually learned how to do this work himself, her attitude remained unchanged. But for once, he was able to show that his legal training and experience meant something in this world, whether she believed it or not. Steve wondered why he should even care about Carol's opinions as he hummed the theme song to Alice to himself. "There's a new girl in town…"

As he basked in his small victory against Carol, the realization that he had just been given a highly important appointment crept back into his psyche. Steve was now Scottie's last chance at avoiding the execution table. Scottie's life was dependent on Steve's legal acumen and diligence; he knew that he would have to put every ounce of his energy and intelligence into the fight before him. He closed the Bohannon file and took a another swig of his coffee.

When he called Parker's office to find out when he could get the case file, her assistant answered the phone. "Oh, the Scottie Pinkerton file… yeah, that's a tough one. You're taking that on? Good luck to you. I'll give Sam the message."

Steve hung up and started searching the internet for background information about the case. He entered "Scottie Pinkerton murder Rogers County Oklahoma" into the search engine, and within seconds, several links to news articles filled his screen. He selected a few and read them over. The facts looked to be as helpful as a mace in a tickling contest.

To be exact, it may have been the worst facts for a defendant Steve had ever read since he'd started in the death penalty business.

The articles painted the picture of an abusive husband who finally went too far. It was a classic tale of despair and heartbreak. One article laid out the amount of uncontroverted evidence against Scottie in twenty-three bullet points; the worst of which stated that, according to all reports, 911 received a call approximately five minutes before Ashley Pinkerton was found dead by a local sheriff's deputy wherein she reported that her husband had just hit her and he was still in their home.

Thirty minutes after her lifeless body was found in their living room, Scottie was arrested with scratches on his face apparently caused by his wife in self-defense. DNA reports confirmed the skin under her fingernails belonged to him. Additionally, there were bloody footprints in the house. The tread matched a pair of his tennis shoes. The shoes were found covered in blood in a field nearby. If that wasn't enough, Ashley's brother and her best friend had testified to a history of abuse in the household.

Several stories included a picture taken by a neighbor shortly after the police arrived. It depicted a sheriff's deputy, covered in blood, holding the couple's ten-month-old baby outside the home. For a while, Steve remembered, the picture had received national attention; the haunting image became iconic nationally - like the child running, naked, from the horrors in Vietnam or New York City firefighters raising the flag after 9/11.

Steve settled back in his chair with a solemn look. I need to call Frank.

CHAPTER 2

Almost every prosecutor and criminal defense attorney in the state considered Frank Ackerman to be the best trial lawyer alive. He was a second-generation practitioner who now handled nothing but first-degree murder cases. Anytime a judge in Oklahoma needed a lawyer to represent an indigent defendant facing the death penalty, said judge's first phone call always went to check Ackerman's availability.

Ackerman, a sixty something year old man with a face covered in a snowy white beard and mustache that matched the hair on top of his head, spoke with the eloquence of a Southern gentleman who'd just stepped out of a History Channel docudrama. He would constantly recite legal precedent from memory, as if the case books were in his hand. In the hallways of the courthouse, he could always be recognized by his trademark—a simple, yet elegant, straw cowboy hat with a colorful band around the base. Sometimes, even when you couldn't see him in the courtroom, everyone knew he was nearby because his hat was resting on the counsel table with a worn leather briefcase underneath it. He was the epitome of class, and his courtroom brilliance was legendary.

Steve had met Ackerman at a fundraising event a couple years ago, and the two formed a unique bond that night. Initially too shy to approach the esteemed lawyer, Steve was startled when Ackerman initiated the conversation.

"So, you're the new habeas clerk working with the federal judges," Ackerman had said, smiling.

"Oh yeah, yeah," Steve stammered. "It's an honor to meet you sir."

"I was a habeas clerk once too, though I have to say, at the time, they were expending a lot less energy trying to give the accused a fair shot. I actually got in trouble for always trying to find a reason to grant relief and let the guys off death row. Those conservative judges didn't take too kindly to it. Got threatened with losing my job even because I tried to push them too far for the poor suckers sentenced to die . You know, judges are supposed to be impartial and all."

"Wow," Steve said, genuinely stunned. "What did you do when that happened?"

"I worked harder, and then, at the end of my term, went to work making sure that the accused had every chance I could provide to prevail against a system that was built against them. That job is why I am doing what I do now, instead of handling corporate matters and hanging out at the country club. Let's have breakfast next week and visit a bit."

Steve nodded his head yes.

Over the next sixteen months, Ackerman became not only a mentor, but also a surrogate father for Steve.

Steve knew Ackerman could help him on the case, but his first call was unfruitful. Ackerman was in court and would not be available until later in the day. He sent a text message asking the old warhorse to call him back as soon as possible. Although Steve knew the law, he would need Ackerman's help to ensure he gave the best possible representation to Scottie.

About a minute later, his phone buzzed. "Mr. Death Penalty Attorney, you have a real lawyer on line three," Carol called out over the intercom. "I'm glad to see you are getting help from someone who actually knows the difference between his ass and the evidence code."

Steve did his best to ignore her and reached for the phone. "Hello, Frank, how are you doing?"

"I'm great, young man. How are you today?" Ackerman asked.

"I was just appointed by Judge Henry to represent Scottie Pinkerton on his federal habeas appeal."

"Congratulations, that is quite the assignment," Ackerman said with pride before becoming serious again. "Son, you do realize you are now that poor soul's last line of defense—the only thing that stands between him and the needle? I assume you plan to work your tail off for that man." Ackerman's voice rose. "You must represent him as if he were your own brother. You understand me?"

"Yes, sir," Steve said. "That is why I called you before I did anything else. I would like to know your thoughts on how to best do this job."

"Well, this is different from working for the Court, analyzing these matters under the auspice of neutrality. First, the most important thing in any death penalty representation is to gain your client's trust. You must get him to tell you the truth. You have to know what happened that day, no matter what it is, in order to effectively represent him. You must get his entire version of events and then try to prove it a lie. That way, you know if you need to argue the facts or the law or both, because if he actually killed her, then you are left with just arguing the law. You understand?"

Steve nodded and said over the phone, "Yes. Can you tell me what you know about the case?"

It was common knowledge among local criminal defense attorneys that Ackerman knew all the publicly available facts of every murder case in the area for the past forty years. All you had to do was mention the name, and he could recite the details of the case with ease. Additionally, due to his favorable relationships with the defense bar attorneys, he usually knew information that wasn't public knowledge.

"Of course, I remember that case; it happened just a few miles from my house. That poor soul had some bad facts. 911 call, DNA evidence, his shoes found covered in blood. I recall he killed his wife while their baby was in the home. I was almost appointed on it. The judge called me when it occurred, but I was in the middle of a double homicide trial in Osage County and couldn't take it. The court ended up appointing Jason Hixon—a lazy, overconfident son-of-a-bitch not qualified to first chair a jaywalking trial, let alone a capital murder. I've always felt bad that I wasn't available to accept that appointment, although with those facts, I doubt Clarence Darrow could have kept that young man from a death sentence."

"Yeah, from the little I have read on the internet, it doesn't look like I'm going to be arguing factual innocence to the court at any point." Steve paused, considering how serious this situation was becoming by the minute. "Thanks for your ti—"

"One last thing before you go," Ackerman interrupted. "There is something you should know—I remember hearing a rumor at the Oklahoma Criminal Defense Lawyers Association convention that your boy originally claimed he didn't do it, but Mr. Hixon didn't believe him and never put up much of a fight on his behalf. Like I said before, you need to find out what actually happened that day to do your job proficiently. Good luck, and work hard for that young man. You never know, you just might be arguing for his innocence someday."

CHAPTER 3

As Steve contemplated what Ackerman had just told him, the intercom buzzed again. "Not sure if you have time for your small fish anymore, Mr. Capital Punishment, but Mr. Hamilton is on line four."

Steve wished he had the authority to fire Carol; however, she was hired by the landlord who ran the office share arrangement where Steve rented. Regardless of how much Carol's quips got under his skin, other client, Steve knew he had to take this call from Hamilton. Jordan Hamilton, one of Steve's many divorce clients, worked in an upper management position at a local manufacturing company.

Steve answered the phone. "Jordan, I have a few questions about the possessions that your wife wants, some of which you might want to reconsider letting go of just to move things forward."

Hamilton responded, breathing heavily, "Steve, I think I'm in big trouble. I was just informed that the state is investigating me for a felony embezzlement charge. There are police officers at my office right now. The owner of the company is with them, and he is giving them my computer. They say I have to go with them to my house and give them my home computer as well. Can you help me?"

"Yes," Steve responded calmly. "I can help you. Have you been arrested?"

"No. Will they do that?"

"Well, I guess it depends on what they find on your computers. Most importantly, at this point, don't talk to them at all about this case, or anything at all for that matter. Tell them that, under the advice of your attorney, you refuse to speak. I am on my way to your house right now. I will meet you there."

Steve retrieved Hamilton's file and typed his address into the mapping system on his phone. He could be there in about five minutes, maybe even before the police and Hamilton got there.

Steve rose from his desk and headed towards the elevator like a firefighter to his truck. As he passed Carol on his way out, she said with a wry smile, "Don't run too fast. I would hate to see you trip and scuff those purty shoes."

Hamilton's house is a modest blue home near downtown with an white porch in front and a detached garage in back. Steve arrived before anyone else so he was sitting in his car playing Words with Friends on his phone when his client and an entourage of police units arrived. He also noticed he had a Snapchat from an unknown number on his office phone. He approached one of the Tulsa police officers and asked politely, "May I speak to whomever is in charge? Can I see a warrant?"

The patrolman pointed to an officer giving out orders nearby. The fiftyish-looking man in a crisp, beige suit noticed the exchange and turned to Steve. "I'm Detective Meyers, and you are?"

"Steve Hanson, Mr. Hamilton's attorney. Are you in charge?"

"I am," Meyers replied. "And we have a search warrant which you are free to review." Meyers handed it to Steve, who began perusing it. This was the first time Steve had ever reviewed a search warrant while in the field. He was nervous, but his knowledge of the law, coupled with his desire to support his client, gave him the courage to appear as if he had done this a million times before.

"Everything looks in order," Steve said to Detective Myers as he handed back the papers. He then took Hamilton aside and spoke softly in his client's ear, "You need to let them in and show them where your computers are located. The warrant gives them the right to take possession of your computers and search your house for bank records. I suggest you show them directly where you keep your bank statements; otherwise, they might ransack your whole house, and you will be the one left to clean up. I had a client busted for drug possession last week who came home from jail to one hell of a mess."

Hamilton pulled the key from his pocket and led the group of officers into his house. While Steve was waiting on the front porch for others to get inside, a white Hyundai Sonata Hybrid pulled up to the scene. Out stepped a woman who was probably in her late thirties. Her jet-black hair was gathered in a bun, her nose was sharp, and her black-rimmed glasses framed a pair of blue eyes that could freeze mercury. Despite the gravity of his client's situation, Steve still felt the "Wow" slip from his mouth.

He immediately knew this woman was all business. She was dressed in a navy-blue suit jacket with matching skirt and plain black heels—a single strand of pearls hung around her neck. She lit a cigarette as she exited the vehicle and walked toward the front porch with the confidence of a champion prize fighter walking into the ring.

As she strode toward Steve, she reached out her hand. "Good morning. I am Dr. Emily Babbage, computer forensic investigator."

Though not a guy with a technical background, Steve had a good grasp of why she was here—to root through Hamilton's computers and other electronics. Steve shook her hand, and a strange jolt traveled through his arm and down to his crotch the moment their hands touched. The sensation electrified his groin and a similar story could be seen behind her eyes.

He gathered himself and, in his best Perry Mason monotone, responded, "Hello, Dr. Babbage. I am Steve Hanson, Mr. Hamilton's attorney." For a split second, he swore to himself he saw a smile on her lips before she returned to her stoic demeanor.

Dr. Babbage exchanged a few courteous pleasantries with the officers waiting outside before abruptly dropping her cigarette on the porch and grinding it out with the toe of her black stilettos. "Myers inside?" she asked them while walking through the front door without waiting for an answer. Steve overheard her instructing Myers on what she needed from the residence, rattling off a laundry list of electronic items and documents. A few minutes later, she walked out with a laptop computer, several zip drives in plastic bags, and an unlit cigarette dangling from her lips. Behind her, a patrolman lugged a desktop computer.

Steve watched as the rest of the police team spent the next several hours searching Hamilton's home for anything they could use against him—opening drawers, looking under furniture, peeking behind paintings, and even tapping on the walls and floor looking for hidden spaces. Eventually, the police finished their inspection, and, drained of both strength and emotion, Steve drove back to his office.

Although he was exhausted from being "on point" during the entire search, he couldn't get Dr. Babbage out of his mind. He simply had to learn more about this woman, not only because she would be key in the prosecution's case against Hamilton, but also because she was smoking hot.

Steve sat down at his desk and typed "Dr. Emily Babbage computer forensics" into the search bar, the smell from the half full coffee cup he left earlier wafted into his nostrils giving him a slight jolt of energy. The first thing he learned was that she'd received her PhD from the University of Tulsa. After graduation, she worked for a large forensic firm before she struck out on her own, mainly working as an expert in court proceedings. He clicked the link for "What is Computer Forensics?" on her web page.

Computer forensics is a branch of digital forensic science pertaining to legal evidence found in computers and digital storage media. The goal of computer forensics is to examine digital media in a scientifically accepted manner with the aim of identifying, preserving, recovering, analyzing, and presenting facts and opinions about the digital information.

Looking next through her biography, he saw that, for the past two years, she regularly testified in federal and state prosecutions. Although her website stated she would provide services and testimony for defense or prosecution, Steve couldn't find a single case where she had worked against the state.

Taking a detour from her professional web presence, Steve checked Babbage out on social media.

Not married. Doesn't even look like she has a boyfriend currently. He smiled to himself and briefly hoped this case would afford another opportunity to meet his new favorite scientist. He wondered how ethical it would be to date someone who was trying to send his client up the river and decided he could cross that bridge when he came to it.

Steve returned his attention to the case at hand, reopened his web browser, and typed in "Oklahoma State Penitentiary." After a few clicks, he found the number of the main line and picked up the phone.

"Oklahoma State Penitentiary."

Steve shifted to his attorney voice again. "Good afternoon, I'm Steve Hanson, appointed to represent Scottie Pinkerton in his habeas corpus proceeding, and I would like to schedule a visit." Without further response on the other end, Steve heard ringing as the call was transferred.

The line picked up. "This is Mrs. Gilcrease," a new voice said in a slight Southern twang. Steve could hear some Waylon Jennings song, that he couldn't recall the name of, in the background.

He repeated his opening litany. "Good afternoon, I'm Steve Hanson, appointed to represent Scottie Pinkerton in his habeas corpus proceeding, and I would like to schedule a visit." Then, he added, "Is this the right office?"

"Yes, it is. Scottie... that's the man who stabbed his wife up by Claremore, wasn't it? That would put him in the H-Unit." Steve could hear papers shuffling and a muffled commercial for what sounded like an ATV dealership. "Let me put you on hold for a minute, that okay?"

The ATV commercial continued while Steve waited. Apparently, the hold music came from the same radio station, but blasts of static kept interrupting the broadcast.

The line picked up again. "Mr. Hanson, the H-Unit is booked solid for attorney visits for a while. I can schedule you for the first Wednesday of the new year at 1:30 p.m. Otherwise, you are looking at the Friday after that."

"I'll take the Wednesday."

"Great, we'll just need written confirmation of your scheduled visit addressed to Warden Reynolds, and please make sure to provide details of your visit. If I don't get the letter a week before your appointment at the latest, it will be canceled, and we will start this process all over again."

"Got it, Mrs. Gilcrease. I will get you the letter." Steve hung up the phone, dashed out the letter, scanned it, and sent it over within minutes. He was now officially scheduled to meet Scottie Pinkerton on January 6, 2016.

CHAPTER 4

Steve walked down the long dark corridor with a man in orange coveralls. They walked side by side, neither one looking at the other. After what seemed like an eternity, they reached a point where a teenager in a fast-food uniform and with a prominent whitehead on his left cheek was waiting for them. The kid asked, "May I take your order?" Behind him was a heat lamp with burgers wrapped under it, and behind that was a 1950s-looking electric chair.

Steve's alarm jarred him out of the dream. It was 4:45 a.m.

When Steve awoke, drenched with sweat, he quickly gathered himself. Today was the day he would meet Scottie. Steve donned athletic shorts and a T-shirt that said, "Elmer's BBQ...It be bad." Continuing his morning ritual, he grabbed some coffee and chewed on a protein bar before heading out the door.

An hour later, Steve sat on the end of the bench between sets with 225 pounds on the bar, the sounds and odor of a busy gym filled the air.

"How's it going?"

Steve turned to see Owen Fasso walking over. Fasso was a newly minted judge and the son of a very prominent one. An affable guy with dark hair and a slight paunch, Fasso had played both sides of the criminal justice system, first as a baby lawyer in the district attorney's office, then going to the private sector and representing primarily white-collar criminals, though he was never afraid to take on a case with some blood, if the facts were right. He was also a scratch golfer, so eighteen holes always presented opportunities for Steve to pick Fasso's brain.

"All good here," Steve said. "Just getting mentally prepared for my first trip to death row."

"I heard you got appointed to represent the guy that killed his wife in Claremore. Is that why you're going?"

"Yeah. Headed to the state pen in McAlester after my workout."

"Good ole 'Big Mac.' They keep the worst of the worst in that place," Fasso said with a shake of his head. "Over the years, I've visited a few clients there myself, though I prefer the federal jails—much better food and more polite prisoners. You ever been before?"

"No. I've been to a few county jails, but never a full-blown prison, let alone Big Mac."

"You'll be fine. Are you prepared to meet this guy? Your client, I mean?"

Steve sighed. "Not completely. I wasn't able to get the case file from his state court attorney until yesterday. By the time I got back from Norman, I barely had time to skim through the sixteen boxes."

"Just explain it to the guy. I've learned over the years that honesty is the best policy when it comes to anyone sitting in prison. They sniff out lies pretty well." Fasso grinned. "By the way, I have a tee time at the golf club this weekend, and we could use a fourth."

"Thanks, but not this weekend. I think this case is going to take over my life for a while."

Steve drove down Highway 75 with a knot in his stomach that grew as he approached the large, white, castle-like structure. He turned off onto a service road and reached a gate surrounded by concertina wire and cement barriers. Heavily armed, muscular men looked out at him from the gatehouse. Overhead, in towers, Steve could see figures standing ready with rifles in hand. Their silhouettes moving like shadow puppets against the clear blue sky. One of the guards walked up to Steve's car. "How can I help you?"

"My name is Steve Hanson. I'm here for an attorney/client visit."

The guard picked up a clipboard and looked at the sheet on it. After a few seconds, he gave Steve a nod and spoke while pointing. "You go down to that area over there, that's visitor parking. Then head over to that entrance and enter through those doors." The guard turned back, and the barrier raised.

As Steve pulled away from the security booth, he surveyed the landscape before him. Soon, that recurring, uneasy feeling floated around in his belly and bubbled up to his mind.

If I don't win this case, my client will die inside this place.

Before him loomed Big Mac. It had been constructed over a century ago, and it looked the part. It was a giant square with a guard tower in each corner. The walls were painted white, but it had likely been decades since anyone had added a fresh coat.

On the exterior of one wall was a giant mural depicting the rodeo that the prison once famously held every year. Back then, most of the inmates were just cowboys who had done wrong, so the prison started holding a rodeo in 1940 with the inmates as contestants. The prison rodeo raised money for charity and gave the incarcerated men something to keep them busy. It reminded him of how, in the 80s, Gene Wilder and Richard Pryor used a prison rodeo as a backdrop in their famous comedy, Stir Crazy.

There were families playing in the park across the street. All of the dads were wearing gray prison uniforms. Steve wondered what type of chance in life those children had—the kids who only saw their dad in that jumpsuit labeled "INMATE" for their entire childhood.

Steve parked his car in the visitors' parking lot near the southwest corner guard tower. He looked up at the twenty-foot-tall chain link fence with more concertina wire snaked around the top. His thoughts wondered about life inside as he traversed the sidewalk to the front door. He saw the sign directing visitors and followed it through the doors the sentry guard had pointed out.

After walking up five gradually sloped concrete steps, Steve faced two large glass doors, each emblazoned with the state seal of Oklahoma. He stopped for a second on the fourth step up, wondering how many people had gone through the doors before him and how many of those never got out. His body slightly shook involuntarily.

When he entered the building, three even larger corrections officers than those at the gate greeted him. The largest of the three spit some Copenhagen into a white Styrofoam cup with a paper towel stuffed inside, then he handed Steve an entry log while another held his hand out and said, "Cell phone." Steve handed him the cell phone and followed the third guard's hand gesture to pass through a set of metal detectors.

The first guard said with a smile, "Don't worry Mr. Lawyer-Man." He paused to raise the cup to his lips and spit. "We won't look at your private photos or emails while you're in there."

The third guard, smallest of the three at maybe 6'2" and 220 pounds, patted Steve down while the second guard thoroughly searched his briefcase. The guards looked at each other, and the largest pointed down the hall to an office. "That way."

Steve knocked on the door with a sign showing the name "Deputy Warden Martha Gilcrease."

"Come in." He recognized the southern twang and opened the

door to see Gilcrease. The deputy warden sat behind her desk, looking at a file, her eyes never leaving the page. Her silver hair was pulled into a severe bun. Steve knew Gilcrease had been deputy warden for about forty years, and she looked like she had been doing it since the day the prison opened.

"Deputy Warden Gilcrease, I'm Steve Hanson, attorney for Scottie Pinkerton," Steve said, voice slightly cracking as he handed his paperwork over.

Gilcrease lifted the glasses hanging around her neck and narrowed her eyes through the thick lenses while she scanned Steve's driver's license and Oklahoma Bar Association card. She pulled out a file. "Yep, you got your letter in. Good first step to getting in the H-Unit. Sounds much homier than death row." She paused, a frown creasing her forehead. "Your letter doesn't ask for a restraint-free, barrier-free visit," Gilcrease said curtly. "You do understand that means you won't be allowed in the same room with your client, and he will have to wear handcuffs during the entire visit?"

"What?" Steve said. "I unquestionably need to be in the same room with him, preferably without handcuffs. This is my first time meeting him. For me to do my job correctly, I need to show him that I trust him so he will hopefully trust me. I am sure you can understand that."

"Well, prison rules require you to clearly state that you want your visit to be barrier-free and restraint-free in order for me to approve this." Gilcrease tapped the offender visitation file on her desk. "We have to prepare for those circumstances ahead of time. Do you want me to cancel your visit today, and you can send us a new letter for a new date with the proper wording on it?"

"I definitely don't want to do that either. I just drove over an hour and a half from Tulsa. Like I said, this is my first time here, and I honestly didn't know." Then, Steve said sheepishly, "It's the first mistake I have ever made in my whole life."

Gilcrease smiled at his facetious statement.

"I'm truly sorry. It was one hundred percent my mistake, but is there not something else we can do so I can see him today and be in the same room with him?" Steve asked in the nicest way he knew how, even giving a flirtatious smile in the hopes that it might help to some degree.

"Well, I suppose I can allow you to have a barrier-free visit in the attorney/client visitation room, rather than a visit separated by the glass partition in the family visitation center. But without the proper letter, there is no way I can allow a barrier-free visit to occur unless the convict is at least handcuffed. I would lose my job if I okayed a completely restraint-free visit without prior approval from the warden."

"Great, thank you! Thank you so much. I don't want you to lose your job because of my oversight. Talking with him handcuffed in the same room is better than talking to him through glass. I promise I will get the letter right next time."

"You will also need to sign this." Gilcrease handed Steve a document that said at the top, "Complete Waiver of Liability for All Dangers and Harm, Regardless of Actual Knowledge, Potential Knowledge, or any other Possible Knowledge of the Danger. This Waiver Has No Exception, even for Intentional Conduct and No Exception for Any Reason." Steve read the rest of the document and realized that he would have to waive his right to sue for any harm done to him in the prison, no matter who was at fault.

Gilcrease, virtually reading his mind, said, "Basically, Mr. Hanson, even if a corrections officer purposely shot you in the back, your family cannot sue the prison—not that any of our highly professional guards would do such a thing, but I can't let you in without you signing it."

Steve scribbled his signature on the waiver. Gilcrease handed him a visitor badge.

"Let me walk you back to the guard station, Mr. Hanson," Gilcrease said, leading him out the door. During the short trip there, she continued on to say, "You know, I do admire something about people like you who have a belief that everyone should get a fair shake. But on the other hand, you set very bad people loose, and they kill or rape or do something much worse again, and then I end up feeding them after they have destroyed more lives—I'm not just talking about those killed or raped, but also the victims' friends and families."

Steve stayed silent.

"Whether this was a crime of passion, or your client is just plain evil, it was absolutely horrible what he did. He deserves an execution or, at best, to rot here until he dies." Seeing that Steve didn't respond to her lecture, Gilcrease turned to the guards. "Please direct this young man to H-Unit." She walked back to her office without another word.

CHAPTER 5

Steve drove around to the special wing for capital punishment inmates, built after Tim McVeigh made the death penalty fashionable again in the 90s. The State of Oklahoma called the place a bunker or H-Unit, Steve would go on to call it a dungeon when he relayed this visit to friends and colleagues in the future.

Gilcrease had told him that he was not allowed to bring his cell phone inside. As he placed his phones into his glove box, he noticed that he had just received a Snapchat message on his work cell from an anonymous sender. He decided he could check it later and walked towards the entrance.

After being screened and searched again, Steve was escorted to a wall of metal bars. He stared at the vertical bars and determined they were each approximately three inches in diameter with a half-inch space between them. Two-inch-thick rectangular metal bars were welded horizontally across the vertical bars every twelve inches, from floor to ceiling. They were the thickest bars he had ever seen.

The officer beside him signaled to someone in the control room. The door in front of them slid open; the dull slow scratching of metal against metal echoed through the corridor. They took two steps forward and were faced with another wall exactly like the one through which they had just passed. Once the door behind them fully closed and locked, the same dull metal sound began again as this door slowly slid open. This sound would forever be etched in Steve's memory, the sound left a scar. As this process happened over and over again, Steve was reminded of an early scene in Silence of the Lambs: the first time Clarice visited Dr.

Lecter in the insane asylum, she went through locked door after locked door to theatrically show the depths at which they keep Lecter confined. Here, however, this containment was not plot-driven; it was simply where the state kept Steve's client and all the other death row inmates.

The pair finally arrived at the H-Unit manager's office, where "Jerome Baldwin" was printed neatly on the door. The nameplate was newer than the one on the deputy warden's office, but even here, it looked like it'd been there for a while.

Steve knocked.

"Come on in!" Steve heard. He opened the door to see a middle-aged man in a red-and-white checkered sweater emblazoned with the University of Oklahoma logo. The man was brandishing a golf putter and standing on a strip of artificial green turf with a hole at the far end of it.

"Mr. Hanson, how the hell are you? Welcome to H-Unit!" Baldwin stuck out his free hand like he was going to sell Steve a car.

Steve shook it politely. "I'm fine, Mr. Baldwin, thank you."

"Call me Jerome. My old pal Ackerman… well, maybe not pal, maybe I don't even like him, but he's a smart egg who says you've got a good head on your shoulders. If you're good in his book, you're good in my book." Baldwin turned his attention back to his putting course. "Anyway, more importantly, word from Fasso is that you never miss within five feet of the hole. I could use a few pointers sometime, as I've kind of lost my mojo here—not today, of course, you have to meet Scottie." He grinned. "But I have a feeling we'll be seeing a lot of each other over the next few months, so let's set aside some time to work on that."

Steve was speechless but recovered quickly. "I've always said putting is like making an omelet. You have to get the spatula in that sweet spot to flip it just right. Otherwise, it goes everywhere but the pan." He cleared his throat. "And I'd be happy to work on putting practice with you, Jerome—as you said, some other time."

"Right, right. That sounds dandy. We actually have a French chef here who killed his wife in a spat. Makes a helluva omelet. I'll treat you sometime," Baldwin chattered on as he handed Steve a paper. "Anyway, I have a waiver for you to sign."

Steve was confused. "I already signed a waiver."

Baldwin laughed. "You signed that waiver, not this one. The first waiver just gets you past the sadistic guards who we can barely control. Now, you will be in the pit with nothing but killers, some of which would love to take another life just for the sake of it. Should things turn bad for you in there, we will try to help, but I'm not going to lose any of my precious, mentally unhinged guards to bail you out. Rather than lose one of our own, we would just gas the area and scrape up what's left of you. But don't worry, I need those putting tips, so we'll try not to let you get killed."

"Or worse," Steve apprehensively joked, not quite reassured by the warden's words.

"Naw, we probably wouldn't stop that. Improves prisoner morale when a cutie-pie lawyer gets sexy time." Baldwin laughed and slapped Steve's shoulder. "Anyway, you have one last sally port to venture through—past those large young men to the right of my door—and your H-Unit cherry will be officially popped."

Steve passed through yet another set of cookie-cutter, massive guards and found himself officially in the bowels of society.

He carefully took in what Oklahoma's death row actually looked like. The interior control booth was constructed from three-and-a-half-inch-thick bulletproof glass, and it was manned by two correctional officers. The bulletproof room was a perfect square inside a square. Three-fourths of the outer square was comprised of the inmates' cells. Steve stood on the fourth side, staring at the open square "C" of cells before him.

From this vantage point, Steve could see the three sides contained two stories of cell doors wrapped around the perimeter. He remembered reading a report from the Federal Public Defenders Office that H-Block currently held one hundred and forty-seven people on death sentences. There was a cell door about every six feet and ten cells on each wall. Inside of each cell was a prisoner or two who faced the most severe penalty and would likely spend a decade or more waiting for it.

One of the guards pushed a button, and the door to Steve's left slid open with the same dull, slow screech he already knew he would never get used to hearing. He walked through, entering the heart of H-Unit for the first time. He felt hollow.

Everything he had previously seen was now on his right. To his left was the outdoor area each prisoner was constitutionally required access to, for at least one hour per day, according to U.S. Supreme Court precedent. The high court had determined that keeping a man locked up in his cell for twenty-four hours a day was cruel and unusual punishment in violation of the Eight Amendment.

The yard consisted of a thirty-by-thirty-foot square of concrete that was surrounded by walls reaching three stories high on all four sides. Steve saw a basketball hoop on one wall and a weight bench in the other corner. As his eyes scanned upward, they stopped at the steel grate with evenly spaced slats each the size of a Hershey's chocolate bar covering the ceiling of this outside area colloquially referred to as "the yard." As Steve looked at the slivers of blue sky he could see through the metal roof, he wondered how exactly one hour out there each day changed their imprisonment from cruel and unusual to something else.

He would later learn that the prison officials sometimes gave inmates their hour in the yard at less-than-favorable times. The law didn't specify when the hour each day had to occur, only that the inmates were entitled to one hour per day. So, when the warden believed a show of control was necessary, he scheduled the hours at extremely inconvenient times for the prisoners.

In the winter, the yard time was set at 3:00 a.m. In the summer, yard time was set at 5:00 p.m. Thus, most of the incarcerated men chose to stay in their cell rather than be woken up to go outside in the cold night or leave the slight comfort of their cell's small oscillating fan to stand in the steam-inducing Oklahoma heat.

As Steve stared at the empty yard, the clang of the door closing behind him signaled that he was now locked in death row. The back of his neck tingled slightly. The door down the hallway opened. He went through one last metal bar door. It closed behind him. To his left, a solid metal door with a small square window clicked open.

Steve entered the eight-by-eight-foot room and noticed first the table and three chairs in the middle. Then, he noticed the window to his right, made of bulletproof glass embedded with steel mesh, which allowed him to see into the unit manager's office he had left just minutes ago. Baldwin looked over, grinned, and went back to his putting practice. Other than the thick metal door, the four walls were uniformly made of some old form of sheetrock. The color reminded Steve of the stained ceiling in his fourth-grade classroom at Lincoln Elementary School back in Pryor, Oklahoma where water had seeped through on who knows how many occasions; the stains in this visitation room appeared somehow dirtier and the walls themselves older than even those decrepit classroom tiles.

He took a seat, pulled out his legal pad and pen, and waited.

CHAPTER 6

After a few minutes, he peeked through the small window in the door facing back out to the H-Unit. There, he saw Scottie Pinkerton standing in the middle of the cellblock. Scottie was a white man a little over six feet tall, slightly overweight, with a belly that pooched out like a starving African child in a late-night infomercial. His black hair was cropped short against his scalp. At the moment, he was being strip-searched.

Steve knew this was for his own safety but wondered how degrading it must be to be searched like that in front of everyone. Not that anyone was looking, but all of the inmates and guards in the cell block had a clear view of the ceremony. He wondered how many times Scottie had to go through this and similar experiences over the past seven years. Steve slowly walked away from the window and slumped back down in his chair.

When the door opened, Steve quickly stood as his client was escorted into the room. Steve reached out, and Scottie tried his best to shake Steve's hand, but the wrist restraints were chained to his waistband. Scottie appeared to be feigning interest in meeting him until the officer left; Steve was certain the man was not happy about something. He sat down and gestured for Scottie to take the seat next to him.

Before Steve could ask what was wrong, Scottie leaned over the table and growled, "Why the fuck are these cuffs on me? Never had these on me before when other lawyers visited."

Steve had to think quickly. He didn't want Scottie to know his inexperience was the reason why the cuffs were on, but he also didn't want his first words with a new client to be a lie. He decided that the best approach was to just be completely honest, considering that is what he wanted from Scottie in return.

"To be honest, this is my first visit to H Unit and I forgot to put the magic words 'barrier-free' on my visitation request letter. So, the prison officials wouldn't let me visit you without handcuffs on today," Steve said. "I promise it will never happen again."

Scottie leaned back and raised his hands up to Steve's eyes. "Good! Because these cuffs aren't protecting you from shit." He placed the cuffs together in a manner that loosened them one notch. If he had continued the maneuver repeatedly, the cuffs would have fallen to the floor. "There, they were way too tight, now I can at least deal with these fuckers while we talk. Plus, I would be in deep shit if I removed them completely." He smirked, leaned back in his chair and said, "You learn a lot of tricks in a place like this."

Steve kept his composure, although internally he wondered if the waivers he had signed were actually based on past events rather than just an overly cautious Attorney General.

Scottie finally sat down and looked Steve in the eye, "So, you are my new court-appointed lawyer. I've gone through three different lawyers over the years and not one of them has been worth a shit. I guess you get what you pay for, huh?" He frowned, making no effort to hide the fact that he was sizing Steve up. "You seem awful young, though. My cellie said you would be super experienced since you're my last shot. You barely look old enough to wipe your ass, let alone to have ever done anything like this before. And the fact I am wearing these cuffs seems to prove my impression."

"Well, as I said earlier, this is my first time here and you are my first capital punishment client," Steve admitted. "However, I just spent the last two years working for three federal judges in Tulsa on these cases. I did nothing but constitutional death penalty work, seven days a week, the whole time. I know this law inside and out. I even know the judge who will be ruling on your case. I promise I will give you my best effort at winning you a new trial."

"New trial? I don't want a new fucking trial. I want out of prison. I want to go home and see my son. I am innocent of these fucking charges. I didn't kill my wife. If I had a decent lawyer at trial, or on my state appeal, I wouldn't be in this shithole. Now, on my last shot, they send some kid younger than me to save me." He almost looked like he would laugh, but he only looked up and grimaced. "Please tell me when this fucking nightmare will end."

"Well, I'm not here to determine your guilt or innocence. My goal is to find some constitutional error that will get you a new trial."

Scottie didn't like that answer. "There you go again saying 'new trial.' Like I said, I'm a god damn innocent man! I've done some legal research to pass the time, and I know that if you show I am innocent I can get out. I can be released based on the fact I didn't kill Ashley. And that's the truth, man. I swear I didn't even touch her at all. I never did. My only chance at getting out of here alive is if you believe me and find the real killer. None of my other lawyers believed me, so none of them tried. They all had other ideas, like you and your fucking new trial plan. None of them wanted to find the person who actually killed my wife." Scottie caught himself and stopped ranting. He finally asked, "Do you believe me when I say I am innocent?"

"If you tell me, you are innocent, then yes, I believe you. But I've also read the news reports. There was quite a bit of evidence against you: the 911 call, the DNA evidence, the scratches on your face, the bloody footprints from your shoes, the fact you showered as soon as you got to the hotel room." Steve listed the points off one by one. "I must admit, all of the evidence is leading to you being the one who did it. That said, I haven't had an opportunity to review your entire file or the trial transcripts yet because they weren't delivered to me until late yesterday, so I don't know everything yet."

"Yeah, yeah, yeah, you sound just like my trial attorney. He never listened when I tried to tell him what happened; he didn't even try to get me a not-guilty verdict. He always said his goal was to keep me from getting the death penalty, that we had no chance at the guilt/innocence phase, and he would get more respect from the jury if he didn't argue for me until the sentencing stage. Now you keep saying you want to get me a new trial, not get me out of here. More of the same court-appointed lawyer bullshit. Man, if only I could afford a real lawyer."

Then something clicked in Scottie's brain, and his expression changed from pissed-off despair to hopeful consternation. He stared a hole through Steve's head. "I'll tell you what, you go read all that stuff and come back here and convince me that you believe I'm innocent. Only then will I tell you the story of what happened that day. Until you do that, I'm not going to waste my time talking to another shitty public pretender. I don't trust you, and you probably won't listen to a word I say anyway, just like all the other lawyers the government has gotten for me. Worthless." He held up his cuffed hands as he said that.

Steve quietly considered his client's words.

"I'll leave you with one fact," Scottie finally said. "When I left the house that day, she was living and breathing without a scratch on her. That's the god-honest truth." He stood up and pushed the intercom button. "We're done in here. Please send Wayne back for me."

While the two men waited in the room, Steve spoke up. "Listen, I believe you. I promise you. I will read everything and come back here and show you that I am different from any lawyer you've had in the past. I'm going to do everything I can to figure out the truth and get you out of here, even if it's the last thing I ever do in my life."

Scottie only stood silently by the door until it clicked open, and a massive guard came in to retrieve him.

The guard said to Steve, "You need to stay in here until I get him back to his cell. No one is allowed in the hall while a prisoner is out of their cell."

Scottie was escorted out. A few minutes later, Steve left the same way he came in, slowly and through many doors. When he signed out, he realized he had been inside H-Unit for almost an hour, even though he'd met with his client for less than five minutes.

When he stepped outside of the facility, Steve suddenly noticed how immense and blue the sky was above him. He had been inside Oklahoma's death row for what was, comparatively speaking, a short amount of time. But the freedom he felt as he soaked up the vastness of the world outside was indescribable. He tried to imagine what it was like to live inside those walls day after day after day. How it would change a person to see only the sky that was visible through the slits in a grate three stories up, to never see the sun set or rise, to never see the horizon.

As Steve stared skyward and slowly turned in place beside his car, he thought to himself that, for some indefinable reason,

Scottie didn't really seem like a murderer. Although his client had opened with a threat, it seemed more bark than bite, almost like learned behavior from having to survive in custody for so long. And despite everything Steve had read in the news about the facts of the case, his gut told him that Scottie was telling the truth; maybe, just maybe, Scottie had left Ashley at home that day alive and without a scratch on her.

Steve decided he would start sifting through the boxes of the case as soon as he returned to Tulsa. Furthermore, he would read through everything from the perspective of innocence, looking for evidence to exonerate Scottie, rather than just looking for constitutional mistakes that would lead to a new trial. Steve knew this was the only way he would gain Scottie's trust and get to hear his version of what happened that August day. That story was key to finding out if Scottie, or someone else, killed Ashley Pinkerton.

CHAPTER 7

By the time Steve returned to his office from his trip to Big Mac, any thoughts about lunch had left his mind entirely. He grabbed a protein bar and an apple from the bottom drawer of his desk and sat down in front of the stack of pink phone message slips that had accumulated while he was on death row.

Each slip relayed a different problem from the myriad of cases he currently had open. Memories from a seminar he once attended filled his mind; the Oklahoma Bar Association's general counsel told the audience that the single most common cause for complaints against attorneys was their failure to respond to client inquiries in a timely manner. Ever since, Steve had promised himself he would do his best to return all phone calls on the same day he received them.

He stared at the pile of messages, then at the boxes containing all of the evidence and documents that may show him the path to liberating Scottie Pinkerton. The sixteen boxes from Scottie's case were stacked in the corner of Steve's office, staring back at him unyieldingly. He imagined they were saying, in the best Glenn Close from Fatal Attraction impersonation that boxes could give, "We are not going to be ignored, Steve."

Steve smiled, briefly thinking how glad he was that the boxes were incapable of attacking him with a butcher knife. He picked up his phone, looked at the first pink slip on the pile, and began returning calls.

The first and second phone calls were to DUI clients and the third was to someone charged with misdemeanor marijuana possession. His office cell phone lit up and he saw he had a Snapchat from an unknown number. He wondered if it was from the same person who sent him a picture of the scales of justice on the day he had visited Scottie.

He decided to open the app and look before he continued. This time it was a video of a car swerving down the road. The car was hitting parked cars on both sides of a city street basically bouncing between them down the road. Then the words "Stay in Your Lane" appeared on the screen.

The next several calls were to divorce clients. These were people whose soon-to-be-ex-spouses had done something to ruin their day, or possibly even their week. Usually, the calls were not emergencies in the legal sense, but to the person on the other end of the line, each situation was more distressing than waking to the sound of a burglar down the hall.

One such call was to a potential new client, Mr. Baxter.

"Thank you for calling me back. I was served divorce papers at work yesterday, and I don't know what to do."

"You called the right person. Situations like that are why you need to hire a lawyer. Whether it be me or another attorney, you need someone who can answer all of your questions and walk you through the horrible experience you are about to undergo." Steve always asked this next question before he continued, "Are you sure your marriage is over? There is no chance of reconciliation?"

"No. We are done," Baxter said, sounding resigned but mournful. "We have been going to counseling for a few months, and she finally said that she is done. She told me that she can't be married to me any longer. She simply doesn't love me anymore."

"I'm very sorry to hear that, and you sound extremely upset about this," Steve said. "Now, not to be cold, but I will need a two-thousand-dollar retainer if you decide to hire me, and I charge two hundred and twenty five dollars an hour. I want you to understand that you are paying me to be smart and rational. You will be torn up with all kinds of emotions during this process; it will be my job to always be the voice of reason. I will be the Spock to your Captain Kirk, and we will get through this together as painlessly as possible."

A small laugh broke through the tearful tone on the other end of the line. After twenty more minutes of talking, Mr. Baxter scheduled a meeting to bring in his retainer the next day.

Steve picked up the next pink message slip. It read "Mrs. Whitehurst—emergency." Mrs. Whitehurst was a mother in her mid-thirties, and her husband had just recently left her for a coworker. She was blindsided by the news and, understandably, had a great deal of anger against him.

She answered the phone immediately and launched into her story. "He checked Nathan and Timothy out of school early today! I texted him, and apparently, he thinks that since it's such a pretty day he is going to take them to the zoo. They shouldn't be missing school for a zoo trip with Dad! This could affect their entire academic careers."

"Okay, Barbara. I know you aren't happy about him doing this, and I agree he should have consulted with you first. But... your boys are both still in elementary school. Do you honestly think missing a day of first or third grade is going to ruin their academic careers?"

"Maybe not, but he can't just take them out whenever he wants! I know it was his day to pick them up, but he has to let them finish school first. I never pick them up early. He is just trying to be the fun dad and make me the mean parent."

"That could be it. Or he could just love his children as much as you do and thought that, with all they are going through, they could use a fun day at the zoo. Either way, you are correct that he shouldn't have done this without talking to you about it first. I will call his lawyer and let her know what happened. We'll make sure this doesn't happen again. Okay?"

"Okay. Thank you." Mrs. Whitehurst chuckled a bit to herself. "Maybe I did overreact a little, Steve. But that's why I pay you, right?"

As the afternoon wore on, the stack of pink message slips whittled down to two. The one on top was from his personal insurance agent calling about quotes for renewing renter's insurance on his personal items at home. The other one was from Jennifer Turner, the assistant district attorney on the Hamilton case. The message referenced another meeting with Dr. Emily Babbage.

Steve closed his eyes. Babbage's face had been popping in and out of his mind ever since that first meeting the other day. He pictured, again, the complex blue of her eyes, a color so unique that he wanted to create a name for it. He remembered the motion of her body as she walked from the house to her car when she left, the way the skirt fit snugly around her thighs, almost clinging to her waist as she strode away. He couldn't forget that electrifying moment when they shook hands. The insurance agent could wait. Steve picked up the phone and called Turner.

After a short pause listening to the chorus of Duran Duran's "Hungry Like a Wolf" played by a string quartet, Turner picked up the line. "Hello, Steve. How are you?"

"Good. I spent the morning down at Big Mac. I had a meeting with my client who is on death row, and I'm just happy they didn't keep me overnight," he said jokingly.

"I'm glad they let you out, too." They shared a laugh before she said,"I didn't know you represented anyone on death row, that's a big undertaking, good luck. I called to let you know that Dr. Babbage has uncovered some evidence against your client. Apparently, Mr. Hamilton tried to delete several pieces of information from the hard drive of his computer."

This wasn't the news Steve had been hoping to hear regarding Dr. Babbage, but it wasn't unexpected either.

"She has recovered all of it," Turner said. "I have no doubt that I can now prove everything we have alleged. I was wondering if you would like to go to her office and look at what she has found. I am pretty sure that once you see the evidence we have against him, you'll want to have a serious discussion with Mr. Hamilton about working out a plea deal instead of going to trial."

"I would love to see what Dr. Babbage has found, but I must remind you, my client has consistently denied any wrongdoing in this matter. Every time I have met with him, he has told me he didn't take any money. He is very adamant about his innocence and his intent to take this case all the way to—"

"I understand that's his position," she said, interrupting him. "However, the law requires me to show you all of my evidence ahead of time, whether your client decides to plea or not, so let's at least go see what Dr. Babbage has found on your client's hard drive. The defendant in just about every case I have ever prosecuted started out by claiming innocence. Hell, your death row guy probably said he didn't do it, too. I think your tune just might change after you see what she has uncovered. When we are done, I'll give you what the state would accept as punishment under a plea deal. If the evidence doesn't sway you, at least we have taken another necessary step toward trial."

"Okay, I agree. We need to do this at some point anyway. Tomorrow might as well be the day," Steve said.

"Are you available in the afternoon?" Turner asked.

"I can meet any time after three."

"Let's say four thirty. The meeting with Dr. Babbage shouldn't take too long. I think we will be done around five or so. Her office is over by Cherry Street. We can go for a drink at The Empire Bar afterward and discuss the case, if you'd like?"

Steve knew that some of the older defense attorneys in town often had lunch or drinks with prosecutors to discuss their cases, but this was the first time he had been invited on such an excursion. He usually dealt with the junior prosecutors, and they were too young, hungry, and out to prove their moxie to ever be seen fraternizing with the defense bar.

However, since Hamilton's case was a more serious charge—felony embezzlement—a more experienced attorney like Turner had been assigned to it. Turner, who had been working as assistant district attorney for over ten years, had long ago moved past having to prove herself; everyone knew she was a career prosecutor and would never question her having drinks with opposing counsel on a case.

"That sounds great!" Steve said. "I'll meet you at Dr. Babbage's office tomorrow."

Steve checked the clock and saw that the day was already getting away from him. It was almost five, and he still hadn't done his final preparation for a preliminary hearing he had set the next morning. Additionally, he needed to prepare for a meeting with a class of high school students, a favor he had agreed to do for a friend. He relaxed back into his chair, closed his eyes, crossed his fingers upon his chest and let out several slow deep breaths.

He reemerged with a decision. No matter how badly he wanted to start on Scottie Pinkerton's case tonight, he knew it was more important that he be fresh when he reviewed everything. Glenn Close would have to wait a little longer.

Steve opened the calendar on his computer. He had a fairly open Friday this week, no court appearances and only two client appointments scheduled in the morning. He marked off Friday afternoon to begin working on Scottie's case.

There was also no set plan for the weekend. This was true on most weekends, as Steve preferred to leave his options open in case a spontaneous adventure presented itself on Friday afternoon or Saturday. This weekend, the adventure would be a trip down memory lane via trial transcripts and court pleadings. He smiled as he realized that he would have over two days of solitude to begin his review of the state court records. He also wondered what that Snapchat message meant and if he could expect more.

CHAPTER 8

All morning the hours seemed to be dragging by slower than the days before Christmas. Luckily, the hearing that morning had gone as expected, and Steve was now headed to Booker T. Washington High School.

Booker T. was a magnet school in the Tulsa Public Schools System that combined local students with kids brought in from all races and socio-economic levels throughout the district based on merit. The end result was a very diverse student body with great academic standards.

Steve was driving to meet one of his friends, John Davis, a history teacher at the school. John recently asked Steve to come talk to his students during their studies of the death penalty in the United States; specifically, Steve was invited in to speak on the particulars of Oklahoma's death penalty system.

When Steve walked into the classroom, he saw couches, recliners, and beanbags arranged in a semicircle facing the smartboard where rows of desks and a chalkboard would have been forty years ago. The handful of candles scattered around the room brought a gentle ambiance to the entire scene.

"I like the way you've laid out your classroom. You must be one of the cool teachers," Steve said with a grin. "I remember one of my favorite teachers from high school set their room up like this."

"I believe a student needs to be comfortable in their learning environment to have the best chance of gaining knowledge," Davis said.

Two minutes later, the bell rang, and Davis began to talk to the class. "Since we have been studying the death penalty this week, I have arranged for us to have a local defense attorney come speak with us today."

Steve smiled and waved as some of the students turned to look at him.

"Steve Hanson spent two years working at the federal court downtown, helping the judges on capital punishment rulings. We are extremely lucky to have someone who knows so much about this area of the law come speak with us, and I ask that you give him the same respect you show me. Steve, you have the floor."

The kids all sat in quiet anticipation as Steve began his presentation.

"Good morning," said Steve. "I plan to give you a short lecture on the particulars of death penalty procedure in Oklahoma. But, at any time, if a question arises, please feel free to interrupt me.

He continued, "In the United States, the only way a person can receive the death penalty is if he or she is convicted of first-degree murder. That means you have to actually kill someone or be an active member of a group of people who kills someone before a jury is allowed to consider the death penalty as a form of punishment. It is a process known around the courthouse as 'filing a bill.'"

A hand shot up from a blonde-haired white girl sitting on a green beanbag to Steve's left. The irises of her curious eyes were a perfect color complement to her seat. A part of Steve wondered if the only reason she raised her hand was to stop him from continuing any longer. "Hi, Mr. Hanson. My name is Alex Wright! Thank you so much for coming to speak to our class today. Have you ever been to death row?"

"Yes," Steve said, unsurprised by the question. "I actually went there for the first time yesterday."

"What was that like?" the girl asked, not missing a beat.

Steve did his best to describe his trip to death row in a school-friendly way; he decided to leave out the part about writing the wrong letter and Scottie being in handcuffs.

Another hand shot up. This time, the hand belonged to a black boy sharing the green beanbag with the girl who had asked the first question. They weren't being too obvious with their body language, but the way the boy had his other arm relaxed behind the girl's back told Steve that the two were in a romantic relationship.

"Hello, Mr. Hanson," the young man said. "My name is Dominick Harrison. Thank you for being our guest lecturer today."

Steve nodded and smiled. Although the young man was more reserved than his girlfriend, they both seemed to be considerate and curious students.

"What if the jury doesn't think the defendant committed the murder?" asked Dominick.

"Well, he or she would be acquitted of murder; they would be released, and the criminal case would be over. From a criminal law standpoint, that's the end of it, whether the person is in fact innocent or guilty. They can go home and will never be tried for that crime again," Steve explained. "For the purposes of this discussion, we will assume the jury finds the person guilty so we can move to the second stage of a capital murder trial—the sentencing stage."

Steve looked around the room. All of the students now seemed engaged in his presentation. The students' attentive expressions gave him more confidence as he continued.

"Once a jury sentences a defendant to death, that defendant goes through the state appeals process. If they lose at all levels in the state, then they have the right to go to federal court. Their federal appeal begins at the district court level.

Steve took a moment to explain, "Generally speaking, there are three federal court levels. There is the district court. Every state has at least one district court, and larger states have several. Then, there are courts of appeal which are mostly regional. Oklahoma, Kansas, and other nearby states are covered by the Tenth Circuit Court of Appeals. Finally, there is the U.S. Supreme Court, which gets to pick and choose which cases it wants to hear. You can't just take a case there.

"Now, the federal district court is where I come in," Steve said, returning to his explanation of the sentencing stage. "I am appointed by the federal court to represent these people on their federal habeas petition. If the case is lost at all levels of the federal court system, ending with the Supreme Court in Washington, D.C., the defendant will most likely be executed, though the final outcome always depends on the state's decision of whether or not to keep the case moving forward to a conclusion in the death chamber.

"Some states execute faster than others, Oklahoma and Texas being fairly quick about it," Steve said dryly. "In California, it can take many years for the execution to occur, if at all."

Another student raised her hand. "Hello, Mr. Hanson. My name is Maria Hernandez, and I appreciate you visiting our class today. What do you do once you are appointed?"

"I read the entire state court record, looking for constitutional error. The record includes every document filed and transcripts of all of the testimony. I then point those errors out to the federal district court, and if I don't win there, I point out the errors to the Tenth Circuit, then eventually to the US Supreme Court."

"So, you basically look for a loophole to get the guy off?" she replied.

"Well, some people might look at it that way, but I believe the U.S. Constitution is the bedrock of our society, and protecting it is more important than executing any one person, even if that person is a murderer. But as long as the police do their job correctly in the investigation, the judge and district attorney follow the law at trial, and the defense counsel does an adequate job representing their client, then the habeas petition will likely be unsuccessful." Steve tried not to think of Scottie's case as he gave this explanation. "The purpose is to ensure that all the rules were followed, and the accused's rights were honored. It is not to retry the case. If all the rules were followed, the appeal will probably fail.

"There can even be what is called 'harmless error.' Harmless error is when a constitutional violation occurs, but the appellate court believes it did not affect the jury's final decision, so the appeal is denied even though there was mistake.

"In summary, the only time a new trial will be ordered is when an error occurred that is so egregious the court believes the jury might have decided differently if the error had not occurred. I think everyone would agree that, in those cases, anybody and everybody should get a new trial. I know that if I am ever accused of something, I pray my trial will be held in accordance with constitutional standards."

The student who'd asked the question nodded her head slowly, accepting and processing Steve's words.

Dominick then asked, "What if everything was done constitutionally, but it turns out the person clearly didn't do it? Not just that he could be found not guilty, but that, with new evidence, he could be proven innocent?"

"In those rare cases, the person is released from prison. To be clear, if I win an appeal on constitutional grounds, that just means my client gets a new trial, a trial where a new jury could still give him the death penalty all over again. The only way someone would actually be released, and the charges dropped, is if new evidence showed they didn't do it at all."

When the class period came to an end, the students thanked Steve for all of the insight he had given them on Oklahoma's death penalty system. He drove back to his office afterward to take care of a few things before his meeting with Dr. Babbage.

Just as Steve was about to wrap things up and head out the door, he heard a fellow lawyer rushing down the hall. The young attorney stuck his head in Steve's office as he passed and said, "You need to come see this."

Steve got up and followed several other lawyers to the break room. All around the small room, he heard snippets of quiet, somber conversation. "Just a teenager... African American boy... was shot... was killed by... a white cop in Claremore. They think the kid was unarmed."

On the television, local newswoman Sandy Shores was reporting live from the front of the Rogers County Sheriff's Office.

"That's right, Tom. We do know the incident occurred at a trailer park outside of town, and the young man is dead. I've been informed there are no witnesses other than the possible victim's sister. She claims it was unprovoked, and the young man was unarmed. At this point, we do not know if the young man was armed or not."

The television cut to a video of a young African American woman screaming hysterically at the several television cameras aimed at her. "That cop shot him! He shot my brother. He killed him dead in front of my trailer! He didn't have no gun or nothin'. That cop just shot him."

"What was your brother doing?" a reporter asked.

"Nothin', he wasn't doin' nothin'. Just standing there, and that cop just shot him."

The young woman broke into sobs again.

The station cut back to Shores live. "The officer involved was Deputy Sheriff Andrew Blackburn. The sheriff's department has not issued any statements other than to say the incident is under investigation, and Deputy Blackburn has been suspended with pay until completion of the investigation."

"Thank you for your report, Sandy," said the news anchor. "We have also just received notice from the Black Lives Matter organization that they are planning a protest in front of the Rogers County Sheriff's Department tomorrow night at six."

The anchor then put his hand to his ear and said, "I have just been told the family of the victim has been informed of his death, so we can release his name. The victim was Dominick Harrison, a student at Booker T. Washington High School. We will have more information about him later tonight."

Steve fell back and put his hand down on the counter he was standing near. He bowed his head and put his other hand over his eyes and face.

As soon as he got back to his desk, Steve called Davis to see how he was dealing with the news. As he rode the elevator from his office to the parking garage, he thought about Alex, the green-eyed girl who had shared a beanbag chair with Dominick just a few hours ago. As he started his car to head to his meeting with Dr. Babbage, Steve wondered how Harrison's family was dealing with the news.

CHAPTER 9

Steve pulled into a spot outside Dr. Babbage's office a little after 4:15 p.m. Her office was in a small strip mall and he parked under one of the many trees lining the street. While he sat in the parking lot, he called Hamilton to let his client know what was about to happen.

"Jordan, I'm sitting in the computer forensics expert's parking lot and am about to go in and see exactly what evidence she has uncovered."

"Look, Steve," Hamilton replied. "I didn't do anything. I have no idea what she could have found on my hard drive. If she says she found something she probably planted it there herself."

"Okay. I'll let you know what I find out."

Steve told the young man at the reception desk that he was there for a four thirty appointment with Dr. Babbage and Assistant District Attorney Jennifer Turner. The man hit a buzzer, and both women soon came out to greet Steve.

Dr. Babbage came over and shook his hand. When their hands touched, Steve felt that familiar jolt and once again he got a little balsa in his pants. He wondered if she felt something, down there, too.

"Nice to see you again, Dr. Babbage," Steve said while trying to keep his cool.

"You can call me Emily, and it's nice to see you again too," she said with a knowing smile.

All three of them walked back to the computer lab where Emily worked. Once in the lab, Steve saw Hamilton's computer on a workbench. Emily walked over to his client's computer and sat down, pointing to the chair next to her. "Sit over here where you can see the screen."

Steve readily obliged and scooted the chair up near her.

Emily began typing on the keyboard and working the mouse. "You see, unless you expertly whitewash your hard drive, nothing you delete ever completely goes away. The computer just moves it to a different section on the hard drive."

Steve watched the incomprehensible data stream flow by on the screen and asked, "So, what's that mean?"

"In layman's terms, everything that is ever typed into your computer stays on the hard drive somewhere, forever," Emily explained. "When you drag an icon to the trash or delete something, the information doesn't magically disappear. Instead, the computer labels the information 'deleted' and then it knows not to worry about those files. The process allows the computer to complete search requests faster than if it had to look through everything that had ever been typed into it, but the computer never truly erases anything from the hard drive itself. Does that make sense?"

"I think so. Do you mean that when I am typing a letter or document, if I type a word, then hit backspace and change the word, all of that is stored somewhere?"

"Yes. Every time you strike a key on the keypad, a record is kept. So, if you typed the letter 'T' and hit backspace once and then typed the letter 'A,' I could find the record of all three of those actions. This is called metadata. Another example is the FBI going through Hillary Clinton's servers to see what emails were sent and received using it. All that information remains on your hard drive, someone just has to know how to find it."

"So that's metadata... I see." Steve could already guess where this was going.

Emily smiled at him. "Unfortunately for your client, I have the training and experience to locate all the files he thought he had deleted. I have thoroughly examined his hard drive and found several files that Mr. Hamilton never wanted anyone to see." As she continued to speak, her smile widened into a wicked grin. "At least, not anyone from law enforcement."

Emily began to show Steve the evidence she had found. There were files that showed Hamilton had written checks for fake invoices. Other documents proved he created the fake invoices. Most damning of all, Emily had found a ledger that Hamilton maintained, showing all the money he had embezzled over the past five years from the company.

Emily pointed to the screen. "This Excel sheet details an embezzlement operation that has been going on much longer than your client's company originally thought, but in the last year, he started taking much larger chunks of money. The bigger amounts are what eventually raised red flags in the accounting department.

"The last part here proves the old adage that pigs get fat and hogs get slaughtered," Emily said. "If he had just kept taking amounts less than a thousand dollars, like he did the first few years, he probably would have gotten away with this forever. Once he started taking thousands at a time, it was just a matter of course that he would get caught."

As Steve mulled over all of the information Emily had managed to pull from Hamilton's own computer, Turner looked to Steve and said, "I am still willing to work out a plea deal for your guy wherein I will only take into account the current charges which amount to $52,347 in stolen funds. If your client doesn't want to plea-bargain, I will add new charges based on the total amount of $123,478 that Mr. Hamilton's spreadsheet shows he has taken. That will not only affect the sentence I think a jury would give him, but it would also be the amount of restitution the court will require him to pay back to his now former employer.

She paused before continuing, "However, I believe the most important issue here is getting some of the victim's money back. If I send him to prison, there isn't much chance of that ever happening. So, if your client will agree to waive his preliminary hearing and plead, I will reduce the charges to a misdemeanor and put him on five years' probation with the understanding that he has to pay back the fifty-two thousand and change during that timeframe. If he pays all of that back, he will never have to spend a night in jail, let alone prison, and he will only have to pay back half of what I honestly think he took. You need to make sure he understands that is one hell of a deal."

"Well," Steve said, "I'll talk to my client, but I can't give you a final answer until then. As you know, it's his case, so it's also his choice."

"Yeah, yeah, I know. You defense lawyers tell me that every day. 'Always the client's decision.' I'll give you till our preliminary hearing to give me an answer. If you waive, you get the deal; if you don't, I will file more charges." Turner shrugged. "Now, enough business. It's five fifteen, and I've been hard at it since eight this morning. I could use a drink, and I imagine you could too after what you just saw.

Steve simply nodded in agreement.

"I'm sure that forty-five minutes ago, you actually believed your client was innocent. You young defense attorneys always believe those lying clients. Trust me, you will get over that in due time." She turned to Emily. "Would you like to join me and Mr. Naïve here for cocktails at The Empire Bar?"

"I would love to," Emily responded with a smile on her face. "Let me just close up this place, and I will meet you two there shortly."

CHAPTER 10

The Empire Bar had been pouring Guinness and serving drinks in Tulsa for over twenty years. When Steve and Turner walked in, they saw people in suits, like themselves, who apparently had just arrived for happy hour. But the guys shooting pool wore T-shirts and looked like they had been there all afternoon. By eight thirty or so, the suits would mostly have trickled out, with the local college students taking over and a band playing later in the evening.

One reason Steve loved living in Oklahoma was the occasional "summer" day in the middle of winter. Oklahoma always gives its residents a couple of sunny, over-seventy-degree days to break up the chill of the coldest months. Today was one of those days, so Steve and Turner each ordered a drink at the bar and went outside to the patio.

The two of them found a table on the lower tier and began discussing different cases each had been involved with to date. Shortly after, Emily approached their table with a Hoegaarden in her hand. Everyone exchanged greetings again, and she quickly joined in the conversation.

Turner had been around long enough to know Steve had only been in private practice a short time and kindly gave him some advice about dealing with different prosecutors in her office. After a while, Turner said she had reached her two-beer limit for driving, and she needed to get home to her family in south Tulsa. As she excused herself, she smirked at Steve and said, "I felt like a third wheel around the two of you anyway."

Steve and Emily ordered another round. All things considered; Steve felt like the two of them were genuinely hitting it off.

Emily started talking about the last time she had been to The Empire Bar. "It was almost two years ago during the 2014 World Cup…"

The Empire Bar was one of Tulsa's top spots for soccer fans. Several local fan groups of different English Premier League teams met at the bar every weekend, during the season, to watch games. The Liverpool group was probably the biggest in town, but Man City, Chelsea, and even Everton had supporters in Tulsa; of course, everyone hated Manchester United.

"I came here to watch the U.S. game against Portugal," Emily said. "This place was packed with all kinds of crazy soccer fans. Everyone was dressed in red, white, and blue. There were even some people who had painted their faces and bodies. It was so much fun.

Then she raised her drink and shimmied her free hand as a nonverbal exclamation point at the end of her statement. Steve could truly see the joy in her this memory produced and it made him smile.

"The inside was people, wall-to-wall, and they had set up extra TVs outside, so it was packed out here too. Everyone was drinking Pabst and singing pro-America songs. When Clint Dempsey scored that goal, putting us ahead so late in the game, the whole place went nuts. People who didn't know each other were hugging and high fiving everywhere." Emily grinned at the memory. "I even hugged some guy I never met. A total stranger and I just exchanged a big happy hug."

"Sounds like you had a great time that day. I remember that game; I watched it at home with some friends. We went nuts when he scored, too. It was a real bummer when Portugal tied it up at the end," Steve said. "Are you a big soccer fan?"

"No, that day was more for the experience and supporting the American team. I've only really watched World Cup games. Oh, I did see the women play last summer and thought it was so awesome that Abby Wambach finally got to win that trophy." Emily leaned forward. "And you?"

"Yeah, I'm a big fan. I played in college, and at one point, I even thought about being a high school soccer coach and history teacher. But ever since I can remember, I wanted to be a lawyer. I had some stuff happen when I was a kid that made me want to fight for the little guy in court."

"What happened?" Emily said.

"It's kind of a long story without a happy ending. I would honestly rather not get into it now." Steve took a quick swig of his drink. "How about I tell you something else about me instead. Pick a number between one and twelve."

"Okay," Emily said, raising an eyebrow. "But, why one through twelve?" Steve could tell she wanted to press him further, but he appreciated the fact that she didn't. He wasn't ready to tell her about his father's death just yet. He had learned over the years that it tended to be a downer topic, and he didn't want anything to spoil the mood.

"Whatever number you pick, I will tell you a story from that grade of school."

"OK. Well, Arrested Development taught me that three is the magic number. So, third grade."

Wow, Steve thought. One in twelve chance and she picks third grade, the year dad passed.

"Hmm. Let's see. Third grade?" Steve sat quietly for a second, trying to remember a third-grade story other than the one thing he didn't want to talk about. He decided on one of his favorite memories about his dad. It had happened a few weeks before the accident and was one of the last memories he had of his father.

"I grew up in a small town about an hour outside of Tulsa, a place called Pryor Creek. It has a large park in the middle of town that lots of people go to when the weather is nice. One day, my family went there for a picnic. It was my mom, my dad, my brother, and me. After lunch, we all went for a little hike around the park. At one point in our walk, we came to a stream that ran throughout the park. There was a sewage tube that ran from one embankment of the stream to the other. The sides were muddy slopes that led down to the stream, and the tube was probably about ten feet above the water at its tallest point." Steve mimed the general layout of the stream and tube with his hands. "Originally, the tube was probably underground, but erosion made it visible over the years. The tube itself was black, about two to three feet in diameter, and very similar to the one Andy Dufresne crawled through to escape prison in -"

"Sorry to interrupt, but I love the Shawshank Redemption."

"Really? It's one of my favorites too. It's the one movie that, anytime I come across it while channel surfing, I always stop and watch it all the way through from whatever point it's at. Do you have any movies like that?"

"Any Harry Potter or Bridget Jones movie. I also love horror movies. But my guilty pleasure is Pauly Shore, so Son-in-Law will suck me in every time."

"Pauly Shore, huh? Okay, interesting to know." Steve smirked a little as he said this, and Emily emitted an embarrassed laugh.

Then she shot him a playful glare and said, "Now, finish your story." She grabbed her beer and brought it to her lips, so Steve picked up where he left off.

"Anyway, we had this pipe in front of us. It was basically a path to the other side of the creek where the playground area was. The original plan when we left camp was to walk over to the swing sets and swing. My mom said we should just keep walking to the footbridge down the way. But my brother, being the adventurer he is, decided to tightrope-walk across the pipe. It was about twenty-five feet across to the other side. After he finished, I decided to try. Of course, my older brother was far more athletic than me; he'd made it look easy. Somewhere around the middle, my nerves got the best of me. I lost my balance and fell."

"Awww," Emily said sympathetically.

"Luckily, I fell into a part of the water that was about five feet deep, so I didn't hurt anything except my pride. But the stream was disgusting. Since it was stagnant in some areas, the water was full of who knows what. The stream bed was several inches of thick black mud. My brother stood on the bank, looking down and laughing at me."

"What did your mom and dad do?"

"My dad walked out to the middle of the pipe where I had fallen off and belly-flopped into the gross pool with all of his clothes still on. He then started splashing and playing in the water with me. We were laughing and having such a good time that, eventually, my brother jumped in too. At that point, my mom ran to the car and went home to get us towels, clean clothes, and a camera. The three of us played in the water for the twenty minutes or so it took my mom to get back. When we finally climbed out, she took a picture of us all drenched and covered head to toe in muck. I still have that picture sitting on a bookshelf in my office."

"Your dad sounds like a good man," Emily said.

Steve checked the time on his phone and pretended not to hear her. "Okay. It's your turn. Tell me a story from eleventh grade."

Emily thought for a second. "Well, it's similar to yours in that something bad happened to me, but the ending isn't so happy. In high school, I was the drum major for the marching band. The way it worked in my school was that one band member each from the junior and senior class was chosen to be drum major. If you were selected, you learned how to do it during your junior year and then lead the band during your senior year. So, usually only seniors performed during football halftime shows."

"I'll assume that you got to lead the band your junior year since I picked eleven," Steve said. "That doesn't sound bad at all."

"Your assumption is half right, counselor. Yes, I did get to lead the band my junior year because the senior got sick before one game. However..."

"Wait, before you finish. There is something I have always wondered. What exactly is the point of a drum major anyway? Doesn't every band member have the music in front of them?"

"Yes. They have the music, but the drum major keeps them on beat. When you are down on the field in the middle of the band, some members can't hear the percussion section. They use the drum major as a visual guide to follow the beat, so everyone stays in sync."

"Okay. That makes sense. I think I get it now. Please continue."

"As I was saying, I was the first junior in who knows how many years to lead the band during the halftime show. We were halfway through "YMCA" by The Village People when a small swarm of bees started attacking me. I started wildly waving my baton in all sorts of sporadic, sweeping motions, trying to scare the bees away from me. Instead, they just got more agitated, and they spread out across the field, attacking the rest of the band. Of course, the entire band lost formation. When the trombones were so panicked that they ran right into the tuba section, it stopped being funny. One girl ended up with a broken arm, and several others were injured.

"I'm sure that was the only time in the history of high school football that more students were injured during the band's half-time performance than during the actual game. It was the most embarrassing moment of my life up to that point. The worst part is that someone offered me a cigarette that night, and I was feeling so crappy that it actually calmed me down. I haven't stopped smoking these damn things since." As if to prove the point, she set her drink aside and lit a cigarette.

Steve couldn't help but laugh a little. "I'm sorry. That does sound embarrassing, but the thought of a bunch of band members crashing into each other is kind of hilarious. I guess I am one of those people that laughs when I see someone fall before I help them up. Plus, it's not like it was truly your fault. You just got super unlucky with that swarm of bees."

"Yeah, yeah, yeah. I suppose I can forgive you for laughing; I do see how you might find it funny. And, yes, it was unlucky, but that seems to be my M.O. I'm always the person that these things seem to happen to."

"Then, would you consider it good or bad luck if I asked you out to dinner?" Steve leaned forward, "I'm getting hungry, and I would love to hear some more of your stories about band, bees, birds or whatever."

Emily's steely blue eyes met his unwaveringly. Her demeanor changed as she took a long drag of her cigarette. She began talking as she stubbed it out in the ashtray. "Listen, I am going to be frank with you. I've completely enjoyed chatting with you the last hour or so. You've got great looks, brains, and that hair. Damn!" She paused to stand up. "Let's just say, I think you are fucking sexy."

Emily grabbed her beer and, in two smooth swallows, finished it without breaking eye contact with Steve. She set the empty glass on the table between them. "But right now, you represent the person whom I am helping the state send to prison. I never mix business and pleasure. When this case is over, give me a call. Until then, it was nice meeting you." She held out her hand, gave him a firm handshake, and walked off.

He followed her with his eyes to see if she would look back, admiring her fine figure as she walked away. At first, he thought she wasn't going to do it. Then, at the last second, as she opened the door to go back inside, she turned her head and gave him "fuck me" eyes over one last smile.

As he sat alone on the patio, slowly finishing his beer, Steve replayed the entire conversation to himself. He felt like he had made a good impression. There was something about Dr. Emily Babbage that made him uneasy. Uneasy in a good way. Unfortunately, any further investigation of this feeling would have to wait until Hamilton's case was done.

As he drove home, Steve thought about calling Hamilton to discuss the offer Turner had given him. He decided it would be best to confront Hamilton in-person with the evidence and plea deal. Steve felt this would give him a better chance of breaking through Hamilton's fortress of denial.

Finally, Steve's thoughts turned to the boxes of Scottie Pinkerton's case files that were still waiting for him in his office. Tomorrow would begin his weekend of transcript review, the first layer of information about Ashley Pinkerton's murder would finally become uncovered.

CHAPTER 11

Steve sat and stared at the volumes of transcripts in front of him. His morning meetings this Friday had run longer than expected, and he had received a couple of emergency calls from divorce clients right after lunch. When he was finally able to truck all of the boxes down from his office, to his car, and then into his house, it was mid-afternoon.

Steve smiled wryly. Another exciting Friday night in Tulsa, America.

When he worked at the federal court, Steve had read thousands upon thousands of pages of transcripts of murder trials. Yet, this time, the process seemed more daunting. In those previous cases, he was merely reviewing the arguments made by the respective attorneys and working with the judges to see whose side the law fell in favor of. This time, he was the one who would have to make the winning argument.

Otherwise, someday, I will have to watch…Steve didn't finish the thought.

Despite the exponential difference in pressure, Steve decided he would use the same procedure he had perfected during his time as a law clerk.

First, he picked up the three-ring binder labeled "Volume One of The State of Oklahoma vs. Scottie Pinkerton Rogers County Case Number CRF-2008-1273" and opened it on his kitchen table. There were seven such binders, and the dates listed below the titles on each told him the trial began on Monday, July 20, 2009, and lasted a little over three weeks.

Next, he got out a yellow legal pad and a pen. He set the notepad to his right. As he read through the thousands of pages, he would create a personalized index of all sixteen boxes, covering maybe thirty to forty pages of his legal pad. It was the perfect resource material for the job ahead.

The first several pages covered some preliminary motions the trial judge ruled on before the court brought in the prospective jurors. He was looking for any constitutional error by the trial court in these preliminary rulings. Sometimes, a death row defendant's best shot at a new trial came from these rulings because they determined what could or could not be presented to the jury.

Unfortunately, he found nothing that gave cause for a reversal of Scottie's conviction. His stomach began to grumble.

Steve made himself a ham and cheese sandwich and sat back down for the next portion of the transcripts. He was finally at the opening statements of counsel.

He took a determined bite of his sandwich. Let the festivities begin.

CHAPTER 12

Thursday, July 23, 2009—Rogers County Courthouse

The murder trial of Scottie Pinkerton was held in the largest courtroom in the Rogers County Courthouse.

In the not-too-distant past, the county jail was housed on the third floor. But shortly after the turn of the century, a new detention facility was built across the street from the courthouse. Once the new jail was completed, District Judge Rodney McClintock remodeled the penthouse to accommodate a new courtroom. No expense had been spared to make it one of the finest courtrooms in the state.

The entryway consisted of two large and finely handcrafted oak doors with the scales of justice carved into the wood of each door at eye level. Upon opening the doors, one could see the jury box on the far left with twelve of Rogers County's citizens sitting inside. Panning right, there were two ornately carved wooden tables on each side of the main floor; both tables were surrounded by leather office chairs, all occupied. After walking through the doors, the large area at the back of the room, containing pews for spectators and the press, became more visible. At the front of the room was the judge's bench where the Honorable Judge Rodney McClintock sat high above the fray.

The table closest to the jury was the prosecutor's table where attorney Ian Battel sat in the first chair. Battel was the Rogers County first assistant district attorney, acting as the lead attorney for the trial. Battel was born to an Irish mother and a German father. Both were first-generation immigrants, and Battel's father taught him German as a child. Consequently, Battel sometimes drifted into German curse words when he was extremely irritated.

Battel had been a prosecutor for more than twenty-five years and had tried hundreds of cases in front of a jury. A salt-and-pepper Fu Manchu adorned his upper lip, and he was rarely seen outside of the courtroom without a cigarette in his mouth. The local defense bar respected Battel's intellect, trial skills, and, more importantly to some, his willingness to laugh at himself just as easily as he could laugh at them.

Next to him was Randall "Buck" Reynolds. Reynolds was the Rogers County District Attorney. He was a handsome man in his early fifties, who had held the office for several years. Since the position was determined by a county wide election, Reynolds was more of a politician than a trial attorney. On the weekends, he ran a cattle ranch in the northeastern portion of the county.

Reynolds sat at counsel table in a bolo tie, with his black felt cowboy hat resting on the table in front of him throughout the entire trial. Occasionally, he would lean over and feign giving advice to Battel, but even the jurors quickly figured out this was Battel's trial to win or lose.

The only reason Reynolds chose to be there was the local news cameras waiting in the hallway. Whenever the court took a break, he always led the prosecution team out the door. Thus, he made himself front and center and easily accessible for interviews with the TV stations in the hallway. Of course, he always wore his hat on TV.

The third person at the prosecutor's table was Deputy Andrew Blackburn, dressed in his brown deputy uniform and with his Carl Grimes-style hat sitting in front of him. Battel had chosen Deputy Blackburn to represent law enforcement because he was the first officer on the scene and the lead investigator on the case.

At the defense table sat two men: Scottie Pinkerton and James Hixon, Scottie's court-appointed attorney.

Hixon was in his late forties, overweight, with a balding dome that he tried to comb over with four long strands of hair. He was wearing a suit similar to the JC Penney's special that Scottie's mother had bought her son to wear during the trial. Hixon did not exude the aura of a great defense attorney to the jurors, or to anyone else in the courtroom for that matter. He had been a public defender in Rogers County for as long as anyone could remember, and if you asked Hixon, he was a great trial attorney. However, his record wouldn't support that boast and neither would the other lawyers, who considered him arrogant and lazy.

Sitting on the bench was the Honorable Judge McClintock. Judge McClintock was a dark-complexioned man of Italian and Native American heritage, sporting a completely bald head and a chiseled jaw. He was known to occasionally lose his temper when attorneys didn't act appropriately in his courtroom, but he was always spot on with his legal rulings—both when he had time to review written briefs and when he had to make the spur-of-the-moment decisions required of a judge during trial.

Judge McClintock spoke first, addressing the jurors. "Ladies and gentlemen of the jury, now is the time for the attorneys on each side of this case to give their opening statements. Please remember that their opening statements are not evidence; after the opening statements, each side will be allowed to present evidence. At this point, each attorney will provide you a synopsis of what they believe the evidence will show. The actual evidence will come from the witness stand, through testimony, and other documents or photos admitted throughout the trial. Once again, please do not consider anything that either one of these fine attorneys says as evidence. Thank you." He then turned to the prosecution table. "Mr. Battel, you may begin."

Battel stood up, grabbed his notepad, and adjusted his blue pinstripe suit. He began by introducing himself to the jury. He then introduced the other two gentlemen sitting at the prosecutor's table. Next, he approached the jury box. Once he stood in front of the twelve jurors, Battel read the charge against Scottie Pinkerton: "Murder in the First Degree resulting in the death of Ashley Pinkerton."

He paused a few seconds before saying, "Ladies and gentlemen, I would like to thank you for being here. I know plenty of people in today's society do not wish to ever sit on a jury panel, much less a panel for a murder case that could result in the death penalty. So, I myself, Mr. Reynolds, the judge, and even the defendant all appreciate your willingness to participate in this case. Without jurors, our judicial system could not work. You are an indispensable part of the American criminal justice system." Battel smiled graciously at the attentive jury.

"As I said earlier, my name is Ian Battel, and I am the attorney for the State of Oklahoma. Right now, we are at the first stage of trial. If you find the defendant guilty of first-degree murder, then there will be a second stage. At the second stage, you will decide the appropriate punishment for the crime of first-degree murder. As you know from the voir dire questioning, the state will be asking you at the second stage to sentence the defendant to death. However, before we can ever get to that point, you must first consider the guilt, or innocence, of the defendant. Hence, the first stage will be purely about whether I, on behalf of the State of Oklahoma, can prove beyond a reasonable doubt that the defendant murdered his wife, Ashley Pinkerton, with premeditated malice in the first degree. At the conclusion of all the evidence of this first stage, I believe the State of Oklahoma will have proven its case, and I will ask you to return with a verdict of guilty against Mr. Scottie Pinkerton."

Steve could imagine Battel pacing slowly while making eye contact with individual jurors, shifting his attention to a different one after four or five seconds, rotating through the jury to let them know of his sincerity but also to eye up which members were paying attention. They would be key when deliberations came.

"I expect the evidence in this case to tell the story of an abusive husband who finally, tragically, went too far. You will first hear testimony from Brent Whitmore, the victim's brother. Mr. Whitmore will tell you that he talked to his sister on the telephone the morning she was murdered. He will tell you that the defendant was not home during this phone call because the defendant played golf every Saturday morning. Mr. Whitmore will tell you that during this phone conversation, the victim informed him that she had recently discovered that her husband, the defendant Scottie Pinkerton, was having an affair. Mr. Whitmore will further testify that the victim told him she planned on confronting the defendant when he got back to the house after his golf game. Additionally, Mr. Whitmore will tell you that he never liked the defendant and always felt like the defendant mistreated his baby sister."

"Next, you will hear from Heather Walters, a close friend of the victim. Ms. Walters will tell you that she and the victim had been friends since they first met as kids at the Justus-Tiawah School just outside of town. Ms. Walters will tell you that Ashley told her she was not happy in her marriage, that the defendant was mean to her. She will tell you that she saw the defendant yell at Ashley on many occasions and that she felt the defendant couldn't control his temper. Ms. Walters will tell you that she never really trusted the defendant or thought he was right for the victim."

"After Ms. Walters's testimony, you will hear from the victim herself. Obviously, Ashley Pinkerton will not be walking into the courtroom because she was found dead on her living room floor on August 9, 2008. What you will hear is her voice on a recording of the 911 call she made just five and a half minutes before Sheriff Deputy Blackburn arrived at her home to find her bleeding from thirty-eight total stab and slash wounds to her chest, back, arms, hands, and torso. In the 911 call, you will hear the victim, Ashley Pinkerton, screaming for help. You will hear the victim, Ashley Pinkerton, telling the 911 operator that her husband, the defendant, had just hit her. You will hear the victim, Ashley Pinkerton, say that she had escaped the defendant's clutches and rushed to the bedroom and locked the door behind her." Battel's voice began to rise, and his tempo of speech quickened as he continued, "You will then hear the victim, Ashley Pinkerton, scream that the defendant was in a violent rage and had just broken through the locked door!"

Battel paused for two seconds, meeting the eyes of the jury. "You will then hear the line go dead." He stood silently for a minute after this last statement to let the information sink in.

"Next, you will hear the testimony of Rogers County Deputy Sheriff Andrew Blackburn. Deputy Blackburn was the first officer on the scene that fateful morning. Deputy Blackburn will describe how he found Ashley lying on the floor in a pool of blood. He will testify that he immediately radioed for an ambulance and more help as he began to search the home to ensure that whoever had done this to the victim, Ashley Pinkerton, was not still present. Deputy Blackburn will tell you that the only other person he found in the home was seven-month-old Gabriel Scottie, the couple's baby boy. Deputy Blackburn will then testify that, once he secured the home for his safety and the safety of young Gabriel, he went back to the victim, Ashley Pinkerton, and attempted to wrap towels around her body to slow the bleeding. He will state that he performed CPR in hopes of keeping her alive until the paramedics arrived. Unfortunately, the victim's wounds were too severe and the victim, Ashley Pinkerton, passed away while Deputy Blackburn tried to save her. Deputy Blackburn will also testify about the seven-inch butcher knife he found covered in blood beside the victim, Ashley Pinkerton. This is that very knife."

Battel held up a sealed plastic bag containing a large butcher knife with a wooden handle. Through the bag, the jurors could see the blade was covered in blackish-red stains. The knife itself was the kind found in any common kitchen block set.

"As the first deputy on the scene, Deputy Blackburn was assigned to investigate the murder. After he explains what he experienced first-hand that morning, he will walk you through his investigation. You will see pictures that he took of the crime scene and the victim. In those pictures, you will see bloody footprints near Ashley's body. He will tell you that the shoes which made those prints were found in a field nearby and that they belonged to the defendant. In sum, he will explain to you how all of the pieces fit together, pointing to the one man who killed Ashley Pinkerton."

Battel turned from the jury to point at Scottie Pinkerton and, with a raised voice, said, "That man, the defendant. Scottie. Wayne. Pinkerton!" Battel stood for a few seconds more with his arm outstretched and finger pointing, glaring at Scottie, before he continued.

"After Deputy Blackburn's testimony, Dr. Pendleton, the state's medical examiner, will take the stand. Dr. Pendleton will tell you that the victim, Ashley Pinkerton, suffered thirty-eight different knife wounds to her torso and upper body. He will describe several slashes to her hands and arms that are what medical experts generally consider 'defensive wounds.' They are wounds that, through proper investigation and training, a medical examiner can testify occur when a victim tries to stop his or her assailant from stabbing or cutting them with a knife. Dr. Pendleton will testify that he is medically certain that the victim, Ashley Pinkerton, attempted to defend herself during the knife attack. This evidence, proving she was alive and conscious during the assault, will be more important at the second stage when you consider whether or not the death penalty is warranted."

"He will also tell you that in addition to the defensive slashes, there were twenty-three actual stab wounds to her body. Dr. Pendleton will testify as to the depth of each wound and the amount of force it took to make said wounds. He will tell you, based on his experience, that it took great force to make these wounds—that this was no accident. Of the twenty-three stabbing points, he will tell you that eight were lethal. Due to the high number of penetrations, he will not be able to tell you which exact wound was the cause of her death, but he will tell you he is medically certain Ashley Pinkerton's death was caused by the stabbings.

Lastly, Dr. Peterson will testify that he found skin tissue from another human under Ashley's fingernails."

"Next, you will hear from Dr. Feinstein, a DNA expert. He will testify that the skin found under the victim, Ashley Pinkerton's, fingernails belonged to the defendant, Scottie Pinkerton."

"The last witness the state will call to the stand will be Officer Glen Matthews. He is the officer who arrested the defendant. Officer Matthews will inform you that he apprehended the defendant roughly forty-five minutes after the original 911 call. The arrest occurred at a local hotel, an approximate ten-minute drive from the murder scene. He will further state that when he arrested the defendant, the defendant had visible scratches on his face and neck. You will see pictures of the defendant taken when he was booked into jail. The pictures will show these marks. Moreover, Officer Matthews will testify the defendant had just showered when they arrested him, which is why the police were unable to find any blood on the defendant."

"These are the witnesses you will hear from in the state's case in chief. The defense may call additional witnesses; that is up to them."

Battel kept his attention on the jury, sparing no glance toward the defendant at this point. "Regardless, ladies and gentlemen of the jury, after you have heard the testimony of all the witnesses and seen all of the evidence, I believe the evidence will show beyond a reasonable doubt that, on August 9, 2008, the defendant, Scottie Pinkerton, attacked his wife with a kitchen knife, slashing and stabbing her over thirty times, resulting in her death! At that point, based on all you have seen and heard, I will ask that you find the defendant, Scottie Pinkerton, guilty of first-degree murder. Thank you."

***

Steve stared down at the transcript. He was beginning to think it was clear Scottie killed his wife. He was only hoping, at this point, the judge or Battel made some constitutional error egregious enough to require a reversal.

But then, he remembered the challenge Scottie had given him—to find a way to believe Scottie was innocent.

Steve reminded himself that opening statements were not evidence; he needed to read the entire transcript and review all of the evidence before making any decisions. Moreover, he remembered from trial practice class that, sometimes, attorneys made statements in opening that they failed to prove later. Steve reread the prosecution's entire opening statement again and again. If Battel had said something he later failed to prove, it might give him an argument for prosecutorial misconduct.

Next came the opening statement of court-appointed defense attorney, Jason Hixon.

***

Jason Hixon stood up and buttoned his ill-fitting jacket. His tie was loosely fastened around his neck and the bottom of it peeked out below the edge of his coat. Hixon began his opening statement by thanking the jurors, then said:

"Obviously there is a great deal of evidence against my client at this stage. I just ask you remember the state must prove beyond a reasonable doubt that my client murdered his wife. After you find him guilty, I ask that at the second stage you pay a great deal of attention to the mitigating evidence showing why my client should not be given the death penalty. In all honesty, this case is undoubtedly about the second stage. Thank you."

Finally, Steve thought. A little something for me to argue in the brief. There may be an ineffective assistance of counsel claim here.

Steve knew that it was every attorney's duty to defend their client, no matter how much evidence may be stacked against them. In his opening statement, Hixon had essentially conceded Scottie was guilty of murdering his wife.

The appellate court might find this to be constitutionally ineffective representation. However, to succeed on a claim of ineffective assistance of counsel, the petitioner must be able to show Scottie would have been acquitted if not for Hixon's poor representation. Although the issue may not be a winner, he thought it was still worth arguing.

Steve tore off a new sheet of paper from his notepad and labeled it "Claims for Relief." He then wrote "1. Ineffective assistance." Steve remembered that most capital habeas briefs at the federal district court level would contain fifteen to twenty claims for relief. He went ahead and numbered to twenty, hoping the empty spots would magically spur him on to decipher more claims.

After the opening statements, as Battel had foretold, came the first two witnesses—Brent Whitmore and Heather Walters. Each fulfilled their role of establishing Scottie as an abuser, and each stated they never trusted Scottie. Next was the tape.

Rather than read the transcript, Steve found the zip drive containing the defense copy of the recording and played it for himself. He wanted to hear what the jury heard.

***

(August 9, 2008, 9:57 a.m.)

911: 911. What is your emergency?

Ashley: (crying) My husband just attacked me. I had to claw his eyes just to get him off of me.

911: What is your address?

Ashley: 5260 E. 420 Road, Claremore.

911: Is your husband still in the house?

Ashley: Yes! Hurry, please!

911: Where are you?

Ashley: After I scratched his face. I ran into our bedroom. I'm in here with the door locked. I need help!

911: Okay, stay where you are. Stay on the line. I am dispatching a Rogers County sheriff to your address.

Ashley: (screaming loudly) OH MY GOD! He kicked in the door. Ple—

(End of call)

***

Steve felt chills run down his spine. How can Scottie think anyone would believe he didn't kill Ashley after listening to this recording?

He ran through the information he got from the recording. The husband and wife were clearly fighting before the call was made. She was audibly upset during the call, and a little more than five minutes after the call terminated, Sheriff Deputy Blackburn found her lying on the living room floor, bleeding to death from multiple stab wounds all over her body.

However, Steve reminded himself of the first rule of jury trials, the plea every good defense attorney always asked of the jury during voir dire or opening statement. It was a simple request:

Each juror should hold off on making any final decisions until all of the evidence has been submitted. Steve knew the state always started with their best evidence to try and convince the jury of guilt before the defense ever got a chance to present evidence. He was now doing exactly what a juror was not supposed to do—making a decision before he heard both sides of the story.

Steve made himself consider the possibility that Scottie hadn't been the one who stabbed Ashley Pinkerton thirty-eight times. He listened to the tape again.

He sat forward when he finally heard it; or, rather, when he didn't.

If they were in this huge fight, why isn't Scottie yelling at her? Why wasn't there a big noise when he kicked in the door?

Steve opened his copy of the transcripts and began reading what occurred at trial after the jury heard the 911 call. The next witness would be Deputy Blackburn. Steve could tell from the Table of Contents that Deputy Blackburn's testimony was well over three hundred pages. He looked at the clock on his microwave. It read 2:38 a.m. His eyes suddenly grew heavy. He yawned.

As much as he wanted to relive Deputy Blackburn's testimony, Steve knew there was no way he could finish the entirety of it that night, and it was not something he wanted to read in parts. He closed the transcript and set his pen down on the notepad. The deputy's story would have to wait until morning.

CHAPTER 13

Steve was startled when he looked over and saw 9:37 on his bedside clock. He rarely set his alarm on the weekend and usually slept in until sometime between 8:00 a.m. and 8:30 a.m. He felt groggy; he brewed a cup of coffee and took it with him as he left for the gym.

A good workout always energized him on days when his mind and body had other ideas. When he returned home, Steve pulled out one of his premade lunches of grilled chicken and asparagus from the refrigerator, poured a glass of orange juice, and sat down at the kitchen table with the trial transcripts. The first line he read was from Battel: "Your Honor, I call Rogers County Sheriff's Deputy Andrew Blackburn to the stand."

Seeing the deputy's name, Steve involuntarily looked up trying to figure out why that name sounded familiar. Then it hit him. Deputy Blackburn was the cop who had killed Dominick Harrison outside of Claremore two days ago.

The shooting caused a nationwide stir. Members of civil rights organizations, alongside their national and community leaders, were on their way to Oklahoma and encouraging others to protest. Some marches and protests had already begun, and press conferences were being held. The small Oklahoma town was heating up and becoming the center of a national debate. Steve turned back to the transcripts.

After Deputy Blackburn was sworn in, he gave his name and testified to his training and experience as a peace officer. Once again, Steve's imagination took him back in time to the Rogers County courtroom.

* * *

July 27, 2009—Rogers County Courtroom

Battel stood near the far end of jury looking forward at Deputy Blackburn, again dressed in uniform, on the stand; thereby nonverbally focusing their attention towards the testimony.

"Now, please tell us what happened the morning of August 9, 2008," Battel prompted.

"A call came in from dispatch that there was a possible domestic abuse situation with the perpetrator still in the home," Deputy Blackburn explained. "At the time, I was sitting in the parking lot of the Racino—the Cherokee Racetrack and Casino. I had just finished up a call where someone was causing a disturbance at the Racino about twenty minutes prior to this dispatch."

"I was sitting in my car, filling out an incident report on my laptop while keeping an eye on the handful of Saturday morning gamblers strolling into the facility. After dispatch gave me the location of the crime, I turned on my lights and drove north as fast as I safely could towards the home."

"A few minutes later, I arrived at 5260 E. 420 Road. The house itself is about a quarter mile up the driveway from the main road. As I drove up the driveway, I saw a one-story ranch-style home. There was a pink Volkswagen bug parked in the driveway and no other cars in sight. I stopped my vehicle and radioed dispatch to let them know I had arrived at the location."

"After confirming that I was at the right address, I got out and approached the house. I could see through the storm door that the main front door was open. I knocked loudly on the screen door and yelled, 'Sheriff's department, anyone here?' After a few seconds, I knocked and yelled again. When I heard no response,

I cautiously entered the residence."

"That was when I saw her. In the middle of the living room, I saw a woman, whom I knew to be Ashley Pinkerton, we had gone to high school at about the same time and we both lived in Claremore our whole lives. She was lying on the floor, covered in blood. I immediately radioed dispatch, told them what I saw, and asked for an ambulance and backup. Before I administered any first aid, I drew my gun and quickly searched the home to see if the perpetrator was still in the residence. Based on my training and experience, I knew that I needed to secure the location before I could help her."

"The only other person in the house was a baby. He was in his crib, crying. I knew it was a boy from the way they had decorated his room. The baby appeared safe, so I went back to the woman on the living room floor. At this point, since I had cleared the house, I holstered my firearm and began performing first aid on the victim. She was bleeding profusely."

"First, I found some towels in a kitchen drawer and tried to slow the bleeding as best I could. I was hoping to keep her loss of blood down as much as possible. It seemed as if she was bleeding from every part of her body. When I began CPR, each pump I made on her chest pushed blood out from the wounds all over her. I soon realized she was dead, likely gone before I even touched her."

"I radioed dispatch to let the ambulance driver know she had passed and that the ambulance did not need to rush. I then went to the master bedroom and pulled the duvet cover off the bed and placed it over the victim. During the entire process, I tried to disturb as little of the house as possible because I knew this was now a murder scene. I didn't want to ruin any evidence that could help later in my investigation."

"Then why did you place a cover on the victim?" interrupted Battel. "Couldn't that affect the scene?"

"Yes, it could," Deputy Blackburn answered. "But the baby was in the house, crying. I had a sense he knew something bad had happened to his mother. Maybe he had heard the fight, the yelling and screaming—the tussle that led to his mom's death. I don't know, but whatever it was, my instincts told me that I needed to get that baby out of the house. I didn't want him to see his mother dead on the floor, so I covered her before I went and got him."

"I carried him out to the street and held him until child welfare workers from the Department of Human Services arrived. For some reason, holding that baby and keeping him calm made me feel like I was helping his dead mother, despite the fact I wasn't able to save her life. It still bothers me to this day that I didn't get there sooner or do something more to save her."

"The only solace I have is that I brought comfort to that little boy for her." The deputy began to tear up during this part of his testimony. He stopped talking, took several deep breaths and then continued.

"After several minutes, the ambulance, other officers, and, finally, the Child Protective Services worker arrived. During this time, officers had run the husband through our databases and determined what type of vehicle he drove through registration records. Every officer in the county was looking for his red pickup truck."

"Shortly after I handed the baby over to the child welfare worker, I received a call that they believed Scottie was in a room at a hotel just east of Claremore. It was the closest hotel between the house and town. Scottie's car had been spotted in the parking lot. A City of Claremore police officer, Officer Mathews, confirmed with the hotel management that Scottie had rented a room the day before."

"The jury will hear from Officer Mathews a little bit later in the trial," Battel said. "Please continue with what you did next."

"I went back inside and began my investigation. I asked some officers to tape off the outside of the house while I began taking pictures inside."

Battel held up a stack of photos and asked, "Your Honor, may I approach the witness?"

"You may," Judge McClintock responded.

Battel presented the photos to Deputy Blackburn. "Are these the photos you took that day?"

"Yes," Deputy Blackburn answered.

"Are they true and correct representations of the house and the victim as they appeared that day?"

"Yes."

Battel took the photos from Deputy Blackburn and handed them to the judge.

"Your Honor, I move to admit exhibits one through fifty-seven into evidence."

"Does the defense have any objections?" Judge McClintock asked while looking through the photographs.

"None, Your Honor," Hixon replied.

"Very well. They will be admitted."

Battel took the photographs back from Judge McClintock and approached the jury box. "Ladies and gentlemen of the jury, since these pictures are now a part of the evidence, you are allowed to see them. I must warn you that some of these images are very graphic in nature."

He handed the stack of photographs to the juror sitting nearest the witness stand. She looked at the first picture and passed it on. Eventually, all of the photos worked their way around the jury box.

＊

Steve imagined how normal citizens would react to the photos. He had enough trouble looking at them despite two years of death penalty work under his belt. Some jurors probably looked quickly and turned away, passing them on without hesitation. Others would take their time to digest the bloody scene.

After Deputy Blackburn's direct testimony was Hixon's cross-examination. As Steve read through the transcript—still following his client's directive to believe he was not guilty—Steve's serious expression deepened into a frown; Hixon's questioning left a lot to be desired. Steve himself had several questions that were simply not asked, and thus, never answered.

Did Deputy Blackburn see anyone else near the home when he arrived?

Did Ashley say anything before she passed that could have pointed them to someone other than her husband as the killer? Did she say anything at all?

Where did he find the knife?

Deputy Blackburn was the first officer on the scene; his testimony should have given clues as to who the real killer was if it wasn't Scottie. Without answers to these questions and many others, that mystery still remained.

Instead of providing new information, Hixon's questions simply allowed Deputy Blackburn to recite his story a second time for the jury. However, this time, Blackburn took the opportunity to mention the knife, saying that he had to move the knife in order to perform CPR on the victim. At least that question was answered—not in a particularly helpful way, but answered, nonetheless.

As Steve flipped through the next several pages of the cross-examination, he concluded that, although Hixon was not doing a great job, the attorney's incompetency likely wouldn't qualify as "ineffective assistance" in accordance with how the United States Supreme Court defined the term.

Steve shot a text to Ackerman: When you have a few minutes, could I run something by you?

Two minutes later, the phone rang.

"How may I be of assistance to you, counselor," Ackerman said.

"I'm reading through the transcripts in this Scottie case, and Hixon didn't even cross the detectives and officers except with open questions that just let them repeat their directs. God-awful representation, but I'm not sure it rises to the level of Strickland v. Washington."

"Well, let's talk through it," Ackerman said. "Explain to me the holding in Strickland. In your own words," he added.

Steve grinned despite the circumstances; he knew this was another quiz by the master. "Well, the Strickland court determined that, in order for representation to be deemed constitutionally ineffective and requiring a new trial, the person raising the issue on appeal must meet a two-pronged test. First, the appellant must show counsel's performance fell below an objective standard of reasonableness. Second, he or she must also demonstrate that if counsel had performed adequately, the result would have been different. I think there is a solid argument for that first prong. Hixon's representation was almost nonexistent."

"I'm not surprised," Ackerman replied. "And the second?"

"Well, as we discussed before, there is a mountain of evidence against him. I don't know if any attorney in the state could have gotten him off."

"No offense taken," Ackerman said dryly.

Steve chuckled. "Present company excluded," he acquiesced before continuing. "Anyway, I have a concern, a real strong concern about convincing the district or appellate judges that anyone, even you, could have kept Scottie from being convicted. Which means the appellate courts will have to deny a request for a new trial based on ineffective assistance of counsel because the result would have likely been the same, even with solid representation."

Steve sighed. The line was quiet for a few seconds while he sat for what seemed like hours and stared into nothingness.

Finally, Ackerman cleared his throat. "Don't ever forget, if you don't win this case, your client will be executed. At the end of the day, it might be that you cannot win this case; it certainly is a tough one. I have lost cases and watched clients be put to death. I assure you that it is a feeling to which you will never get accustomed and, despite handling cases with insurmountable odds, if your client dies, you will suffer guilt that will never leave you."

Steve nodded somberly to himself.

"To minimize the time spent lying awake and replaying your every move and decision, which will be inevitable if you continue to take on these cases, you must scrutinize every scrap of evidence, every word in the transcripts, every word not in the transcripts. Every corner of every photograph. If the second prong is out there, you have to find it."

Steve looked over at the box of photographs. "Understood. I'm on it."

During his two years working for judges, Steve dreaded this

part the most—detailed photographs from all angles and ranges of the surroundings, the murder scenes, the victims.

The pictures of Ashley Pinkerton's dead body covered in blood were as gruesome as Steve had imagined, and the blackish-red stains splattered throughout the living room made the room look like a bad Jackson Pollock forgery. Steve thought back to all of the pictures of dead bodies he had looked at over those two years—exactly twenty-four cases, with two of them including separate murder scenes, for a total of twenty-six murder scenes and thirty-two dead bodies. Scenes where it appeared that the perpetrators had rushed away quickly. Scenes where he could tell the murderer had lingered after their victim's death. Some with lots of blood, some with none, but always with a body and a face contorted with death.

The images had looked eerily fake to him, almost like a Hollywood movie scene, as if the body and blood had been staged to lay in just the right manner, yet at the same time they were unmistakably real because the cold reality was that they weren't fake. The pictures Steve had seen were of real people.

As much as a part of his mind wanted him to think the scenes were staged, the visceral truth of the pictures always surfaced. The reality often hit him in the middle of the night when, for one reason or another, Steve just couldn't sleep. Now, he wondered if Ackerman would also lie awake at the same time, for the same reason, and if, despite their best efforts, the two of them were merely two legal ships struggling to stay afloat in unforgiving seas.

Despite his apprehension, Steve knew he had to look closely at every detail in every picture. He had to study each one to see if something stuck out to him which would even hint that his client was not the murderer. Any chance of winning this case depended upon it.

Steve had been trying to persuade himself to believe Scottie's words, but the truth was, deep down, Steve was nearly convinced his client had killed his wife that summer day. The evidence was overwhelming. The 911 call proving there was an altercation minutes before the police arrived, the scratches on Scottie's body, particles of his skin and blood found under Ashley's fingernails, even the fact Scottie had showered before police arrived. Additionally, the pictures showed the bloody footprints on the floor matching the pair of bloody shoes that Scottie owned and that were found near the crime scene. It all added up to Scottie Pinkerton being the killer. There was nothing tangible to support his client's claim of innocence, except his word.

Then, Steve saw it! He wondered how no one had noticed it before, but then he realized that he was probably the first person to truly look for something other than proof of Scottie's guilt. He knew perspective often replaced reality in these investigations. He turned to his computer and excitedly pounded on the keys.

First, he prepared a motion asking the court to appoint him an investigator to assist him on the case. If Scottie had not committed the crime, then he needed to find out who did. Although Steve felt confident in his knowledge of death penalty law, he had no investigative training whatsoever. Moreover, as much as he preferred to work alone, in this instance he knew that he needed help.

Second, he typed a letter to the prison requesting a barrier-free and restraint-free visit with Scottie as soon as possible. Steve knew that, with this evidence, he could convince Scottie he believed in his innocence, and Scottie would tell him everything he knew about that day and the events leading up to it.

CHAPTER 14

As Steve finished typing his request to the court to appoint an investigator, he realized that, just like how all attorney appointments were not equal, investigator appointments were not equal either. He wondered if Ackerman had any advice on this front.

Too fired up to text and wait, Steve picked up the phone and called Ackerman. "Hello, Frank, this is Steve again. How have you been? I know it's been ages since we last spoke."

Ackerman chuckled. "I'm great, just sitting here in my great room, in front of a roaring fire, playing board games with a few of the grandkids. You know how much I love getting to spend time with them."

"Yes, very sorry to bother you again on a Saturday, especially since you have your favorite little visitors," Steve said. "I won't keep you long. I just have one quick question."

"Don't be foolish, as I've told you before, I'm always willing to help a fellow lawyer in his attempt to find a little justice in this damn state. You sound better than you did on the last call, fire away?"

"I think I might have something on the second prong of Strickland. Going back through the photos, I honestly think there is a good chance he is innoce—"

"You mean you didn't get scared off by the DNA, 911 call, bloody shoes, and all the other evidence the state presented?" Ackerman asked, sounding more amused than confused.

"Well, it certainly scared me, but not off. There is a ton of evidence pointing to him, but I honestly believe he didn't do it," Steve continued. "Based on what I have found so far, I plan on asking the court to appoint me an investigator. I need someone who can go out and try to find the real killer. I know you have worked with every investigator in the state, and I am hoping you could give me a name to request in my motion."

"Well, you can't officially request a specific investigator. If you ask for a name the judge will give you someone else just to prove who is in charge. That said, you need Harold Thomas," Ackerman said emphatically. "Most everyone calls him 'Booger,' though the reason for that is a story you must hear from the man himself. Anyway, he is the best in the business. Not afraid to get his hands dirty, if you know what I mean. Moreover, if you convince him of Scottie's innocence, he will put in extra time for free beyond the court's limited budgeted amount. You know the court will only pay those guys for a few hours of work. If you get the wrong one, then that is all the time they will put into your case. Booger, on the other hand, is one of the real good guys in the business. If your boy is innocent, he won't sleep until he finds the truth."

"Thank you very much, Frank. I knew you would know the person I needed to request. Take care and enjoy the rest of your weekend."

"No problem, son. One last thing, I would suggest you go talk to him before you file the motion. He runs an auto body repair shop just north of Pine Street on Lewis. If he wants in, he can find a way to make sure he gets appointed and you just file the motion without naming anyone. Not sure how he does what he does, but that man is a real wizard. Good luck."

The call ended, then Steve immediately searched "Harold Thomas Auto Body Tulsa" on his phone. Nothing but chain body shops came up. Then he tried "Booger Auto Body Tulsa." Sure enough, Booger's Auto Body and Detail Shop came up with an address on

North Lewis Avenue. The business was open on Saturdays until five. Steve rushed to get ready and properly dressed. In a matter of minutes, he was in his car and heading to the location on his GPS.

On the drive over, he rehearsed the pitch he was about to make to Harold "Booger" Thomas. Steve knew, based on Ackerman's emphatic recommendation, that he must get this man to work on the case.

When he pulled up, Booger's Auto Body and Detail Shop looked much like Steve had expected. It showed signs of being an old, full-service gas station before Booger had turned it into an auto body repair shop. Steve parked next to a concrete island out front, where the pumps clearly used to be located.

He observed the front of the station, which had been transformed into a building containing four garage bays. The two middle ones were open. The back and side yards were fenced in by an eight-foot-tall chain link with four rows of barbed wire angled outward along the top. Several wrecked cars were parked within the fenced-in area.

As Steve approached the open garage bays, the odor of Bondo and paint flooded his nostrils. Standing at the front end of a red 1982 Camaro Z28 was a tall black man wearing a mask and holding a spray gun in his right hand. He was focused on the job at hand.

"Hello!" Steve yelled to get his attention.

The man calmly lowered the mask and looked up from his work at Steve. Booger was much older than Steve, being in his late fifties or early sixties, with gray curls interspersed throughout his head and facial hair. Despite his great age, the man still looked wise beyond his years.

"How can I help you?" he asked.

"Hello, Mr. Thomas, my name is Steve Hanson. I am a criminal defense attorney here in Tulsa," Steve said as he walked forward and extended his hand. "I need an investigator on a death penalty case, and Frank Ackerman said you are the best in the state. Would you like to help me save the life of an innocent man?"

Booger accepted the handshake even as he shook his head and chuckled. "I haven't had anyone call me Mr. Thomas in a long time. So, you know Ackerman, do you? One hell of a lawyer he is, and an even better man" Booger said with a smile that showed his appreciation and respect for the old warhorse. "But I'm out of the investigating game. Excuse my language, but I've simply gotten too old for that shit."

"Well, I promise not to get you into any danger," Steve said. "I just need someone to do some snooping around for me."

"Steve, was it?"

"Yes."

"Steve, that is what you damn lawyers always say before I get involved in something that ends up landing me in some precarious situation a short while later. If it's not an outright despicable situation, it's usually some type of physical danger to my person. If I end up helping you, I'll bet you a dollar you have to eat those words someday."

"Okay. Fair enough. It's a bet," Steve said with a grin. "Does that mean you'll help me?"

Booger sighed. "I'm not saying that just yet. I still need a little more information. You look a little too young and clean-cut to be working this type of a case. You look more like the type to be charging the oil companies big bucks for writing up contracts and eating at Mahogany's on the firm expense account every week. I suppose that means something happened to you when you were a kid to put you on the right path. Do you even have any idea what the hell you're doing?"

Steve was taken aback by Booger's quick assessment of him, "I am young, and, I'll admit, I did want to look put together when I met you. This is not my usual Saturday afternoon attire. That said, Judge Henry appointed me to represent a gentleman by the name of Scottie Pinkerton who is currently on death row. I worked as the capital habeas clerk at the federal court my first two years out of law school, so I know death penalty law inside and out. And I honestly think my client is innocent. But I don't have the investigative skills needed to find the real perpetrator and save Scottie's life."

"Damn, young man, there isn't an adult in this world truly innocent. I agree there are lots of people sitting in prison for crimes they didn't commit, but nobody is innocent! Besides..." a twinkle lit in Booger's eyes as he continued, "isn't that the dude that stabbed his wife about five thousand times?"

Steve nodded. Booger pulled his mask back up and turned to return to his work. Steve walked around to where Booger could see him and waved his arm.

"Please, just give me five minutes and if you still say no, I'll leave in peace."

Boogers shoulders dropped, "Tell me what you think you know about what happened,"

Steve asked, "Do you want the good news or the bad news first?"

"I've always considered myself a bit of an optimist, so give me the bad news first. That way, I have something positive to look forward to. Do you want something to drink? I have cold soda and beer."

"You have ginger ale?" Steve asked.

Booger just stared at him like an old man watching a child touch a low voltage electric fence.

"How about root beer?"

"That, I have. Take a seat." Booger went into the building to work the soda machine, and Steve sat down on a car seat from an old Rambler that was rigged-up out front. Booger came back with two opened bottles and sat down on a bench car seat. Might be from the back of an Oldsmobile 442, Steve thought.

"So, what do you have?" Booger asked.

"Well…" Steve took a swig. "Starting with the bad, like you asked. They have a 911 call from the wife saying he had attacked her, and the call was cut off after she said he was breaking down the door."

Booger took a drink. "And?"

"Bloody footprints matched his shoes, he took a shower right before the cops grabbed him so there was no blood on him at the time of arrest, scratches on his face, and she had his DNA under her fingernails—"

Booger held up a hand to interrupt him. "Stop, I don't want to hear any more right now. Mr. Hanson, when you said 'bad news,' you were putting it lightly. You were just getting started, and those are already the most damning facts I think I've ever heard in over thirty years of handling murder investigations—and I had one where the guy shot one of my young brothers while calling him the word I hate to hear more than any other. The whole thing was in front of five witnesses gassing up their cars, and all of it caught on the gas station camera."

He folded his arms, tilted his head back, and looked down his nose at Steve with his eyebrows raised. "What's the good news? Someone else confess? Because short of a confession from some other idiot, you aren't going to be able to convince me to waste my time helping you. And if you do have a confession from someone else, you don't need me anyway. Either way, sounds like I'm still retired." Booger stood up, put his mask back over his mouth and nose, and turned to face the red Camaro.

"Wait!"

Booger turned back toward Steve but didn't remove the mask again.

"I have two things that make me think he didn't do it," Steve said hurriedly. "Number one, when I met him, he said that he didn't do it. My whole life, I have been a very good judge of people, and when I talked to him, he just didn't seem like a murderer. There was something about the way he acted that made me believe deep down he didn't do it."

Booger pulled the mask down and interrupted Steve. "How many murderers you met in your life, young man? I would bet good money this was the first, because I have met several and only one seemed like a murderer; the only time I have ever truly been scared in my life was sitting in a room with that man."

He began to tremble and shake as he said, "I was on his side, he knew I was on his side, and it still scared the heck out of me to be anywhere near him. Thought he might snap my neck at any minute. He was a true sociopath. All the rest of them seemed like normal, everyday folk, even the ones where there were eyewitnesses and confessions. The guy I told you about earlier, he ended up crocheting me a real nice afghan. A decent guy on certain levels, he wasn't even a racist. Tough upbringing and a lot of other issues. Just had a very bad day, and that poor kid was unlucky enough to run into him at that moment."

Booger stared Steve down. "Your second issue better be stellar. I don't mean to be rude, but I've got plenty to do around here, and I would like to get back to it." He waved his hand at all the cars that needed work done in his shop.

Steve pulled three pictures out of his pocket. The pictures showed different angles of the interior of the Scottie's home taken by Deputy Blackburn during the investigation of Ashley's murder. As he showed Booger the pictures, Steve said, "Look closely. You remember I mentioned the 911 call? This morning, I was listening to the tape again and happened to be looking at these pictures at the same time. On the call, she says that Scottie had hit her, and she was locked in the bedroom. Right before the call cuts off, she screams that he had just kicked in the door."

Booger's jaw dropped. "The bedroom door in all of these photos is completely intact. Not a scratch. It's shut in this one and open in these other two. Are you sure there wasn't another room in the house she might have been inside during the call?"

"Yes, I'm positive," Steve replied. "The house only has three bedrooms: the master, the baby's room, and a guest room. I've looked at all the pictures and none of the doors in the house were busted. I just brought these three because they show the master bedroom door the most clearly."

"If your boy never busted a door in, then why did she say it on the call?"

"I don't know, but if she lied about the door, maybe she lied about him hitting her too? And who knows what else isn't as it seems with this case," Steve said.

You sure do have some interesting information, but like I said, I'm out of the investigation game. I would recommend you contact Mark Bailey or Glen Holden, they are both excellent investigators.

Steve continued for several minutes to try and convince Booger to join his team but eventually realized it wasn't going to happen.

CHAPTER 15

Steve spent Sunday finishing his review of the state's case in chief. As expected, Battel followed the script he had presented in his opening statement.

Dr. Peterson gave what amounted to a dry and boring recitation of the injuries sustained by Ashley. Since death was an element of every murder charge, the state had to prove beyond a reasonable doubt the victim died and how she died. Over the course of two hundred pages, Dr. Peterson left no doubt that Ashley's cause of death was loss of blood from the numerous knife wounds she sustained to her body.

Next was the DNA expert, Dr. Feinstein. Once again, the tedious nature of this testimony seeped through the court reporter's type-written recreation. She spent what was probably more than an hour detailing her own training and expertise. Following her self-introduction was two more hours explaining the procedures used to examine the skin discovered under Ashley's fingernails. The results confirmed that the skin beneath her nails came from Scottie's body.

Last to take the stand in the state's case in chief was Officer Matthews. After being sworn in, he testified that he found Scottie at the motel with wet hair and only a pair of shorts on. Matthews also testified that he could see scratches on Scottie's neck and face. Finally, Officer Matthews testified that Scottie didn't seem surprised they were there to arrest him.

There was nothing constitutionally defective about the testimony thus far, but there was one section that caught Steve's attention: the only time during the entire trial that Hixon had actually seemed to be defending Scottie.

***

August 4, 2009—Rogers County Courthouse

Officer Matthews sat on the stand, dressed in his Claremore Police Department uniform. By this time, he had been testifying for a couple of hours, but the young cop still appeared fresh and excited to be contributing to such a high-profile murder case.

"Was Scottie dressed when you arrested him?" Hixon asked.

"Yes. We knocked on the door. Announced who we were. He came out willingly," Matthews replied.

"What was he wearing?"

"As best I can recall. He had on an orange Oklahoma State Cowboys T-shirt and blue jeans."

"Was there blood anywhere on his clothing?"

"No."

"Did you find any clothes with blood on them?"

"Clothes? No. But a few weeks later, we did find a pair of bloody tennis shoes in a field near the home. A local rancher found them in a plastic Walmart bag. During the investigation, we were able to ascertain the shoes belonged to the defendant, Scottie."

"But no clothes? Correct?"

"Correct."

"No shirt?"

"Correct."

"No jeans or pants?"

"Correct."

"Did you search the hotel room and his vehicle for bloody clothing?"

"Yes."

"Let me show you what has been marked as state's exhibit thirty-six. This is a picture of the victim lying in the living room of her home." Hixon handed the photo to Matthews.

"Would you agree with me that there is a lot of blood around Mrs. Pinkerton?" asked Hixon.

"Yes," responded Matthews. "And you can even see in this photo the prints that matched the soles of the shoes we found in the field."

"Okay," Hixon continued. "And the shoes you found had blood on them?"

"Correct."

"Okay. So… what I want to know is if you would agree with me that, with that much blood, whomever did this would have had blood all over them? All over their clothes. Their shirt. Their pants. Wouldn't that be the case?"

"Objection," interrupted Battel. "That calls for expertise beyond what this witness has testified to. We would need a blood splatter expert to answer that question."

"Your Honor," Hixon said, "I am merely asking this man's lay opinion from looking at the pictures. When you look at this photo, I believe it is clear we don't need an expert to tell if blood would have gotten on the person who committed this crime."

"I am going to sustain the objection," McClintock said. "The jury has seen the photos; they can form their own lay opinions. I believe an expert would be necessary to give an opinion from the witness stand. I'd ask the jury to disregard the question as to this witness. Continue, Mr. Hixon, with a new line of questioning."

"Regardless of whether or not you think the perpetrator of this crime would have been covered in blood, the only clothing you found with blood on it was the running shoes discovered in the field?"

"Correct." Said Officer Mathews.

"No more questions, Your Honor," Hixon said as he sat down.

Battel stood up next. "How did you determine the tennis shoes you found were the same shoes that left the bloody footprints at the scene?"

"We were able to match the pattern from the shoes with the pattern in the floor," Matthews answered.

"How were you able to determine the shoes belonged to the defendant?"

"We found pictures of him wearing the shoes a week before the crime. Also, the shoes in the picture were never discovered in the residence."

"Anything else?" Battel prompted.

"The shoes we found were size nine-and-a-half. All of the other men's shoes found in the home were the same size. From this information, we deduced the bloody shoes belonged to Scottie."

"Since you found the shoes in a field near the home, would you assume the defendant disposed of the shoes and his other clothes on his way from the murder scene to the hotel?"

"Objection," interrupted Hixon. "Calls for speculation."

"Sustained. Members of the jury, you shall please disregard the last question," said Judge McClintock.

"No more questions, Your Honor," Battel said.

***

Of course not, Steve thought. You already made your point despite the judge's instruction. The jury is now thinking Scottie ditched the bloody shoes and clothes on his way to the hotel.

Steve added a number twelve to his list of possible claims for relief. Steve believed Judge McClintock's decision not to allow the testimony of Matthews regarding blood on the assailant's clothes was an error. The officer should have been allowed to give his lay opinion about the subject.

Will it be enough to win a new trial? Steve scrutinized the transcript. He didn't know if it was enough, but he did know that, at this point, he needed to look for even the slightest issue that might turn out to be the winning argument. He knew that in this line of work, it was his job to throw everything possible at the federal court and hope something triggered a favorable decision from the court. He remembered one case, when he was a clerk, where the judge he was working with made him thoroughly research an argument he himself did not think was very strong, but the judge ended up being right.

It was now late Sunday night, and Steve's review of the second stage of the trial would have to wait until another day.

A little over two weeks had passed since Steve had filed for the Court to appoint him a private investigator. As he sat in his living room hoping he would hear something soon, his doorbell rang.

"Mr. Thomas, what are you doing here? And how did you find my house?"

"First, did you forget I'm a private investigator? Moreover you don't cover your tracks at all. It took me about two minutes to find your address."

"Second, after you left thoughts of your case have been rattling around in my brain. This weekend I finally had time to do a little independent research. Once I discovered that racist asshole Deputy Blackburn was the investigative officer, I decided to take the case. Nothing I would love more than to show the world how incompetent he was in his investigation. You will be getting the order with my official appointment tomorrow, but I decided to swing by and get started."

Steve grinned widely and reached his hand out to welcome him to their new team. Booger entered and Steve started the process of bringing Booger up to speed on everything he had found.

The next morning Steve was able to amend his appointment request with Deputy Warden Gilcrease to add Booger to the list. Once she heard she was going to get to see Booger, she acquiesced immediately.

The team was now almost to the prison for their visit. "How many times you been to death row?" Booger asked as they veered right off of the Indian Nations Turnpike and followed the exit ramp that led to the prison.

"To be honest, this is only my second time. My last meeting with Scottie was my first time ever."

"Pretty amazing how they can legally keep these fellas in a modern-day dungeon. Everything but a stretching rack, huh?"

"Yeah," responded Steve, recalling the dismal conditions of H-Unit. "I know they call it a bunker, but I agree 'dungeon' seems to fit a lot better. I was more than a little disturbed by the conditions when I was last there. I can't imagine living in a cell underground, with the only sky you ever see being through those overhead grates for only an hour a day."

"Well, that is a legal fight for you to have another day. Today, we need to get Scottie's story and see how the pictures, testimony, and other evidence fits in with his version of what happened. I want you to do all the talking; that way, I can observe his body language freely. When I told you I can spot a lie a mile away, I wasn't kidding."

Steve nodded in agreement. There was no doubt in Steve's mind that the retired investigator was the equivalent of a human lie detector.

CHAPTER 16

When Steve and Booger arrived at the gate, the guard set his clipboard down, walked up to the window, and smiled broadly. "Booger! Haven't seen you here in a while. I saw your name on the list this morning and got excited to see you again. Thought you'd committed fully to your body shop?"

Booger smiled back. "Clarence, been a while. You still have that old Javelin? I don't recall you bringing it by my shop in the last few years."

"Yeah, well, that thing was a labor of love, and at some point, the labor exceeded the love. Sold it off to some guy from Texas." The guard shook his head before continuing. "Well, you know the drill, Booger. Park over there."

"Thanks, Clarence. Shame about the car."

Steve and Booger went through the same checkpoints, searches, and waivers that Steve had done the last time; but this time, instead of cold stares and little to no conversations, they got smiles and chit chat from at least one guard at each checkpoint. Booger greeted them with a smile and friendly conversation. Deputy Baldwin offered to catch up with Booger over some coffee, but the two of them wanted to get in with Scottie as quickly as possible so they declined.

Eventually, Steve and Booger were escorted into the same small room where Steve had met Scottie for the first time. Soon thereafter, the lock on the door clicked open, and Scottie Pinkerton walked in with his official escort; his hands and feet were free of chains, and he had a smile on his face. He became even happier when Steve introduced Booger, realizing the court had appointed an investigator to his case.

"So," Scottie said enthusiastically. "Maybe you aren't just another lazy, court- appointed lawyer. Getting an investigator is more than anyone else ever done."

"You said you would tell me what happened that day if I convinced you I believed you were innocent," Steve said as he reached into his briefcase. He pulled out the three photos he'd used to persuade Booger to join the case.

"Looking at these pictures is what made me believe you. As you can see, the bedroom door is still intact, which means you never kicked it in, which means if Ashley lied about that, maybe she lied about everything on that call."

"Ah!" Scottie exclaimed as he slammed his hand on the table. "You've got it! I tried to explain that I never harmed my wife to that bum, Hixon, but he wouldn't listen. You are exactly right, and Hixon would have found that out if he'd been paying attention. I told you I'm innocent."

"Well, now that I know you didn't bust down the door, tell me what happened the day your wife was murdered."

Scottie sat up in his seat and began to talk calmly. "I got up early that morning and went to the golf course for my usual Saturday morning round of golf. After I was done, I went straight home and—"

"That's a lie, Scottie!" Booger interrupted sharply. "If you lie to us one more time, I will drop this case. Don't you understand we are trying to save your life here, young man? The only chance we have to win this is if we know everything you know. Everything down to the smallest detail."

Booger stood up, as if he was going to leave, but stopped and glared at Scottie. "Do you understand?"

"Yes..." Scottie lowered his head. "Okay, okay. Please just sit back down. I will tell you the whole story, but I've never told anyone some of this, not in my whole life."

Booger sat back down.

Scottie's eyes fixated on his own shoes. "After I finished nine holes of golf, I went to see a woman. I was having an affair when all this happened."

"My entire adult life, I had a Saturday morning routine of playing a round of golf. For several months before Ashley was killed, I would meet this woman when I was supposed to be golfing. A round usually takes four hours, so I would play nine to make sure people saw me at the golf course and then meet her for the last two hours before I went home. I had rented a motel room the day before; we hooked up Friday afternoon and again that morning since checkout wasn't until noon."

Booger looked knowingly at Steve.

No one is truly innocent. The words Booger had spoken, when they first met, echoed in Steve's head as Scottie continued to speak.

"When I returned home from my little rendezvous, Ashley was on the phone with her brother. She was mad as all fuck. He'd gotten her all worked up. When she saw me, she immediately got off the phone and confronted me about the affair. She asked if I had been playing golf or been gone all morning to meet the other woman. I couldn't even answer before she was yelling and screaming and throwing stuff at me. She came at me and scratched my face and neck all up. I was scared she was going to hit me, or worse. It wouldn't have been the first time; she'd attacked me before, but I swear I never touched her. Not that day, not ever."

As Scottie said this last statement, he looked up to meet their watchful eyes.

Steve looked at Booger, who nodded to signal he believed the statement was true.

"She scratched me up pretty good, and then she got on the phone," Scottie said. "She screamed that she was going to punish me for cheating on her, that she was going to get me thrown in jail for the weekend. She called 911 and acted like I had attacked her. She ran to the bedroom with her phone in her hand and slammed the door, all while screaming hysterically to them that she was in danger."

Scottie took a deep breath "I just stood there in shock; I didn't know what to do. So, I left. I went to the hotel room and took a shower. The shower is where I like to think. Sitting in there with the hot water beating down on my head and just sort of letting everything go… it's how I focus on my problems. I planned on giving her time to calm down before going home to talk to her. I decided that I was going to end the affair and try to save our marriage. Ashley and I had drifted apart over the years. 'Maybe this is rock bottom,' I thought—the event that would wake us both up and get us back on track. The next thing I knew, the police were knocking on the door. When I opened it, they threw me down and arrested me for murder."

Steve asked, "Anything else you can remember from the fight?"

"No, not right now," Scottie responded.

"Who was the lady you were having relations with?" Booger asked.

Scottie squirmed and then looked up at Booger. "Heather Walters."

"The same Heather Walters who testified against you at trial?"

Steve asked as his voice rose.

"The same one," Scottie mumbled.

"Okay, so we have our first suspect," Booger mused. "Anyone else you can think of who could have done this?"

"Suspect?" Scottie started shaking his head. "There is no way Heather killed Ashley."

"Well, the fact she was your mistress is reason enough to make her a suspect. Any other ideas?"

Scottie scowled. "I have thought about this long and hard for the past seven-and-a-half years, and my best bet is Ashley's brother, Brent Whitmore. He knew she was mad at me. She may have even planned the 911 call with him. He has always been a manipulative fucker, and he lived very close to our house."

"You see, their parents were wealthy cattle ranchers. They owned almost ten thousand acres. After our marriage, Ashley's parents built our house on their property. They built her brother and his wife a house on the same property. Their place was not that far, and he regularly drove his four-wheeler over to visit us. It would only take him about five minutes or so. If he left his house shortly after they hung up, he would have arrived about the time I left. He could have killed her and gotten away. That way, he takes out both his sister and me for her half of their inheritance. He could get it all, especially if he ended up being Gabriel's guardian, which he has become since all this happened."

"Interesting theory, Gabriel is your son right?" Steve said. "Any-one else you think could have done it?"

"Yes, he is my son. And, no I can't think of anyone else, I am sure it was her brother," Scottie said.

"All right, well, thank you for being honest with us. We are going to go talk to Walters and Whitmore. We'll be back in a few weeks to let you know what we find out," Steve said as he stood up and pushed the button to let the guards know the visit was over.

Scottie stood and walked toward the locked door. As he waited for the click of the deadbolt sliding open, he pleaded to Steve, "Please don't tell anyone about Heather. She is still with her husband—they have two kids now. I don't want any more lives ruined by Ashley's murder."

"I won't," Steve promised. "Even if I wanted to, I'm bound by attorney-client confidentiality, and Booger is bound by similar rules of ethics for investigators."

"Thank you." Scottie's eyes teared up as he reached his arms out to hug Steve. "Thank you for believing in me. This is the first time since I got here six years ago that I have felt like I might not die in this godforsaken place with a needle in my arm. Scottie released his hug but held one hand on Steve's shoulder, "Thank you."

After they got into the car and out of earshot from any prison guards, Booger turned to face Steve. "The more I think about it, the more I am certain he didn't tell us the whole truth about what happened that morning. I think he has been telling the same lie for so long that even he believes it, which makes it more difficult for me to figure out what is and isn't true."

"I still believe he didn't kill her, though," Steve said.

"I don't think he killed her, either, but I also don't think he told us everything. I believe everything he told us is true, but I guarantee you, he left something out of the story. Regardless, like you told him, we need to go talk to everyone involved in this thing. Starting with Whitmore and Walters. I'm ready to get moving on this ASAP. I've got stuff at the shop the rest of the week, but do you have time to go to Claremore with me on Saturday?"

"I will make time," was Steve's only response as he grabbed his office cell phone to check for messages.

CHAPTER 17

Steve decided it would be best to reread the portions of the trial transcript containing the testimonies of Whitmore and Walters. He wanted their words fresh in his mind when he met them the next day. Steve pulled out the yellow legal pad with the index he had created previously. He found where he had noted the testimony of Walters.

* * *

July 24, 2009—Rogers County Courthouse

"For my next witness, I would like to call Heather Walters to the stand." Ian Battel walked to the rear of the courtroom and opened the small swinging door that separated the gallery seating from where the action happened.

Walters strode through the large oak doors and into the courtroom as if she were a fashion model. She graciously smiled and thanked Battel as she passed him holding open the small door and finished her runway walk to the witness stand. Walters was wearing a blue dress with white polka dots that showed off her toned and well-endowed twenty-three-year-old figure, a dress that was fashionable and yet would have been appropriate for Sunday service. Her blonde hair came down in waves just above her shoulders, and her face reminded people of Charlize Theron with a slightly turned-up nose, a distinct jawline, and a crisp smile. She had classic, small-town beauty and charm that caught the attention of everyone in the courtroom.

Walters sat and smiled at the judge as he swore her in to testify, then she turned to face Battel.

Battel asked, "Could you please state your name for the record?"

"Heather Walters," she responded promptly.

"Could you please tell the ladies and gentlemen of the jury your relationship to the victim, Ashley Pinkerton?"

"She was my best... friend." Her charade of confidence and stoicism cracked halfway through her first line of testimony. She reached for the tissue box near her and began to cry.

Battel approached her and placed his hand on her arm. He comforted her by, speaking in a low voice according to the transcripts, "It's okay. This won't take long. Remember, I just have a few questions to ask you, and then this will all be over."

A few seconds later, Walters regained her composure and continued, "We had been best friends since the day we met in fifth grade at Justus-Tiawah Elementary School. We remained friends through high school and were best friends up until the day he killed her." She pointed her tissue in Scottie's direction.

"During your friendship, did you have a chance to see her around her husband, the defendant, Scottie Pinkerton?"

"Yes, of course. On several occasions."

"How would you describe their relationship?"

"In the beginning, it was merely puppy love, two high school kids finding their way. Then, she got pregnant right after we graduated. Of course, they immediately got married. Unfortunately, they lost that child shortly after the wedding. I think both of them regretted getting married, especially Scottie. He always seemed like he wanted something different, like he was stuck with Ashley."

"Did you ever see him act out violently?"

"Yes, I remember one time, when we were playing this game. I guess you would call it a game. We had a book called The Book of Questions."

She turned to the jury. "It was exactly what it sounds like. A book containing maybe a hundred or so questions about life, sex, morality, etc. We would go around the room asking each other different questions from the book and talking about our answers. It was a great way to get to know people and discuss deep issues. Anyway, the deal was everyone agreed to answer honestly, otherwise, what was the point of playing? One time, and I don't even remember the question, Scottie thought Ashley was lying."

"We were on a ski trip in Colorado, and we were all sitting in the living room of the house we had rented. There were probably ten of us staying there. I was sitting right next to Ashley on the hearth in front of the fireplace. Scottie was sitting across the living room from us, probably fifteen to twenty feet away. Anyway, when she denied lying, he lost all control. He stood up, screaming at her, and threw the book as hard as he could at Ashley's head. It zinged by my ear, falling behind us. I was scared to death, so I can't imagine how Ashley felt. She ran out of the room crying. That was the first time I saw him lose his temper. Then, over the years, his responses became more and more abusive and aggressive."

"Did you ever see him hit her?"

"No, but I imagine he probably did. I saw him yell and berate her and throw other things at her. I would call it abusive treatment. He is a smart man. He wouldn't hit her in front of anyone, but I can only imagine what he did when no one was around. Like I said, he was not happy with her. He always acted like he wanted something else. I think they got married too young, and he never truly loved her, like he knew she wasn't the true love of his life."

"What was your first thought when you heard she had been killed?"

Walters sat still, looking off into space for maybe ten seconds, before calmly stating, "That Scottie finally lost it and went too far."

"Thank you," Battel said. "I have no more questions for this witness, Your Honor."

Hixon stood and approached the lectern. "To be clear, you never actually saw my client physically harm Ashley, correct?"

"Well, there was one time when I saw him grab her arms. They were screaming at each other about something, and she began to pound on his chest and maybe even hit him in the face once. He locked his hands around both her wrists and forced her to the ground. She was crying and screaming that he was hurting her. He didn't seem to care. He just kept her arms pinned to the ground while he lay on top of her."

"But he was defending himself then, right?"

"I guess you could call it that, but she was five-foot-three and weighed barely over a hundred pounds. He is over six feet tall and weighs more than two hundred. She could have clobbered his chest all day and never literally hurt him."

"But he was stopping her from hitting him, correct?" Hixon asked.

"Yes," Walters responded begrudgingly.

"You testified that you think he may have abused her when people weren't around. If that were true, why would she ever hit him?"

***

Steve grimaced as he read this question. It seemed Hixon had made the classic litigation rookie mistake.

In law school, Steve had learned that one of the first rules of trial practice was to never ask an adverse witness a question to which you didn't know the answer. It only gave the opposing party room to fill in the blanks with whatever fit their agenda.

***

Walters' smile was cold. "Probably because it was her one chance to hit him back. She knew he wouldn't hit her in front of people, so she hit him when I was there because she had been beaten so many times before that she wanted to get him back just once. She was scared and sad. She didn't think leaving him was an option. Just this one time, she took the opportunity to hit him back. This happened about two weeks before she was killed. I guess he got back at her for trying to hurt him. Wouldn't you agree?" Walters asked in mocking anger.

"Ma'am," Judge McClintock interjected. "Please just answer the questions asked of you. You are not allowed to ask questions of the attorneys. Please show that last statement stricken. The jury is ordered not to consider Ms. Walters' question to Mr. Hixon as evidence."

"No more questions, Your Honor," was all Hixon could muster as he slunk back to his chair.

Next, Mr. Whitmore was called to the stand. As Brent Whitmore walked into the courtroom, he removed his cowboy hat. He was about thirty years old, but his weathered face made him look at least forty. He was wearing a work shirt, denim jeans, and boots. The dried mud caked on the hem of his pants left a trail of dirt as he walked to the witness stand.

***

Steve noticed in his outline that he had only made a handful of notations during Whitmore's testimony. After he reread it, he remembered why. There wasn't anything particularly eventful about the testimony. Whitmore had never seen Scottie do anything abusive; he just "never liked him" and "always thought he was bad for Ashley."

Steve wondered why Battel had bothered to call Whitmore to the stand at all. Probably just wanted the jury to see the victim had a brother.

After finishing the testimony, Steve decided to call it a night. He wanted to get a good night's sleep before he and Booger interviewed their two suspects in the morning.

CHAPTER 18

Steve and Booger were on the freeway, making the thirty-minute drive to Claremore. Steve fiddled with the radio a bit; however, nothing came in clearly except for a country station. He turned it off completely.

"So, what's the game plan for the day?" Steve asked. "Start at the Scotties' old house?"

"Yeah," Booger replied, taking his turn at the radio. "I think we pay Mr. Whitmore a visit before heading over to the Walters' home. What do you think about this rancher brother?"

"Well..." Steve scratched his jaw. "I don't know. He didn't try and nail Scottie to the cross at trial, basically just said he didn't like him. It'd be interesting to hear his take." He glanced over at Booger. "How about Ms. Walters... mention the affair or play dumb?"

Booger gave up on the radio and leaned back. "Play nice and play dumb. Try to get as much as we can with a smiley face before she ices us. Then we drop the bomb."

The address, 5260 E. 420 Rd, was on the southeast corner of the Whitmore Flying W Ranch. They pulled up to the gate, which was basically a long metal pole stretched across the entryway. A barbed wire fence extended from each side of the pole. It was padlocked closed; perfect for keeping vehicles out, but someone on foot could easily pass.

From the county road, they could see the house where Ashley was killed. It was about a quarter mile up a gravel driveway and appeared to be abandoned. There were boards nailed over the windows in a shoddy fashion, as if someone had rushed the job.

"Doesn't look like anyone is around," said Booger as he opened his door. "Let's go have a look inside."

Steve hesitated. "Are you sure?"

"If you want to solve this crime and save Scottie, you are going to have to get your hands a little dirty. Come on."

There was enough room for Steve to park the car in front of the gate and still be safely off the main road. They got out of the car, hopped over the gate, and walked up to the empty house. As Steve peered through the boarded windows, Booger jimmied the back door with a tool from his body shop and entered the cave-like darkness of the abandoned structure.

Upon entering, the first thing Steve noticed was the smell of neglect that wafted throughout the house. Light sliced through the dusty air from the gaps between the planks covering the windows. Then, he noticed the silence. The house was eerily empty. Clearly, no one had been here in several years. Steve recognized the furniture from the crime scene photos. The only items missing were Ashley Pinkerton's body and the blood stained carpet.

The pair's first priority was a detailed examination of the door to the master bedroom. There was not even a scratch on it. Booger took several pictures of the door to have more proof for their file. He also made a video of himself opening and closing the door. He took more pictures of the living room and of other rooms throughout the house.

After a few minutes, the aura of the house began to bother Steve. "Don't you think we have seen enough?" he asked Booger.

"Probably. You can step on out if you want. I'll sit here and digest the place a bit. May sound hokey, but sometimes just sitting in a place where someone was murdered can give you a feeling about what happened. I'll be out in a minute."

Steve went back to the car, opened Words with Friends and was excited to get to play "Zippy" on a double word square against his anonymous arch nemesis while he waited. About fifteen or twenty minutes later, Booger hopped back over the gate and got in the passenger seat.

Steve looked over at the investigator. "Anything?"

"I had some thoughts—some kind of crazy ones. Nothing I definitively want to get into just yet. Let's go talk to the brother."

Although it may have been a five-minute drive across the ranch as the crow flies, the drive around the perimeter of the acreage, along the county roads, took a little longer.

As their car pulled through the southwest entrance to the Whitmore Flying W Ranch, they saw the house built for Whitmore and his wife, Julie. It was similar to the one built for Scottie and Ashley but slightly bigger. It also was a classic one-story ranch-style home with several bushes and flowers in front, a three-car garage attached on the side, and a long gravel drive connecting the house to the county road. Unlike the vacant yard of the Scotties' old house, the front and side yards here were strewn with different children's toys, and there were children playing on a wooden playset out back.

Mrs. Whitmore was the first to see the car. She had been sitting on the porch, watching the children play. She immediately rose from her chair and went inside. Within seconds, Steve and Booger could see Whitmore come out of the house. He was briskly walking toward them. Steve put the car in park and rolled down the window.

"Is there something I can help you two with?" Whitmore asked.

"My name is Steve Hanson, and this is Harold Thomas," Steve said as he got out of the car and approached Whitmore with his hand outstretched. "We represent Scottie Pinkerton in his federal appeals case."

Whitmore took his hand and shook it fiercely. He then pulled Steve close to him without releasing his grip on Steve's hand. Whitmore spoke quietly, "If you represent that bastard, then I've got nothing to say to you. Please leave my property now. You know, in this county they give rewards instead of prison time for shooting trespassers." He released his hold.

"We don't want to cause any trouble, Mr. Whitmore," Steve said, keeping his tone polite and friendly while raising his hands peacefully in the air. "We just hoped you might be able to help us. We have found evidence that we believe might exonerate Scottie and help prove he didn't kill your sister. We are looking to find the real killer."

Whitmore's eyes darted away and back to Steve. "Listen here, buddy, the person who killed my sister is in prison and will get his due soon enough. I'm not talking to you, and neither is my family."

During this time, Booger had gotten out of the car and now stood a few feet behind Steve. "Mr. Whitmore, we don't want any trouble. We will leave, but can you tell me if one of those kids over there is Gabriel?"

"Yes," Whitmore snapped. "The one in the blue-and-white-striped shirt, but you best stay away from him, too. He doesn't need to be reminded any more than is needed that his daddy killed his momma." Raising his voice, he demanded through clenched teeth, "Now get the fuck off my property!"

The two men slowly turned and walked back to their car. Steve put the car in reverse and began to cautiously back out of the driveway.

Steve spoke first. "Well, that didn't go so well."

"No, he didn't seem too excited to hear that we think Scottie didn't kill Ashley." Booger retrieved his camera and telephoto lens from their bag. "Don't pull away until I get some pictures of Gabriel."

When they stopped to get the photos, Whitmore turned and rushed into his house. Booger got some photos just as Whitmore walked back out of the house carrying a shotgun.

Steve put his foot on the gas. He was driving so fast backward down the long gravel driveway, all the while looking back and forth between Whitmore and the direction the car was headed, that he almost ran into the county sheriff's patrol car that was turning onto the property as they were leaving. The officer inside was none other than Deputy Andrew Blackburn.

When Deputy Blackburn saw Whitmore walking down the driveway with the shotgun, he flipped on his lights and gave one burst of the siren. Steve pulled over but made sure he did outside Whitmore property line.

"Brent, these gentlemen bothering you?" Deputy Blackburn yelled as he exited his patrol car.

"I just wanted them to leave, which it looks like they were finally doing before you stopped them."

Steve rolled down his window. "We were just leaving, officer, if that's okay with you?"

"You sure you don't want me to arrest them for trespassing or anything?" Deputy Blackburn asked Whitmore.

"No, let 'em go," Whitmore said gruffly.

"All right. I don't know who the hell you two are or what you are up to, but the property owner seems good with you leaving.

So just get the hell out of here," Blackburn commanded.

Steve put the car in drive and sped off.

Booger glanced back at the receding figure of Deputy Blackburn. "Wonder why the deputy was going by Whitmore's place on his day off?"

"I assumed the wife called 911, and he was here on official business. Why do you say it was his day off?"

"Because he wasn't wearing a uniform."

"I didn't even notice that," Steve said. "I was too worried about getting shotgun pellets in my car or spending my weekend in the Rogers County Jail." The two men shared a "thank god that didn't happen" laugh and drove on.

The next stop on their investigative journey was the Walters' house.

"Here we go," Booger said. "Remember. Let's put on our nice faces and see what we can get before we play the ace in the hole."

CHAPTER 19

Walters and her family lived in the Fieldstone housing addition just east of Claremore Lake. Fieldstone was a nice upper-middle-class neighborhood with large houses on acre lots, and the addition was a fairly recent expansion to the Claremore realty market. Every house had a wooden swing set or a trampoline in the backyard; some had both. Now, just a few years after the neighborhood was originally developed, only a couple of empty lots remained, and sold signs were erected on both of those.

The Walters lived in a two-story beauty near the back of the addition. There was a six-foot-tall wooden privacy fence around the back half of the acre lot and several tall trees dispersed around the property. From the size of the trees, Steve determined that this was one of the older houses in the neighborhood.

As they walked to the front door, Steve noticed heat upon his arms from the sun now beaming down through a few clouds on this beautiful Oklahoma spring morning. Walters' husband answered in sweats and a T-shirt that looked slept in, his hair still a mess. He scratched his round belly and asked, "How may I help you gentlemen?"

"I'm Steve Hanson, and this is my colleague, Harold Thomas. We represent Scottie Pinkerton in his federal appeal."

"Oh. I thought he was all done with appeals and off to death row."

"Well," Steve said, "after the appeals in state court, he gets an appeal at federal court. But yeah, it doesn't look good for the fellow when it gets to this point. We're just doing a standard investigation as part of our due diligence at this phase."

"You can come in then, have a seat on the couch. Can I get

you some coffee?" Mr. Walters turned toward the hallway. "Hey, honey, there are some men here about Scottie Pinkerton."

Walters came around the corner dressed in a pair of yoga pants and a tight-fitting, peach-colored workout T-shirt. Her blonde hair was styled as if she had been to the salon, and her face was perfectly made up with eyeliner and lipstick. The outfit fully accentuated the curves of her athletic body; now in her thirties, she was still an attractive and fit woman.

Steve looked at his watch; it was 10:25 a.m. He wondered if this was common attire for her on a Saturday morning in March or if she was truly on her way to or from the gym.

Walters raised her arms in the air with a smile on her face and said, "Welcome to Walters Inc. I am president and CEO of this fine establishment! How can I help you today?"

Steve and Booger stood up, and Steve extended his hand. "Good morning, Mrs. Walters. Sorry to bother you on a weekend. I'm Steve Hanson, and this is my colleague, Harold Thomas. We represent Scottie Pinkerton in his federal appeal."

Steve looked around the room and noticed everything was "in its place," not a mess anywhere to be seen—not even on the kitchen counters in the adjoining room. He then said, "We are interviewing everyone that testified at his trial, as well as anyone else we believe might have useful information."

"Well, I don't know what I can tell you that would be helpful, and to be honest, I still haven't gotten over the fact he killed my best friend. I know he had a temper, but until that day, I never thought he was a murderer." She said the last sentence with a look of disappointment and heartache.

"That's interesting. As I recall from your testimony, you kind of thought he might be the killer," Steve said.

"Well, that was seven years ago, and I just testified the way the prosecutor asked me to. It seemed clear from the evidence Scottie had done it. So, I did what I was told to help them get their conviction. I do remember Mr. Battel telling me that I had done an excellent job on my testimony." She smiled proudly.

"Can you tell us what your exact relationship with Scottie and Ashley was?" Steve asked.

"Ashley was my best friend. We had known each other since we were little kids. We went to elementary school at Justus-Tiawah together. I'll never forget the day we met. One day during recess, in the fall of fifth grade, some boys were making fun of my clothes. I lived in the trailer park just west of the Racino, although it was still just a horse racing track at that time. The people of Oklahoma hadn't yet voted to allow slot machines in the racetracks. Anyway, those boys were making fun of my cheap clothes, and then up walks Ashley. She told them to shut up and even pushed one of them down. That girl had no fear. The boys ran off, and we were best friends from that day forward. I always looked up to her and appreciated her standing up for me that day. She was my hero." Walters began tearing up as she told this story. Her husband brought her a tissue, sat down, and put one of his arms around her.

"What about Scottie?" asked Steve.

Walters's attitude quickly changed to one of disdain. "He was her high school love and was never much more than that to me. I mean, I was around him a lot, but never without Ashley. So, I can't really tell you a lot about him." Steve noticed she subtly glanced toward her husband with apprehension as she said this.

"The two of them started dating our sophomore year," Walters continued. "Other than a brief time when they split up in our junior year, they were together ever since. She got pregnant when we were all eighteen. It was right after we graduated from Claremore High School in 2004. He proposed as soon as they found out about the baby, and they got married shortly thereafter. Sadly, she ended up miscarrying that child. As far as I knew, they were going to wait awhile before trying to have a baby again after that happened, but she ended up pregnant three years later. That is when Gabriel was born."

"When was the last time you saw Ashley alive?" asked Steve.

"It was the morning of her murder."

Steve and Booger glanced briefly at one another.

"I started my morning at the gym like I do every Saturday."

Steve thought Every Saturday, she said, the same as Scottie's weekly round of golf. That part of his story lined up, then.

"When I was done there, I went by Ashley's house to see how she was doing. She had confided in me the day before that she thought Scottie was cheating on her. I went by to see what she knew and console her if she had found any real proof. When I got there, she told me it was just a hunch based on the way he had been acting. She didn't have any concrete proof. She was going to confront him when he got home from his golf game. I left and wished her good luck. About an hour or so later, I got a phone call from her brother, Brent; he told me the news."

"Is there anything else you think we should know?" asked Steve.

"No," Walters said with a shake of her blonde head. "That is pretty much all I know."

As he began to stand up, Steve thanked Walters and her husband for their time. Booger stood as well, and they all exchanged pleasantries. Just as they reached the doorway, Booger turned and said, "We were just out at the Whitmore Ranch visiting Whitmore. Deputy Blackburn pulled in while we were leaving. It looked like he was there on his day off. Are the two of them friends?"

"Well, I wouldn't say they are friends. Of course, we have all known each other for years and went to high school together, but Andy was probably out there to visit Gabriel. Ever since the day Ashley was killed, Andy has kind of been like a big brother to him. Andy says he feels some responsibility to take care of Gabriel since he is the one who carried him out of the house that day. He goes out there almost every Saturday, I think, and takes Gabriel places. I think Brent and Julie honestly appreciate the break with one less child in the house."

"Do you know what they do?" Booger asked.

"I think they just go to the park at the lake most days, or just whatever. I'm honestly not sure about all the details."

"Okay," Booger said. "Thanks."

After the two men got into the car and began to pull away, Steve looked over at Booger. "What do you think?"

"Well, she was definitely hiding something. I could tell that clear as day. The only question is, was she just hiding her affair, or did she kill her hero to take her place on the mantel? I've seen it several times over the years. You have two best friends, one with a strong personality and the other a follower. Over time, the idolization turns to something else, and the follower wants not only to start having a say in the relationship but to also take over the other person's life. It definitely explains why she started sleeping with Scottie, but I'm not sure if it makes her a murderer."

Booger turned and smiled at Steve, "One thing I do know; this sure is going to be an interesting journey, my friend. I'm glad you got me involved. Let's go to that park."

Steve turned right on Blue Starr Drive and drove toward the park. As they neared the parking lot adjacent to the playground, they saw the sheriff's patrol car. Steve pulled his car up next to it. Both men got out. Booger took a few pictures of Deputy Blackburn pushing Gabriel on the swing before they approached.

As they got within earshot, Deputy Blackburn left his position behind the swing and headed toward them. By the time they met up, all three men were a considerable distance from Gabriel.

Deputy Blackburn calmly said, "Hello, gentlemen. I know why you are here. Brent told me who you are and what you are up to. I would be happy to meet with you sometime when the little man is not around." He turned and gave a nod toward Gabriel still on the swing. "I don't like to talk shop around him, especially not this case. I'm sure you understand."

Steve spoke first, "Yes, of course, there's no reason for him to hear about it. Is there a time next week you'd be available?"

"My on-duty hours are Monday through Thursday from 6:00 a.m. to 4:00 p.m. every week, but I would be happy to meet with you anytime that Gabe is not around. Brent told me about your theory, and I would love to find out what you have uncovered. As a lawman and the first officer on the scene, I would hate it if we got the wrong person. However, I must tell you that I find it highly unlikely we made a mistake. Considering all the evidence that pointed to your guy, there is no doubt in my mind the right man is in prison. That said, I'm extremely curious to see what you think my department missed in the investigation."

Steve looked at Booger and said, "I have a court hearing on Monday. Can you do Tuesday?"

Booger nodded. "I'm fairly open at the body shop this week and I got a text earlier the Javelin I expected on Monday won't be coming in. I can be wherever whenever, young man."

Steve turned back to Deputy Whitmore. "How about Tuesday morning around nine thirty?"

"Can you do 4:00 p.m.? That way, I don't have to worry about being called away if something comes up, since I will be officially off-duty."

"Four sounds perfect. We will see you then," Steve said.

CHAPTER 20

When they arrived back in Tulsa, it was a little after 1:00 p.m. Steve turned to Booger. "All that lying and evading we heard today has got me real hungry. Do you like traditional English food?"

"What do you consider traditional English food? Internal organs and French fries?" Booger frowned. "Probably not."

"You'll love this place. The White Lion Pub near 71st and Yale. I love the 'Lancashire Feast'—a steak and mushroom pie. No intestines. I promise."

"Okay, I'm game. I'm sure I can find something to eat."

At the pub, a waitress brought Steve a Guinness and Booger a Bud Light. Booger took a swig from his bottle and asked, "How can you drink that stuff? It looks like tar."

"Well, I'll admit it is a bit of an acquired taste," Steve said with a shrug. "But once you get used to it, there is not another beer in the world that can compare to its complexity. I actually started drinking these in law school at Georgetown in DC. The law school campus is downtown, not out in Georgetown proper where the main university is situated. There were two Irish bars/restaurants within walking distance of the campus."

"The Dubliner was located on the ground floor of a posh hotel. It had leather chairs and cloth napkins, and they served a nice pint of Guinness. A lot of businesspeople, as well as students who had a few bucks, ate and drank there. Right next to The Dubliner was The Irish Times. It was more of your hole-in-the-wall type of Irish pub. There was always the smell of stale beer stuck on the floor with the occasional whiff of puke on the wrong nights. The rest of us went there. The Irish Times served the best Guinness I have ever had in the States, and that is pretty much what everyone who went there ordered. Grew to love this stuff in that place, and I hope one day to visit the brewery. I think I would be in heaven if I ever got to have a pint there."

"Georgetown, huh?" Booger said. "That is a top-shelf law school. You must be some kind of intellectual. Not that I've picked up on that thus far." He said jabbingly.

After lunch, they drove home without much conversation, each man quietly pondering their morning's activities. As Steve pulled up to the body shop, Booger said, "Spend the next couple of days thinking about what all happened this morning. Not just what was said, but also what wasn't said, and how everyone reacted to our presence. Plus, we need to go see Scottie again. Something has been eating at my gut ever since our meeting with him. There is still something he isn't being completely honest about. I know it, and we need to get it out of him."

"Okay," said Steve.

"Lastly, I remember you told Deputy Blackburn you have something Monday. Can we meet at 1:00 p.m. on Tuesday and go over our thoughts before we go back to Claremore to meet him?"

"Yes," Steve said with a nod. "Can you meet me at my office? If you have the time, we can even plan on meeting about noon and have lunch first. If that works for you?"

"Sounds good. By the way, just out of curiosity, what type of case do you have Monday?" Booger asked.

"Oh, it's not the juiciest of cases, but it was the most important case in my filing cabinet before I got this one. I represent a guy accused of embezzling tens of thousands of dollars from his company. The preliminary hearing is set Monday afternoon, but after all the evidence I've seen, I think our best bet is to take a plea. I am meeting with him Monday morning to discuss all of our options."

CHAPTER 21

Monday came all too quickly for Steve. He had spent so much time thinking about Scottie's case that he had neglected the Hamilton matter. He started early that morning by going back over the entire file. He wanted to be completely prepared for his meeting with Hamilton at 11:00 a.m, so he spent most of the time reviewing the information contained in the zip drive that Emily had provided him. It contained all of the data she had extracted from Hamilton's hard drive. Some of that time Steve spent thinking about Emily herself, but he did his best to focus on the zip drive information.

Steve had told Hamilton today's meeting was so they could go over any final questions before their preliminary hearing at 1:30 p.m. before Judge McCuan. But Steve's real plan was to present Hamilton with the new evidence and see if Hamilton would fess up. At this point, Steve knew that Hamilton's best option was to plea; however, that would never happen as long as the man kept denying his guilt.

Hamilton arrived on time, and Carol showed him to the conference room in the back. After leaving him with a soda, she went into Steve's office.

"Hey, Mr. Death Penalty, your embezzler is here to see you. I put him in Conference Room B—assuming you still have time for your other clients."

Steve said, "Thanks, Carol," before shaking his head and muttering something under his breath as he got up. He walked to the conference room, and the two men exchanged pleasantries before Steve got down to business. Steve sat at the end of the long wooden table near Hamilton who had been placed in the first seat along the side earlier by Carol.

"Okay, we are set for your preliminary hearing this afternoon. Before we go forward with that, I want to make sure you understand all of your options. Most importantly, I want to make sure I have answered any questions you have."

"Sounds good," replied Hamilton. "My first question is: What exactly is a preliminary hearing?"

"A preliminary hearing is a gate-keeping procedure wherein the state must prove that there is probable cause to believe a crime has been committed and probable cause to believe you are the one who committed that crime," said Steve. "If the state is unable to meet that burden, then the case is dismissed. However, you should understand that, at this point, they only have to show probable cause, not proof beyond a reasonable doubt as they will at the final jury trial."

"I'm not sure I understand. What is the difference between probable cause and beyond a reasonable doubt?"

"Probable cause simply means the evidence shows it probably happened. Beyond a reasonable doubt means there is almost no doubt in the jury's mind you committed the crime charged. A simple analogy would be to think about two children playing in the other room, and a lamp falls over and crashes. The mother could meet the burden of probable cause against both children because she was in the room next door, heard the crash, and immediately came in to see the broken lamp. But she would only have proof beyond a reasonable doubt against either child if one of the two confessed, and the other agreed. Without the confession, she does not have proof beyond a reasonable doubt against either of them," Steve explained.

"So, the state could win a preliminary hearing against both children, but couldn't win a jury trial against either?"

"Correct, unless they got more evidence against one of them, like a confession, or maybe the dad saw what happened from outside or whatever."

Hamilton frowned. "It sounds like it doesn't take much evidence for them to show probable cause."

"Correct again, the state wins probably 90 percent of all preliminary hearings because, if the prosecutor knows he or she can't meet the burden, they usually dismiss the case without wasting time having a hearing. But if they think they have enough evidence to get past the low burden of probable cause, they proceed.

"Also, the law in Oklahoma assumes that the prosecution will continue to gather more evidence after the hearing and make their case even stronger before trial. So, yes, it is a very low burden, and they almost always win at this stage. You should understand that most defense attorneys never put any evidence on for the defense at these hearings, and I don't plan on putting on any evidence today myself."

"Why not? Shouldn't we prove my innocence now?"

"No. The main purpose of this hearing, from our perspective, is not to win the hearing, but to hear the testimony and evidence the state has available so that we can begin to come up with a strategy to defeat them at trial. They are basically forced to show their cards while we are able to keep ours tight. If we put on evidence, we would give them an idea of our strategy. Make sense?"

"Yeah, your plan sounds good to me," Hamilton said.

"However," Steve continued, "we have another option. We can

waive this hearing, should you choose to do that."

"Why would I waive the chance to see their evidence?"

"Well, the first reason is that I already know what evidence they plan on producing. They are required to show me the police reports and other documentation they have gathered. I just haven't been able to ask questions of any officers involved or cross-examine them about their actions, which, in your case, wouldn't truly produce much more information. Your case is not like a traffic stop or something similar where the officer is a key witness. In those cases, we might be able to catch the officer lying or admitting to doing something wrong that would let us keep evidence out of the hearing."

"And what's the second reason?" Hamilton asked.

"The second reason is that Ms. Turner, who is the prosecutor in your case, tends to look kindly upon defendants who do not force her to put on a hearing that we all know she will win. At this point, she has made us an offer for a plea deal that would let you stay out of prison as long as you pay the money back. I think—"

"I'm not taking a plea deal!" interrupted Hamilton. "I didn't do anything. I didn't take any money."

"While I understand that is your position right now," Steve said in an understanding manner, "I have to tell you that the evidence against you is quite substantial. Their star witness is a woman named Dr. Emily Babbage. She is a computer forensics expert. What that means is that she knows how to search the hard drive of a computer and find files and information that the person who owned the computer had previously deleted. You see, nothing deleted from a computer is truly gone unless you wash the entire hard drive. If a person simply removes items by clicking delete or dragging them to the trash, it doesn't completely erase them. They will still be somewhere on your computer, and Dr. Babbage is trained in finding those files."

Hamilton began to shift in his chair, looking very uncomfortable as Steve continued.

"Dr. Babbage took your computer and searched it for deleted files. The United States Constitution requires the prosecution in every case to provide defense counsel with all of the evidence the state has procured against a defendant. This is because the courts want transparency in prosecutions so that no defendant is ambushed at trial with a bunch of evidence they knew nothing about. Plus, the defense should always be given an opportunity to rebut with evidence of their own."

Steve opened the box of documents he had printed from the zip drive provided by the state. He began pulling certain marked pages out from the stacks of paper.

"When Dr. Babbage went through your computer, she found all of these documents that you thought were deleted. There are a few specific ones I would like to ask you about. This one, for instance, shows a transfer of money from the corporate account of Phillips Industries to an unknown account on April 23 of last year. Here is another from April 27 and a third from May 8. There are several more of these. Can you tell me how they got onto your computer?"

"I have no idea… I promise I did not take that money," Hamilton responded, his voice quivering.

"Did anyone else have access to your home computer?" asked Steve.

"No."

"Let me show you a few more documents she recovered from

your computer. These are spreadsheets showing your accounting ledgers. This page shows the ledger that you turned into the company, and this page shows all the changes that were made to that document from the time it was first created and all the way through to the final version you submitted. Here you can even see where you misspelled the word 'account' and went back and added the second 'c.' Here the ledger shows that $2,689 was originally transferred to the same unknown account as all the other transfers. Plus, on this one, your name is listed as the recipient, and then, in the document turned into the company, your name is replaced with one of Phillips Industry's suppliers to make it appear as a legitimate expenditure. It seems when you first made transfers, you put your name on it so you would know how much and when the transfers were made. Later, you went in and changed those transfers to names you thought no one would notice when reviewing your ledgers."

Hamilton's head slowly drooped as he continued to listen to Steve.

"I should also let you know, although they haven't tracked down the information yet, Ms. Turner has requested the judge allow the state to send a subpoena to the bank where the unknown account is located. They will get all of the bank's records relating to this account, including the name of its owner." Steve paused, laying the stack of evidence on the table.

"Now, this is what my mentor, Frank Ackerman, would call a 'come to Jesus' moment. All this information is pointing directly to you, so if your name is going to appear as the owner of that bank account, I need to know that right now in order to best represent you in this case."

At this point, tears were beginning to form in the corners of

Hamilton's eyes.

"Is your name going to be listed on the account? Is your signature going to be on the enrollment documents for this account?"

Finally, Hamilton cracked. "I'm sorry... I'm so very sorry... I never meant for it to get this far. I just borrowed a little that first time and was planning on paying it back. There is something I haven't told you, and it is a big reason for my divorce as well. I have a serious gambling problem. I simply love playing slot machines at the casinos around town. The Osage Casino north of town is my favorite. The excitement I feel in my bones when I hit a bonus on those machines is the most exhilarating feeling to me. When they spin red. The biggest problem was that I actually won a lot of the time. That was how I paid your retainer; I came in right after winning over ten thousand dollars on one spin. It makes me think I'll win every time I go play. So, when I didn't win, I just kept putting more and more money into those damn machines, thinking I would eventually win. When I won five hundred, I thought I could get one thousand. When I won a thousand, I thought I could get two thousand. No matter how much I won, it was never enough, so I'd keep trying to win more until I checked my pockets, and there was nothing left. Not the one thousand I'd won, not the five hundred I'd won, not even the money I'd originally brought with me. I would realize I'd given it all back to them. Then this awful feeling would start in my stomach, and I'd sometimes want to kill myself."

The tears slowly tumbled out of Hamilton's eyes; Steve removed a tissue from the box sitting on the table and offered it to Hamilton as he continued, "Afterward, I'd go home and fight with my wife because I was so mad at myself that I wanted to yell at someone.

She became my victim…" He paused, looking wracked with guilt.

Steve leaned over and put his arm around Hamilton. "I understand. I am very sorry you have had to go through this."

"But now, I've decided that I need to stop gambling, and last week, I went to my first Gamblers Anonymous meeting. They say you have to hit rock bottom before you can begin to get better, and I think this is it. I've lost my family, my job, my savings, my self-respect, and now possibly my freedom because of those damn machines."

Steve nodded encouragingly. "The good news is that if we take the deal today, you won't have to go to prison or even spend a single night in the county jail. The deal Ms. Turner has offered is this: First, that she will only take into account the current charges, which amount to $52,347 in stolen funds. When Dr. Babbage searched your computer, they found evidence of over a hundred thousand dollars' worth of embezzlement. If we don't take the deal, Ms. Turner will amend the charges to reflect the higher number; however, to be clear, if we do agree to plea, then she won't add any more charges. Second, if you waive your preliminary hearing and plead to the charges as filed, she will even reduce the charge from a felony to a misdemeanor. You will then be placed on what is called a five-year deferred sentence."

"A deferred sentence?" asked Hamilton hesitantly.

"This means you will be on probation for five years with the understanding that you have to pay back the $52,347 as restitution. The balance must be paid in full before your probation is up. If you pay it all back and don't violate your probation, then you will never have to spend a night in jail, let alone prison, and the charges will be dismissed. You won't even have a conviction on your record."

"Wow. That sounds great," Hamilton said as he wiped away his last few tears. "I can't believe I might get through this without a conviction on my record... But how in the world will I pay all that money back?"

"First of all, by staying out of the casinos and going to those meetings. But that doesn't matter right now, to be honest with you. The first thing you need to worry about is how to solve the problem of these charges hanging over your head. Did you see that movie from last year, The Martian?"

"Yes. Why?"

"Do you remember how Matt Damon's character focuses on solving the problem in front of him? He knows that there are several problems that have to be fixed before he will get home, but he understands that the most important thing for his survival is to solve the most important problem facing him first—food—before he can even worry about getting on a ship back to earth. That is similar to your situation. You need to solve the problem of having felony criminal charges pending against you. We can do that today by pleading guilty and taking a deferred sentence with the knowledge you will have to pay back the money. Once that is resolved, you can start trying to figure out how you will come up with $52,347. Does that make sense?"

"Yes," Hamilton said.

"Does that mean that you now believe it is in your best interest to take a plea deal today? Should I call Ms. Turner and let her know we will be waiving the preliminary hearing and taking the deal? As I have said before, the final decision is always yours. As your attorney, I am just here to give you advice on what I think is your best option. Should you decide you want to maintain your innocence, I will do my best to fight the state and poke holes in their case."

"Yes, I understand, and, yes, I want to take the deal," Hamilton said with a slight nod. "It honestly feels better to have admitted what I did. You don't understand how much guilt and angst I have felt lying to you and everyone else about the money. Not to mention the feelings I have from hiding my gambling addiction… I want to call my wife and finally tell her the truth."

"Well, I would recommend you don't tell her that today. As your attorney—and not to sound heartless or uncaring—it is my job to protect you. Let me talk to your wife's lawyer, and maybe we can set up a meeting where you can discuss all of this with her. She could use this against you if she chooses. Like The Martian character, let's just get through this criminal part and worry about the rest later."

"Okay," replied Hamilton with his chin to his chest. His crying had stopped, but he still sat motionless, staring at the floor.

As Steve rose from the table, he said, "It's almost lunchtime. Go get something to eat, and then meet me in Judge McCuan's courtroom at one thirty. I will call Ms. Turner and let her know what's up. We can do the plea this afternoon, and you can begin the process of putting your life back together."

Hamilton finally looked up. "Thank you. Thank you so much. I already feel better just knowing I am going to admit to everything. Knowing I won't go to prison. Knowing this part of it is all over. The lies, everything. Thank you!"

Steve went to his office and phoned Turner. It was professional courtesy for defense counsel to let the assistant district attorney on a case know as soon as possible if a client was going to waive the preliminary hearing. This was done so the prosecuting attorney could contact their witnesses and let them know they didn't have to come to the courthouse. Although Steve knew this was the right thing to do, he was a bit hesitant because, deep down, he had been looking forward to seeing Emily again that day in court; however, he knew what was best for the client always came first in this job.

After Turner answered the phone, Steve began with, "I'm calling to let you know that I just got out of a meeting with Jordan Hamilton. He has decided to take the deal. We are going to waive prelim today and go ahead with the plea this afternoon."

"Wait, I thought he was innocent," Jennifer said with a smirk that Steve could practically see through the phone line.

"Turns out he wasn't. Listen, don't be too hard on him. He has been through a lot. It seems he has a serious gambling problem that has not only cost him his job and put a mark on his criminal record, but also cost him his family. I am handling his divorce, too."

"All right, all right, calm down. I was just giving you a little grief. I know you are fairly new, but if you can't handle a prosecutor giving you a hard time about your client, then you won't make it long in this business. See you in court."

That afternoon, Hamilton plead guilty to the embezzlement charges filed against him. As part of the deal, the state reduced the charge to a misdemeanor so he would not be a convicted felon. He was given a five-year deferred sentence with orders to pay back the fifty-two thousand dollars and reform himself.

After court, Steve pulled Turner aside and asked her if she would kindly give him Emily's cell phone number. He explained that he had asked her on a date back when they all went for drinks at The Empire Bar and that she had told him she never mixed business with pleasure. Now that Hamilton's case was over, he hoped she would reconsider his offer.

Turner said she didn't feel comfortable giving him her number without Emily's consent, but she did agree to pass his number on to her. She also told Steve that she would tell Emily she thought he was a catch and that she should jump on the opportunity to go out on a date with him. Steve appreciated her willingness to help.

Steve was glad Hamilton's case had resolved in a manner that worked out well for his client and now gave him an opportunity to date Emily; most importantly, it closed the file, which meant he now had more time to focus on Scottie's case.

He spent the rest of the day wondering what Deputy Blackburn would have to say at their meeting the next day.

CHAPTER 22

When Steve walked into the Monkey Tree Diner in downtown Tulsa, Booger was already seated at a table in the middle of the restaurant. On either side of the investigator were groups of well-dressed men and women discussing office drama while munching on their strawberry pecan spinach salads and chicken Caesar wraps. A tile outlay depicting a jungle scene graced the wall behind them. Steve sat down, opened the menu and flipped through it.

"Have you been to this building before?" Steve asked.

"I know the BOK Tower, never eaten here. I remember when they first built it they used a famous architect—what was his name?"

"Minoru Yamasaki of Yamasaki and Associates."

"Yeah, that's it. I remember hearing he was the same gentleman who built the Twin Towers in New York and our little building here is an exact replica of those, just shorter. It didn't mean much at the time; didn't mean much until the real ones were gone. But now I'm kind of proud of our city to have it. You notice the tourists taking pictures outside?"

"It's become quite the draw for visitors," Steve said. "Not sure if they consider it a lasting tribute or a spectacle. Something to visit I guess."

Booger scanned the menu, slightly frowning. "A lot of vegetables and smoothies and things here."

"Sir, I wouldn't ask you to a place that lacks animal protein," Steve promised. "They have the juiciest burger in town." To the waitress who approached their table, he said, "I'll have the kale salad with a blueberry, strawberry, and almond milk smoothie."

"I'll take the cheeseburger, ma'am, medium rare, with French fries. No kale. Please and thank you."

After their waitress left, Steve asked, "What do you think Deputy Blackburn will tell us this afternoon?"

"I doubt much. I would bet my left arm he will tell us that he is 100 percent sure Ashley's murderer is sitting on death row. I don't expect him to be very receptive to our alternative theory."

Out of nowhere, a large older gentleman stopped by their table and slapped Booger on the back in an aggressive yet friendly manner. The man had just placed his finely tailored suit coat on the back of a nearby chair. His tie hung down perfectly over his round belly, which stuck out between his suspenders. "Booger!" he boomed. "How the hell are you?"

"I'm good. How have you been, Jim? How is Wilma?"

"I've been great, and Wilma is good too. She is still spending too much of my money too fast, but what the hell. I love her. What are you up to?"

"I'm here with a young man who hopes to follow in your footsteps." Booger rose and gestured for Steve to do the same. "Steve Hanson, meet James Ferguson." He turned to Mr. Ferguson. "I'm working with Steve on a capital habeas case. So far, it looks like he cares as much about finding justice as you and some of the other true heroes in your profession."

Steve stood and extended his hand. "It's an honor to meet you, Mr. Ferguson."

Steve had recognized the man as soon as he had walked up behind Booger. Jim Ferguson was known throughout the Tulsa legal community as an incredible trial attorney. Everyone knew that if you ever got into trouble, and Ackerman couldn't take your case for some reason, you hired Ferguson. Although some less-informed people might put one above the other, no one doubted they were the top two attorneys in their field.

Ferguson shook Steve's hand firmly. "Well, kid, if Booger here thinks that highly of you, then you are top-notch in my book. Here's my card. If I can ever help you with something, don't hesitate to call. Us good guys have to stick together."

"Thanks," Steve said. "I just might take you up on that someday."

"I heard you are taking on the Southern Hills Slasher pro bono," Booger said.

"That's a fact. His wife just so happens to be my cleaning lady. We have him, his wife, and his kids over for dinner every year at Christmas. I know these people." Ferguson's jovial tone turned grim. "It is the perfect example of racist cops going after the little guy. Four golfers are found dead on the course, all hacked up with a garden tool, and they go after the Mexican immigrant who works at the course. I've known that man for many years, and there is no way he is a murderer, but those lazy cops are trying to pin it on him rather than do a thorough investigation to find the real killer. You know—with all the anti-immigrant sentiment brewing—going after a Mexican on a criminal charge is like picking the low-hanging fruit."

"You really don't think he did it?" Steve asked. "From everything I have read in the paper, it looks like they have a lot of evidence against him."

Ferguson shook his head. "I obviously can't get into all the details, but let's just say I think the police have failed to do a thorough investigation. I plan on putting a lot of time and money into the case to get to the bottom of it. Anyway, I have an important motion hearing this afternoon on the matter, so I need to get a quick bite and get out of here. Great seeing you Booger! Take care." Ferguson walked back to the table where he had left his jacket.

Steve turned to Booger. "That brings something to mind that I have been meaning to ask you. Why does everyone call you Booger?"

Booger settled back into his chair with a grin. "Young man, the best way for me to explain it to you is with a joke I heard awhile back."

"Over a hundred years ago, there was a traveler who made his way into a wee Scottish village on the western coast of Scotland. As the traveler enters the town, he sees a wee sign that says, 'Welcome to Sheamustoun.' He doesn't think much of the sign and eventually works his way down to the docks where he finds a small pub. The traveler goes into the pub, sits down at the bar, and orders a pint."

"As he is drinking his pint, he notices the bar is a beautifully handcrafted piece of wood with ornate carvings running up and down it. The traveler gets the bartender's attention and asks who made the bar. The bartender responds by saying"—Booger switched to the most perfect Scottish accent, which he continued to use for every Scottish character in the story— "'Aye, a made this bar wi' ma ain hans, that's why am known as Sheamus the Barmaker aboot toon.'

Booger continued, "the traveler thinks that is nice and settles into drinking his pint. He then looks out the window and sees the most majestic, well-built pier he has ever seen in his life. He turns to the gentleman next to him and asks if he knows who made the pier. The gentleman responds, 'Aye, a made that pier wi' ma ain hans, that's why am known as Sheamus the Pier Builder aboot toon.' The traveler next notices an amazingly crafted ship docked at the end of the pier, and he asks who built the ship. A gentleman sitting at the end of bar says, 'Aye, a made that ship wi' ma ain hans, that's why am known as Sheamus the Shipbuilder aboot toon.'

"At this point, the traveler asks why they all have the same first name. Sheamus the Barmaker responds, 'This toon is known as Sheamustoun, an' aw through history aw wee boys wur named Sheamus. Then, at a point in the wean's life he gits a title based on whit he did to be known aboot toon so we dinnae get mixed up speakin' aboot him.'

"The traveler then notices a man sitting in the back corner of the pub, keeping to himself and clearly trying to avoid the conversation. The traveler yells to this gentleman, 'Sheamus, what are you known for?' The man angrily finishes his beer, slams the glass down on the table, storms over to the traveler, and shakes one finger in his face"—which Booger acted out as well— "while saying, 'Ye shag wan sheep!' and stomps out of the pub."

Steve began to laugh, as did the group of young professionals seated near them who couldn't help but here the joke. Once he regained his composure, Steve asked, "That was hilarious, but what does it have to do with why they call you Booger?"

"Well, one day in the second grade, I ate a booger that I had just picked out of my nose. Anthony Anderson saw me and told everyone in my class about it. Before long, all the kids were calling me Booger, and the name has stuck ever since. At this point, to be honest, I kind of like it," he said with a shrug. "No one else I have ever met is called 'Booger.' Since we are now friends, you should call me Booger, too."

"Okay, Booger," Steve responded with a mix of awkwardness and joviality. "I'm glad you've changed your diet from boogers to burgers. Let's finish lunch and get on with our investigation."

After lunch, Booger and Steve spent a few hours back at Steve's office, going through reports and discussing what they had learned on Saturday. On the drive to Claremore, both men agreed there was something Walters seemed to be trying to hide from them. The question to be answered was whether it was the affair with Scottie or something more. They also made a game plan for their meeting with Deputy Blackburn.

They arrived at the Rogers County Sheriff's Office a little before 4:00 p.m. Steve approached the receptionist who sat behind a bulletproof glass wall with a two-way intercom system in the middle of it. Steve pushed the button and said, "Hello, we have a meeting with Deputy Blackburn at four."

The receptionist led them back to Deputy Blackburn's office.

Blackburn stood and approached them with an outstretched hand as they entered. "Nice to see you both again. Please, come in."

"Thank you for taking the time to see us," Steve said.

Steve looked around the deputy's office as he sat down. Deputy Blackburn showcased several awards on the walls from his service in the Rogers County Sheriff's Office, and a degree from the University of Oklahoma hung on the wall behind his desk. The bookshelf to Steve's left contained various knickknacks and a few photos. Steve noticed there were no pictures of a wife or family. He also noticed the desk was clean, and everything seemed to be in its place. Another section of the bookshelf was devoted to University of Oklahoma football memorabilia; there were a few team pictures and a game ball on the shelf.

Steve asked, "Did you play for OU?"

"Yes, I was a walk-on for Coach Stoops. I played my way into a scholarship and was eventually voted a captain by my teammates." The deputy picked up a picture from the shelf and handed it over. "This one was from one of the greatest days of my life—six receptions for eighty-seven yards and a touchdown against Texas. I'm there, in the center of the team, wearing the Golden Hat; that's the trophy for winning the Red River shootout. Whenever we won the game, everyone on the team took turns getting a picture with the trophy on their head."

"But enough about my football days," Deputy Blackburn said abruptly, taking the framed photo back and shifting the conversation to more serious matters. "I would love to hear what evidence you have found that exonerates your murdering client." He said with a smirk.

"Well, Deputy Blackburn," Steve said as he pulled the photos out of his briefcase. "If you take a close look here, I think the evidence will speak for itself."

Steve stood and spread the photos out on the desk in front of Deputy Blackburn. "This one shows it best. You can see here, here, and here. The bedroom door in the Scottie home was not broken on the day in question. That means Ashley Pinkerton lied on the 911 call, and if she lied about that, then maybe there is more to this story than meets the eye."

Deputy Blackburn began to chuckle under his breath. "And?" he asked loudly.

"What do you mean 'and?'" asked Steve, somewhat flustered. "These pictures—"

"I know you aren't about to disparage the victim in this case and start calling her a liar to save your murdering client from the needle, are you?" the deputy interrupted him sharply. "We saw those pictures in our original investigation. Hell! I took the damn things. In every crime scene investigation, there is something that doesn't fit, but when you take all the parts that fit and they all point to one thing, you disregard the outlying evidence as germane. Whether or not he broke the door doesn't matter. Maybe he just opened it and barged through. Maybe she said 'broke in' on the call because she was scared, he was about to kill her. Either way, it doesn't matter when you look at all of the other evidence that points to your client as the one who did it."

Blackburn scowled at both men in turn. "If this is all you have, then you really need to go back to arguing about some bullshit constitutional loophole you damn defense lawyers are so good at and quit trying to be an investigator. If there isn't anything else you have discovered, then this meeting is over, and I am going home. It's been a long day."

Steve was troubled by this response. He thought everyone would see the case his way, that this evidence created doubt in the state's version of the story. He hadn't considered the possibility that others had figured out the same thing and disregarded it as immaterial. Steve internally gathered himself. "Then, can I see your notes from the investigation?"

"As a matter of fact, I told First Assistant District Attorney Battel you were snooping around the case and planned to meet me today. He told me to let you know that if you want to see the police investigative files, you will have to get a court order. He told me not to turn them over without one. He actually didn't even want me talking to you at all. I told him that, with my experience in interrogation, I could get out of you whatever information I needed without telling you a damn thing, which I think I just did," Deputy Blackburn finished smugly.

"I see. Thank you for your time, Deputy Blackburn," Steve said as calmly as he could, considering the anger that now surged through him. The two men quickly exited the deputy's office.

As Steve and Booger walked back to their car, Steve said, "I was a bit surprised about how quickly he rejected our theory."

"I wasn't," Booger said with a snort. "Did you honestly think he would admit a mistake? Remember, a lot of the time the police do an investigation, they already have a perpetrator in mind. Then, as they investigate, they gather evidence that points to that person and ignore evidence that doesn't. There was a good podcast recently called Serial that discusses what I call the 'police blinder's mentality' pretty well. You should listen to it."

Steve drove away from the sheriff's office, still thinking over the less-than-pleasant exchange.

Booger patted the young attorney's shoulder. "Anyway, this is the main reason you defense barristers hire me to do the exact opposite of the cops. I find the exonerating stuff and put the incriminating information aside. I honestly don't blame these police detectives, though. They are overworked and underpaid. You just need to remember they are human and make mistakes sometimes, just like the rest of us. Hell, you might even be wrong about something someday."

"Very funny. Regardless, we need to see his file. I'm not 100 percent sold he ever noticed the intact door before, and I want to see if he is lying. First thing in the morning, I will file the motion asking the court to order him to provide the material. I should have it done by noon."

"Sounds like a plan," Booger said. "Since it is not quite five yet, let's go see Frank. I bet he has some insight on our case."

CHAPTER 23

Sharyn Harrison, a seventy-two-year-old woman, was sitting behind the reception desk just inside the entryway. She rose to greet them as soon as she saw them enter, giving them both a hug, "Booger, I haven't seen you in forever! How have you been?"

"I've been great. I can't believe you are still working. Isn't it about time you retire and take some time for yourself?"

"Thirty-six years and counting," Harrison said proudly. "The old warhorse back there needs me too much. As long as he keeps going, I'll keep going. You know he couldn't do anything without me here."

"Truer words have never been spoken," Booger said.

The three of them shared a laugh.

"Not that I don't like seeing you, Sharyn, but we were hoping to have a word with Frank. He available?"

"Right now, he is in his office, going through police reports on the triple homicide that happened last week in Osage County. I'll go tell him you two are here." Harrison came back a few seconds later, followed by Ackerman.

"Booger, how the heck are you?" Ackerman asked as he went in for a big hug.

"I'm great, other than having to deal with this rookie over here."

"He's young, but that just means he still has a lot of fight in him." Ackerman turned and hugged Steve. "And how the heck have you been, Steve?"

"Doing well. Always good to see you, Frank," Steve said.

"You boys come on back to my office." Steve felt his office cell phone vibrate in his pocket as Ackerman led them down the hallway.

The office itself looked like that of a traditional country lawyer portrayed in a Norman Rockwell painting. Bookshelves full of statutes and legal treatises lined the south wall. Numerous plaques, awards, and signed jury verdict forms from winning cases covered the east wall. The north wall contained two large, framed pieces. One was a lithograph depicting Abraham Lincoln giving the Gettysburg Address. The other was a copy of the United States Constitution on weathered and torn paper.

Ackerman's desk, a large piece of glass held up by metal replicas of two deer antlers, was positioned to the west. The leather chair behind his desk was covered in a cowhide print, and behind where Ackerman sat was a sketch of him giving the closing argument in his first death penalty trial. Before judges started allowing cameras in the courtroom, a sketch artist had rendered the drawing to be used by the media to show courtroom action. After Ackerman had won the trial, the artist gave him the original as a trophy of sorts for his victory.

"To what do I owe the pleasure of your company this afternoon?" Ackerman asked as they all sat down.

"We just left Deputy Blackburn's office while investigating the Pinkerton case," Steve said, "and we wondered if there is anything you might be able to tell us about the case or Deputy Blackburn that we couldn't find in the record."

"I doubt there is much I can tell you about your case that you don't already know, but I can tell you something about Deputy Blackburn. He is one of the bad cops," Ackerman said seriously. "I'm sure you heard about him shooting that young man last month. I would bet he was in the wrong on that one. There is no doubt in my mind that man is racist. On top of that, he is one of the few cops I have caught lying on the stand. He believes that the end justifies the means. Doesn't matter what rules or laws he has to break to put the 'bad guys' in prison as long as they end up in prison. He somehow thinks that is good police work—that the Fourth Amendment and other laws don't apply to him because he is a 'good guy.' Mind you, not all police officers act that way, but I'll tell you the ones who do are what drive me to get out of bed every morning and come in here to this office to work my tail off for the downtrodden."

"Never ceases to amaze me," Booger said with a slow shake of his head, "the number of police officers who think the law doesn't apply to them. They think that because they are putting away the bad guys, as you called them, then they can do whatever they want to make sure that happens."

"Exactly," Steve said. "Don't they realize the Constitution is the most important law in the land? It is what makes our country great, and without it, all these other laws wouldn't matter."

"Just make sure you keep your eyes on him," Ackerman said. "He is capable of just about anything. That case is what made his career. The investigation and subsequent conviction put him on the map in the police world as a big-time cop. I would bet the farm that Deputy Blackburn will do anything to protect his reputation and make sure your client is executed—whether he truly believes Scottie did it or not."

After some time discussing the other details of the case, Steve and Booger thanked Ackerman for his advice and returned to Tulsa. They decided to go downtown to the Main Street Lounge for a drink and strategy session.

CHAPTER 24

The Main Street Lounge was an upscale bar in the Blue Dome District of Tulsa that featured mixologists rather than bartenders. It was just dark enough to still be swanky and the odor of cedar barrels prevailed. Steve liked their version of an old fashioned. Booger ordered a Bud Light. On the television above the bar, the big news of the day was the Department of Justice's decision to drop their lawsuit against Apple to unlock the San Bernadino shooter's iPhone.

"Have you gotten anymore Snapchat messages." Booger asked.

"Yes. A few more. All still vague threats but nothing substantive."

"Make sure you start keeping an eye out around you."

"Got it. So, at this point in the game, what do you think of our case, my friend?" Steve said.

"The way I see it, we have four suspects: Walters, Whitmore, Scottie, and the X factor."

"Scottie?" Steve said, shocked.

"Yes. He still has the most evidence against him. Now, don't get me wrong. I believe him when he says he didn't do it. But I also think there is something he is not telling us. It would be foolish of us to completely discount him just because we want to believe him."

"What do you think he is hiding?"

"I don't know. I just have a gut feeling he is hiding something. The more I think about it, if it wasn't Scottie, whoever it was had to be in the house, or very close by, at the time Scottie left for the hotel. According to the police radio logs, it was exactly six minutes and forty-seven seconds between the time Deputy

Blackburn received the call to respond to a domestic violence situation at the Scottie house and the moment he radioed for assistance with Ashley. Now that we've been to the house, if you consider the length of the driveway and the fact he would have cautiously entered the residence, I think we can reasonably deduce he would have seen a car leaving the residence at least a minute before he radioed for help. That leaves approximately five minutes and forty-seven seconds for whomever it was to kill Ashley and leave without being seen by Deputy Blackburn."

"But if it was Whitmore on his four-wheeler," Steve said, "he could have driven off from the back of the property. Deputy Blackburn may not have seen him as he pulled up to the front of the house."

"Good point. If it was Whitmore, then he may have had an extra thirty seconds or so. Either way, I think the person was in the house when Ashley called 911 and before Scottie left. Then, he or she killed Ashley and got out of there quickly... I also think that our killer is the one who talked Ashley into making the fake 911 call in the first place. It was a total setup for the murder." Booger said this as if he had just put this piece of the puzzle together at that precise moment.

He continued after a swig of beer, "You know, young man, the only way to get away with murder is to have a fall guy. You have to give the police someone to arrest and the district attorney's office someone to convict. There has to be a picture on the front page of the local paper showing they got the guy. Otherwise, they will keep looking until they find you."

"How do we figure out who else may have been in the house?" Steve asked.

"Short of a surveillance video, we have to do some hard work. I think we start with who we know for sure was there: Scottie and Ashley. We have to go back to prison and talk to Scottie," Booger said. "I told you I think there is something he isn't telling us, and it is high time we find out all of his secrets."

"Okay. Back to your list," Steve said. "Why don't you have Deputy Blackburn on it? He was the last person to see her alive and Ackerman said he is crooked. He could have done it."

"Yes. I would put him in the X-factor column. I'm not quite ready to call him a clear suspect. Him being a dirty cop doesn't make him a murderer of young white women. Of course, if he killed that young man a few months ago in cold blood, maybe he could do it in this case too. Only problem is there is no reason. I can see a racist cop taking the opportunity to kill a black man just because he thinks he can get away with it. But I don't see him killing a white woman in her home and then blaming the husband without some additional motive."

As Booger finished, a phone rang. Steve patted his pockets and pulled out a phone, then pulled out a second phone, checked it, and paused. Seeing Booger's expression, Steve explained briefly, "It's my personal phone but an unknown number." Then he answered the call. "Hello, Steve Hanson. How can I help you?"

"Hello, Steve Hanson." The woman on the other end gave a slight laugh. "Wow, that sounded very official and lawyerly. This is Dr. Emily Babbage. Jennifer told me your guy pled to the embezzlement charge and gave me your number. Case closed, right? Which means I'm available for dinner, assuming you are still interested."

"Of course!" Steve said a little too excitedly. He tried to calm his voice down and asked, "Is tomorrow night good for you?"

"Tomorrow is great. Pick me up at my office around six thirty. See you then." Emily hung up without giving Steve a chance to respond.

Booger looked at Steve and raised an eyebrow meaningfully. "You look happier than a fox loose in the hen house. Good news?"

"Yeah, a girl I have a little thing for. She agreed to a date tomorrow night," Steve said with a wide smile on his face and a flicker of mischief in his eyes.

CHAPTER 25

For Steve, the next day dragged on like a poorly acted monologue. As soon as he arrived at his office, he wrote and filed the motion asking to see the Rogers County Sheriff's Office's complete investigation file. In the pleading, Steve laid out his theory about Scottie's innocence, weaving in other legal jargon he hoped would sway the court to grant his request. Upon receipt of the motion, the court gave the state three weeks to respond and set the matter for a hearing three weeks after that date. Steve had hoped the issue hearing would be set sooner but knew from experience that the wheels of justice turned slowly.

Steve also set up a meeting with Scottie. Luckily, Gilcrease was able to get him in quickly because another attorney had called earlier in the day and canceled his appointment for next week.

He spent the rest of the day working on other cases and planned to spend his weekend catching up on more of them. He had nearly a hundred files that had been mostly ignored because of Scottie Pinkerton's case. They definitely needed attention, but tonight, Steve finally had a date with Emily. As the evening drew close, his growing excitement made it hard to concentrate.

Steve arrived at Emily's office around 6:15 p.m. In college, his soccer coach at Oklahoma City University, Brian Harvey, had drilled the need to be on time into all the players' heads. It only took a few times of running extra sprints for tardiness for Steve to learn that it was much better to be fifteen minutes early than one minute late. Since then, he always arrived fifteen minutes early to every appointment, date, meeting, or whatever he had on his schedule.

He played Chess with Friends on his smart phone while sitting in his car. Although he liked to be timely, in this instance he didn't want to seem overanxious to Emily. At six thirty on the dot, Steve walked up to the entrance. Since the office closed at 5:00 p.m., the glass door was locked. He peered through it and couldn't see anyone in the reception area. He knocked. Shortly after, Emily came out and said hello. She locked the door behind her and walked toward his car. Steve hurried ahead and was holding her door open when she arrived.

"Wow, an old-fashioned gentleman," she said with a look of pleasure and surprise. "Thank you."

From there, he took her to Mi Cocina, an upscale Mexican restaurant on Cherry Street. The restaurant had a modern interior, giving it a very different vibe from the other Tex-Mex restaurants around town, all of which had sombreros and Mexican blankets on the walls. Mi Cocina was the type of place that sold specialty cocktails made from top shelf tequila or mezcal rather than pitchers of premixed drinks that tasted more like a green Gatorade than a true margarita.

After they were seated, Emily placed her cell phone upside down to her right, and Steve placed his two cell phones upside down to his left.

"Why do you have two phones?" Emily asked.

"One is my work phone, and one is my personal cell. In this day and age, clients expect you to give them your cell phone number when they hire you. So, I use this phone for them. It actually does make it easier to communicate with them. I can call one from the courthouse if he or she isn't there on time and find out why they are late. Also, on days when I am just one of many lawyers on a judge's docket, I can step into the hallway and make calls for other cases while waiting my turn in court. I'm sure you know how it is at the courthouse. All the hurry-up and wait."

"Right? You have a hearing set at 9:00 a.m. You rush to be there on time, and then it turns out there are fifty other cases set on the same docket. And you don't actually have your hearing until lunchtime. Or sometimes after."

"Exactly," Steve said. "In those situations, I can go in the hallway and make calls. That way, it is not such a waste of time waiting my turn. I have the personal one so that on weekends or vacations—assuming I get to take one of those someday—I can turn the office phone off and still get calls from my friends and family."

"I guess a first date with an amazing woman isn't cause for leaving your work cell at home?" Emily asked teasingly.

Steve, somewhat oblivious to Emily's flirtation, flatly stated, "The truth is I can never bring myself to turn it off or leave it behind. I should probably just have one phone and tell my clients the number. But for whatever reason, it makes me feel good knowing I could turn it off."

Steve was afraid he had been too short in his response or possibly offended Emily by bringing both phones so he was happy to be saved when the waiter came up to their table. Steve ordered a top-shelf margarita with a Cointreau floater, and Emily requested a Mezcal on the rocks and a slice of orange.

After some first date small talk, Emily said, "Tell me something about yourself unrelated to your profession."

"Hmm. Like what?"

"I don't know. Tell me the craziest thing you have ever done in your life."

"Okay. Let me think." Steve stared into space for a few seconds, thinking to himself. He perused the card catalogue of his memories and thought, Crazy story suitable for a first date. Not that one. No, not that one either.

"You okay?" Emily said.

"Oh, got one," Steve said. "I jumped out of a perfectly good airplane once. Is that crazy enough for you?" he asked with a grin.

Emily's eyes widened. "Wow? That is a pretty good one. Tell me about it!"

"It was a few years ago, back when I was still an undergraduate at Oklahoma City University. Every year, the school organized an auction to help cover the cost of running the athletic department. As a member of the soccer team, I always had to attend the event because the school would introduce each team on stage to show the donors the faces of the kids they were helping. You know, make it more human. Anyway, during my junior year, one of the silent auction items was a certificate to skydive at a local facility. It was a $150-value, and I got it for the minimum bid of thirty dollars. I got it so cheap because I was the only one in the room who was crazy enough to bid on the thing."

"Or dumb enough," Emily said, laughing.

"True," Steve said, laughing in agreement. "I scheduled my session for a few weeks later. Because I had a certificate for one jump, the parachute facility said that I could either go tandem or do what's called a static line jump. If I tandem jumped, then I would get to free fall because the person I was strapped to would pull the ripcord for us whether or not I panicked. On the static line jump, I would be all by myself, but the rip cord would be automatically pulled as I fell away from the plane, so I would not get any of the free fall sensation. Since I chose to do the solo jump, I had to show up early in the morning and train for six hours before they would take me up in the sky.

"At the end of the day, I got in the plane with my instructor and a couple of other classmates—all of whom had gone through the class with me that day. We got to put on jumpsuits, and then I strapped the parachute on my back and climbed into the belly of the plane. We flew up to a little over one thousand feet above the ground. I happened to be the last one to jump, so I had to sit and watch my five classmates jump out of the plane one by one before I got to do it."

"Were you scared?"

"Definitely! Once it was my turn to jump, my instructor linked a carabiner hook to the static line and my ripcord. Anytime someone goes on their first jump, any reputable jump company will connect a static line. The static line is attached to you on one end and the fuselage of the airplane on the other end. Its purpose is to ensure the ripcord is automatically pulled as you fall away from the plane. It is set up to save those people who might otherwise panic and forget to pull the cord as they plummet to their death."

"For our first date, let's try to keep the topics light and stay away from dying. Okay?" Emily said jokingly.

"Sorry about that. Other than my poor attempts at humor, there is no death in this story. No one dies, I promise," Steve said, sharing another laugh with her. "The scariest part was when I had to get out of the plane. The plane had a propeller on the front of the fuselage. The wings were on top and there were two struts, or bars, sticking out from the under the wings connecting down to the bottom of the fuselage." As Steve described it, he made the outline of the plane and wings with his hands.

He continued, "I had to lean out, hold onto one of those struts, and then shimmy out away from the plane, hanging on with just my bare hands and with my feet literally dangling a thousand feet up in the sky. I had to scooch out far enough from the fuselage that I would not fall back into the side of the plane. Once I was three or four feet out from the plane, the instructor told me to let go. It was scary as all get out, but I let go and fell back from the plane.

"Thankfully my chute opened immediately. I also didn't have any trouble with twisted ropes or have to pull my secondary ripcord or deal with any of the other emergency situations they had gone through with us in the training. My chute opened perfectly, and, after that, I just floated for a while."

"Wow, that is crazy!" Emily leaned forward. "It also sounds extremely exhilarating. Did you love it?"

"It was honestly one of the coolest things I have ever experienced in my life. Just floating down to earth. It was very peaceful and quiet up there," Steve recalled, before he grinned. "A friend of mine asked me to do one thing for her when I was up there. So, as I floated, I screamed, 'Excuse me while I kiss the sky!' and puckered up to the air."

Emily chuckled at the mental image of Steve parachuting with his lips puckered. Her arm brushed against his as she set her drink down; they shared a smile.

"All right, your turn," Steve said. "What is the craziest thing you have ever done?"

"Me?" Her face flushed for a moment. Steve figured that she was doing the same drill that he did before telling his "craziest thing ever" story. He wondered what she wasn't ready to tell him about yet.

"Well, I'm not sure if this counts as crazy to someone who has jumped out of a perfectly good airplane," Emily said, "but for a computer forensics geek, it tops my list. The graduate program I was a part of, the University of Tulsa computer forensics, is one of the top three in the nation, so there were people from all over the country attending school with me. Not sure if it was like this in law school, but in every class, there was always one jackass who sat in the front row and tried to outsmart the professor."

"Definitely had those in law school too," Steve said with an eye roll and a smile.

"Well, the one in our class had spent a year at MIT. When he showed up the first day of class, he actually thought he knew more than the professors at 'podunk' Tulsa University. He was so annoying! Anyway, as I am sure you can imagine with a bunch of computer nerds, we all took notes on our laptops and used them for everything in class.

"One of our classes was about computer security—firewalls, restricted access protocols, etcetera. The assignment was to create a firewall for your own laptop, and the professor would grade you on its functionality. I figured out a back door to the brainiac's firewall and secretly downloaded a virus to his laptop. Needless to say, me breaking through the firewall he had created for his assignment didn't help his grade much."

Emily's smile widened into a mischievous grin. "But that is not the crazy part. The program I created caused his computer to make fart sounds whenever he hit the enter key. I inserted the virus one day during class using the school's Wi-Fi system we were sharing. It took him about three strokes on his enter key to realize he was the one 'farting' in class. Once he understood what was happening, he got super mad and stormed out of the lecture hall. Everyone died laughing as he left. I'm pretty sure I even saw the professor crack a smile as the door shut behind him."

"Did he drop out?"

"No. But he stopped acting so pompous to everyone. Not sure if that counts as crazy compared to skydiving, but all of my classmates loved it."

"Of course, it counts. That's a hilarious story!" Steve said laughing all the while.

As dinner continued, Steve and Emily shared many more anecdotes from their lives. When the sopapillas hit the tables, Steve's phone buzzed. It was another random Snapchat.

"Duty calls?" asked Emily.

"It's a Snapchat from an unknown number."

"Do you regularly get Snapchats from unknown numbers?" Emily asked, curious.

"I have been getting some weird ones recently. My website has my work cell number on it, so I often get calls or texts from unknown numbers." He flipped his phone back over and turned his attention back to Emily. "I'll look at it later. Even if it's a new client, the courthouse is closed until Monday; there is not a lot I can do at eight o'clock on a Friday night for whomever it was, anyway."

After dinner, they walked across the street for a few drinks. Steve opened the door for Emily to go in first. Inside, they saw a wooden bar which ran down the length of the place on the right, and there were probably a hundred beer taps lined along the wall behind it. Eight tables with four chairs each were positioned along the left wall. Most of the tables were occupied, but they found an open one in the back corner. Emily sat down, and Steve went to the bar and got them each a beer.

When he returned, Emily looked anxious. "As an investigator, I have to tell you that your unknown Snapchat is driving me mad. Although I appreciate you putting it aside for our date, would you mind checking it for my sanity?"

"Sure," Steve said as he picked up his phone. He leaned over and held it in front of him so they could both see the screen. He opened the application and began to press play.

Emily pushed the phone toward him gently and said, "I know I'm not the first girl you ever went on a date within your life. That might be an old fling trying to get your attention. I don't want to see it. I just want you to check it and tell me what it is, if it is not too personal."

Steve turned the phone screen toward himself and pressed play.

Emily saw his face turn from happy to ashen in an instant. "What was it?"

"I don't want to say," Steve said.

"You look like you just saw a ghost. Was it some crazy ex who stalks you or something? Do I need to be concerned?" she said while jokingly looking around the room and crouching down as if someone was going to jump out at her any second.

"No. You have nothing to worry about," Steve said, smiling faintly at her antics. "I don't know who it was from, but it wasn't about you… I think it was a death threat."

Emily sat up straight, completely serious now. "What? What do you mean? You think? What was it?"

"Let me show you." Steve started turning the phone toward her.

"No." Emily put her hand over his, stopping him. "You know

you can only play a Snapchat message twice, and then it's gone forever. Don't show me. Just tell me. If it is what you say it is, we can take it to my lab where I can work my magic and save a copy that will give us the ability to re-watch it as many times as we want without them knowing we saved it. Plus, I might be able to determine who sent it."

"Wow! Really, you can do all of that?"

"Yes. Now tell me what it was," Emily said.

"It was a video of a huge pig being slaughtered," Steve said, grimacing as he remembered what he'd just seen. "The animal was hung upside down by its feet, and a butcher sliced its throat to drain the blood from its body. The words 'the only good lawyer is a dead lawyer' were written in red on the screen."

"Oh my god, that is demented. That definitely sounds like a death threat to me. Does this type of thing happen to you a lot?"

"Not before I got appointed to this new case. Since then I have been getting them here and there. Each one is a little more demented than the last, but this is the first one that seemed to be a true threat."

"Well, you are one lucky guy. In the future, you can tell people you were on a date with a computer forensics expert when you got your first death threat," Emily said, trying to lighten the mood. "You can talk about how lucky you were to have the threat come via an electronic device and that your date ended up helping you find the person who threatened you. That should make for a good story. Now, let's get out of here. Take me back to my office and let me see if I can figure out who wants to kill you."

They downed their beers, gathered their belongings, and left for Emily's forensics lab.

CHAPTER 26

Once they returned to her lab, Emily hooked Steve's phone up to her computer. Using one of her many forensic programs, she was able to make a copy of all the data contained on Steve's phone and transfer the information to her hard drive.

While they were waiting on the transfer, Steve noticed a small wooden wand sitting on a stand on the workbench next to Emily's computer. "What is that?"

"That is Hermione's wand." Emily gestured to the bookshelf behind Steve. "I have all the other main characters' wands over there; I keep Hermione's near me for inspiration. I hold it whenever I am stuck on trying to crack into a locked program, firewall, website, computer file, or the like. It always seems to send me magical thoughts and outside-of-the-box ideas. Are you a Harry Potter fan?"

"Yeah, I loved the story, but I'm apparently not as big of a fan as you. I have read all of the books and have whole-heartedly enjoyed them, but I don't own any wands. Maybe I should get one for my next jury trial," Steve said half-jokingly.

"You definitely should. They truly are magic wands," Emily said with a smile. "I'm obviously a huge fan. They are my all-time favorite books, and I have a whole costume at home—complete with a robe, yellow and burgundy tie, and a Gryffindor scarf. I'm going to London in the fall to see the new play, which tells a story about one of Harry's children. It's called Harry Potter and the Cursed Child. I've got front row seats too."

Her blue eyes were gleaming with excitement as she recounted the tale of acquiring tickets. "I set my alarm and woke up at 3:00

a.m. last summer to get online when the tickets went on sale at 9:00 a.m., London time. The tickets to several months' worth of performances were sold out in a matter of hours. However, I've created a program that refreshes the Ticketmaster feed in less than a nanosecond, with a new window for each one. The program can identify the best seats and highlight that window. I just had to make sure I logged in and started my program about two minutes before the tickets went on sale to the public; that way, I always get great seats to every concert or performance I want to see and always at face value. So that's how I have two front row seats in the middle orchestra section to a performance in September."

"First, that's awesome! Now I know who to contact next time a concert that I want to see comes to town. Second, a trip to London and front row seats to a Harry Potter play sounds like a lot of fun. Who is going with you?"

"I haven't decided yet," Emily said. "Maybe I'll take you if you play your cards right, and this nut job doesn't kill you first."

They both smiled at the thought of traveling together, then sat quietly, thinking what a trip together in September would mean about their relationship five months from today. Steve happily realized the silence didn't feel awkward for either of them.

"All right, the transfer is complete. I now have a mirror image of your phone's memory on my computer. You did know your smart phone is actually just a small handheld computer, right?"

Steve nodded; because he did now.

"Anyway, without getting super technical on you, I can go through everything on your phone using my computer, as if I was actually on your phone. Except, I can do a lot more fun stuff with the information because I have several computer programs that give me the ability to analyze the metadata contained in your messages. This technology would be too complex to even attempt to download onto your phone's simple operating system."

"I must say, it is amazing and a little scary how much information you can get about me from my phone. Can you see everything I have on my phone on your computer now?"

"Yes, but don't worry. I give you my word I won't go through any of your personal stuff, and I will delete the entire copy as soon as we are done. As I said earlier, I know this is our first date. I can tell by how calm you've been that you have been on your fair share of first dates in the past and might even be seeing other women right now. When I tell my friends about you, I will tell them that I even consider you a bit of a ladies' man," Emily said teasingly. "However, I'm not interested in your number, not yet anyway." She looked him in the eyes for a brief second and then turned back to her computer screen.

"Tonight, I'm only interested in opening your Snapchat message to see what I can discern from it and, hopefully, figure out who sent it. Like I said, I have several programs that allow me to find the metadata contained within your message. I think I told you once, but in case you forgot, metadata is information buried within all computer files. It contains all sorts of information about the file—when it was created, where it was created, etcetera. Mirroring your entire hard drive is the only way for me to get the Snapchat message to my computer. I will delete everything except that message once I get it saved properly."

"I thought you also told me once that nothing is ever really deleted?"

"Yeah. That's basically true, too. I'm impressed you actually paid attention to some of the things I've already taught you," Emily said with a playful smirk. "I guess you will just have to trust me not to look at it. If it helps, I can promise you that I have absolutely no desire to see pictures of your ex-girlfriends or whatever else you may have saved on your phone. Not yet, anyway."

She said "yet" again, Steve thought. A part of him actually looked forward to the time when she would want to know about his romantic past. Possibly by the time they went to London together.

Emily disconnected Steve's phone and handed it back to him. "All done with that," she said as she pulled up what looked to be a mirror copy of Steve's phone data on her computer. Steve watched Emily click on the Snapchat application and open the most recent message. With a few more clicks, she was able to find the phone number associated with the unknown sender's message.

"Looks like a local number," she said. "Do you recognize it?"

"Unfortunately, no," Steve said.

She wrote down the number, then opened a separate web browser. In her favorites, she clicked on a website that contained a reverse number directory. After she typed it in, the result showed the number was registered to the Roach prepaid cell phone company. She then hacked into Roach's database and determined the phone had been purchased two years ago at one of their South Tulsa locations, but it was only recently used. According to the sales contract, the person who bought the phone was named Taylor Gains and had a Tulsa address.

"Do you know her?" asked Emily.

"No. I don't know him either. Taylor could be male or female. Does the contract have a place where the person checks a box declaring their sex? We could at least eliminate roughly half the population if we knew that."

Emily moved the mouse so they could examine the entire document. The portion for sex of the individual had been left blank.

"Well, one thing is for sure: whoever sent you this is no idiot. He or she used a gender-neutral name and didn't mark their sex on the application form. I'm sure the address at the top will lead us nowhere, so I won't check it until later." Emily returned to the Snapchat application. Before she played the message, she opened another program.

"What is Groundhog?" Steve asked, reading the program's name.

"It's one of my many fancy investigative tools. It will allow me to pause the message while it's playing and dig into the embedded metadata." She opened the video from the unknown number and clicked play. Then, she began typing and clicking the mouse feverishly. Shortly thereafter, she found what she was looking for.

"Do you see this number here?" She pointed at the screen.

"Yes," Steve said.

"That is the IP address of the cell tower the person was connected to when he or she sent the message. With this number, we can find out the location of your new friend, within a twenty-to-fifty-mile radius. Watch." Emily opened her web browser and went to another site.

Steve was able to read over Emily's shoulder that this newly opened website could give IP locations for any location in the United States. She typed in the IP address and up popped a location—Claremore, Oklahoma.

Emily looked back at Steve. "Any idea why someone in Claremore would be threatening you?"

"Yeah. I've got a pretty good one. That is where my new death penalty case happened. I guess my recent investigations have drawn more interest than I realized. Can you get me a more precise location than Claremore? Like an address or part of town?"

"Hold on." She began typing away at her keyboard some more. After a few seconds, a map appeared on her computer screen with a blinking dot just to the east of town. There was a red circle about an inch in diameter with the blinking dot in the center of it. Around the red circle, there was a bigger green circle.

"The blinking dot is the tower. The red circle around it is the radius where a phone can only get a signal from that specific tower. The green circle is the maximum distance the tower can pick up a signal, period. Sometimes, your phone connects to a tower farther away even if there is one nearby. That is why you get dropped calls and bad connections on occasion. However..." Emily paused to click on something, and several dots and circles showed up on her screen. "The person was likely in the red circle. Looking around, there are enough towers out there for all of those red circles to cover areas outside of our tower's red circle. So, if you were outside this red circle," she said, pointing to the original red circle and tower, "you would fall into one of these other red circles and most likely get a different tower. Does this make sense?"

"I think so. Basically, if you are in a red circle, you will almost always get the tower closest to you, but in the places where there is no red, the green circles overlap, and you may get a tower close to you or one farther away?"

"Exactly. Looking at this map, I would say there is a 90 percent chance your new friend was within this circle when he or she sent the message." As Emily said this, she clicked her mouse again, and all of the other dots and circles disappeared, leaving only the original dot and red circle.

Steve leaned forward to look closely at the map. According to the key, the red circle encompassed an area approximately thirty miles in diameter. He could see the Claremore Racino, the Whitmore Flying W Ranch, and the Fieldstone housing addition, all located within the red circle. Although he couldn't pinpoint the threat, at least now he knew he was on the right track in his investigation.

"Thank you for your help," Steve said. "This map at least lets me know who probably sent the message, and I obviously never could have obtained this much information about where this message came from without you. Thank you so much."

"Not a problem. I'm just sorry I couldn't get you a more precise location. A fifteen-mile radius is not exactly small." Emily glanced at the time in the upper right of her computer screen. It read 12:38 a.m.

"It's late," she said. "I will come up here tomorrow and try to get more metadata out of this message. I know, at a minimum, I can figure out where the video was filmed. But I am not sure how much that will help us. I would guess your new friend just downloaded the file from the web. But if he or she recorded it themselves, then we will know at least one place this person had access to."

She handed Steve a zip drive. "This contains a copy of the Snapchat message and everything we discovered tonight: the Roach phone application, the cell tower map, etcetera. Follow me out."

Steve stood nearby as Emily locked the door to the lab behind them. After she tested the door to make sure it was locked, she turned, leaned in, and gave Steve a short, soft kiss on the lips. After she was done, she immediately walked away, saying over her shoulder, "I had a great time tonight, Steven Hanson. Call me if you want to try a second date."

Steve watched as Emily got into her car. When she drove by, she gave Steve a quick wave goodbye and sped away with a smile on her face. From the time she kissed him until her taillights sped away, Steve had stood in the same spot, dumbstruck. The aftershocks of the kiss still ran up and down his body. He couldn't believe how much attraction he felt toward her after just one date. She is truly one amazing woman, he thought.

A second or two after she drove off, Steve regained his composure. He needed to focus. He texted Booger to let him know something major had happened in the case. The message told Booger to call him first thing in the morning.

Steve went home and fell asleep thinking about Emily, then dreamed about what the future might hold with her. But occasionally, Steve's dreams were interrupted by the waking realization that he was now at risk of losing his life at the hands of a psychopath.

CHAPTER 27

The phone rang at 6:30 a.m. Steve sleepily reached for it.

"Good morning, young man," Booger said dryly. "What momentous piece of information arose in the wee hours of last night that required this morning's urgent phone call?"

Steve quickly explained what happened the previous night with Emily.

Booger said, "Okay, I'm on my way."

After they met up and Steve had shown the investigator the contents of the zip drive Emily had given him, Booger said, "Well, we definitely got someone's attention. Too bad all of our suspects live within a few miles of each other."

"True. What do you think our next move should be?" Steve said.

"I think we definitely keep it our secret for now. Can you trust Dr. Babbage not to tell any of her friends at the district attorney's office?"

"Yes, I think so. I will ask her to keep this on the down low. I do think the threats might help us in getting the police file though. I would like to prepare a second motion to the court including this information."

"Good idea, just make sure you get the court's authority to file it under seal in order to keep it out of the public realm. You know that, otherwise, everything you file can be found online from the court's website," Booger said.

"Yeah, I know," Steve said, nodding. "I will definitely ask the court to let me file the motion and exhibits under seal. That is the only way to let the judge know what is going on, but make sure no one else knows what we know."

"Damn lucky you were on a date with a computer forensics expert when you got this threat," Booger said with a chuckle.

"Yeah. Especially since they sent it via Snapchat. Not sure if you know this, but once you watch the video twice, it's gone forever, and it's gone in twenty-four hours even if you don't watch it twice. I doubt many people would have even believed I got this message if not for Emily's quick thinking and expertise."

"True." Booger paused, then said with a grin, "I don't suppose you want to give me five numbers between one and thirty-six and your favorite number? I'm thinking a dollar for the purchase of a lottery ticket might be in order."

After Booger left to work on some cars, Steve hunkered down to prepare his motions. First the motion to seal and then his addendum to the motion to see Blackburn's police file. He asked the judge to move up the hearing. He used the threat to support his argument that he needed the file as soon as possible for his own safety, as well as for the fact he now strongly believed an innocent man was sitting on death row.

Steve persuasively told the court that since there was no possible way Scottie sent the threat, someone else must be worried about the investigation. He further alleged that the unknown someone could be the person who actually killed Ashley Pinkerton. There was no other logical reason for anyone to be concerned enough about their investigation to issue a death threat. Moreover, that unknown someone might kill Steve if he or she wasn't apprehended quickly.

Steve finished the brief by late Saturday evening; he then filed everything that day using the court's online filing system. As he clicked through the process, Steve thought about how frustrating it must have been to be an attorney in the past. Less than ten years ago, he would have had to wait until Monday morning and taken copies in person to the court clerk's office to file his motion. Now, thanks to technology, he could relax for the rest of the weekend, work on other cases, and wait to see what Judge Henry had to say about his motion on Monday morning.

Early that morning, Steve was in the office, trying to occupy himself with work that needed to be completed on his other files. He had caught up on the majority of them Sunday but still wasn't comfortable with where he was on a few of them. Mostly though, he wanted to stay busy to keep his mind off the motion he filed Saturday evening and what response he thought it might garner from the judge. Shortly after 11:00 a.m., Carol buzzed his intercom. "Judge Henry's office on line three, big shot."

Steve picked up the phone. "Hello, this is Steve Hanson."

"Hello, Steve. Gail from Judge Henry's office. The judge reviewed your motion to seal, your motion to obtain the police file and your application for emergency hearing that you filed over the weekend. He is granting your request to keep the second motion under seal. He is also granting an expedited hearing on your motion requesting access to the police file. He is going to stay through lunch and hear your case tomorrow at noon."

"Thank you, Gail. I will see you tomorrow."

"See you then." Before Gail hung up, she said under her breath, "One more thing, Steve… Stay safe. You know we are all fans of yours around here. We wouldn't want anything to happen to our favorite young attorney."

"Thanks," Steve said. "Will do."

As soon as he hung up with Gail, Steve called Booger.

"We are set for a hearing tomorrow at noon," Steve said.

"Noon?" Booger asked.

"Yes. I guess that threat got the judge's attention. He often skips lunch when he has a matter he wants heard quickly but can't find any open time slot on his docket otherwise. Also, we still have our trip to McAlester on Wednesday to visit Scottie. Hopefully, we will have some good news for him."

"Well, that worked out mighty nicely. I think I am definitely going to run to the corner market and buy that lottery ticket. Can you give me the numbers to pick?

"In all seriousness," Booger continued after they'd shared a laugh, "it sounds like you have a lot of work to do in the next twenty-four hours. You know the state is not going to just roll over and let you get that police file without a fight. This threat may have gotten you a quick hearing, but the state won't care. They will still fight you tooth and nail on this one. They don't like turning over investigative files in any case, let alone a murder investigation."

"Yes, I know. See you tomorrow at the courthouse."

Steve had a divorce mediation set that afternoon and some DUIs set for plea the next morning. He was able to move them to a later date by telling the state court judges he had just been informed that Judge Henry, a federal judge, had set an expedited hearing the next day, and he needed to prepare. It was common for state court judges to defer to federal court judges when it came to conflicting schedules. Steve went home to his war room, which until the Scottie appointment had merely been his dining room. He spent the rest of the day preparing for the hearing.

First, he printed copies of the relevant case law he wanted to use in support of his arguments. He had done all of the necessary research while preparing the motion, so it was easy to find the cases. Next, he highlighted and tabbed the specific sections of those cases he wanted to read to the court.

Having read numerous briefs while working for judges, Steve knew that, oftentimes, rather than making up the wording of your entire argument from scratch and citing cases, the most effective way to persuade the court was to use direct quotes from a similar case or situation, especially when the case had come from a judge who was superior in the judicial system to the judge you were appearing in front of. Luckily, Steve had already found a few cases that he thought fit squarely behind his position.

He finished his oral argument preparation by outlining his thoughts and organizing the quoted material in conjunction with his outline. He did this so he could easily shift from the specifics of his case to the quoted material in support without delay.

Once he had his argument in focus, he put an empty box on his dining room table. He arranged his notes and copies on it to simulate the lectern he would be standing behind in the courtroom. He practiced over and over until he essentially had the entire argument memorized.

Steve did not usually practice this much for a simple motion hearing, but he knew the police file contained the key to finding the true killer. If he and Booger were not allowed to see the file, all would be lost. It would be almost impossible to investigate the murder seven years later without knowing everything that had been discovered when the investigation was still fresh.

If you don't win this case, your client will die. This was the thought that kept popping up in the back of Steve's mind; this was the thought that drove him to work as hard as he could. He had to win tomorrow.

CHAPTER 28

Steve arrived at the federal courthouse at 11:45 a.m. He checked in with the clerk's office and made his way to Judge Henry's courtroom where he saw Booger sitting on a bench in the hallway. The investigator mockingly looked at his watch as Steve approached him.

"Are you always this late to court, son? Or is it just when you appear in federal court?" Booger asked with a grin.

Steve smiled back as they shook hands. "I guess my 'early' is not everyone's early," he said as Booger opened the door to the courtroom.

Judge Henry was the senior federal judge at the courthouse for the U.S. Federal Court of the Northern District of Oklahoma. His courtroom was on the third floor of the federal building in downtown Tulsa—the same floor Steve worked on for two years just before going into private practice. The courtroom itself was a much larger and more ornate version of the floor plan used in the Rogers County courtroom where Scottie was originally convicted. But instead of the seal of Oklahoma above the judge's bench, there was a large seal of the United States of America.

Because of the size and aura of the courtroom, some lawyers were intimidated by federal court and would never practice there. If they secured a client who needed help in federal court, they would refer it to a colleague. Steve, on the other hand, actually felt more comfortable in this setting because of the countless hours he had spent working here with these judges. The federal court would always be his first home.

As he walked down the aisle between the rows of pews in the

gallery, Steve saw a well-dressed woman sitting at the opposing counsel's table. She appeared to be in her mid-thirties, with auburn red hair, glasses, and a frumpy build. She looked up and stood when he came in. As Steve crossed through the small swinging doors separating the gallery from the courtroom, she approached him with her hand out.

"Hello, Mr. Hanson," she said. "I am Assistant Attorney General Julie Bass. Nice to meet you."

"Nice to meet you, Ms. Bass," Steve said as they shook hands.

"I heard you were young but didn't realize how young. Of course, I should have guessed when I read your motion about a 'threat.' Only someone as inexperienced as yourself would make up some Snapchat threat to try to persuade the court to give him a police file from a case that was about as open and shut as they come." Ms. Bass gave him a disapproving frown. "Scottie Pinkerton killed his wife. That is clear. Why are you wasting time trying to pin the case on someone else?"

Steve started to answer, but Ms. Bass interrupted by raising her finger at him. "Don't answer. That was a rhetorical question. For the record, your brash exuberance and your 'emergency' are causing me to miss my son's science fair."

Then, while continuing to glare at him, she said, "Let me give you a little free advice. When there is this much evidence and the jury has already convicted your client, you are better off making constitutional arguments about some alleged trial error rather than trying to find a ghost killer. And more importantly, always ask opposing counsel before you get anything set for hearing. Some of us have lives outside of the courtroom and, occasionally, activities occur that actually take precedence over our careers. It's called 'professional courtesy.' You should ask Ackerman about it sometime; I hear you know him." With that last jab, Ms. Bass briskly turned and walked back to her seat.

Well, ain't she a peach, Steve thought as he sat down at his counsel table. But I guess I should have called her Monday morning to make sure she didn't have any time conflicts this week. He made a mental note to never make that mistake again.

Steve opened his briefcase and removed the outline he had prepared. As he reviewed the argument one last time, he heard the door open at the back of the courtroom. In walked Brent Whitmore, Ashley's brother. He glared at Steve, then at Booger as he walked down the aisle toward them. He sat in the first row directly behind the defense table, his eyes never leaving either of them.

A short time later, the door behind the judge's bench opened and the bailiff called out, "United States District Court for the Northern District of Oklahoma, Case No. CJ-2015-347, is now in session. The Honorable Judge Michael W. Henry presiding." Judge Henry walked through the door and took his seat on the bench, which was positioned several feet above the courtroom floor.

He looked down at the people present and said, "Good afternoon, counselors. Thank you for coming during the lunch hour for this hearing. It was the only time this week I could get you on my docket, and after what I read yesterday morning, I felt this needed to be heard sooner rather than later.

"Before we begin, I notice there is someone in the audience. Sir, normally these hearings are public record, but today, one of the motions to be considered was filed under seal. That means there is a good reason to keep it out of the public forum until further consideration. Can I please ask you to leave the courtroom? You are welcome to wait in the hallway, out of earshot of these proceedings, but I am afraid you cannot stay."

Whitmore stood up. "Your Honor, my sister was the one killed in this case. I don't want to do nothin' to upset Your Honor. I just want to know what's going on, and I feel like I have that right. Doesn't the Constitution or some law give me some rights?"

Judge Henry answered in a compassionate tone, "Sir, you probably have more right as a human to know about these proceedings than even myself. Unfortunately, the law has certain rules in place that give me privileges I probably don't deserve and takes rights away from people like you that it probably shouldn't. However, these laws do exist, and I have sworn an oath to uphold them. So, I am going to have to ask you to wait outside until we finish the sealed portions of this hearing. Marshal, please escort this gentleman into the hallway at a far enough distance from the doors that he cannot hear what is being said and stay with him until we have concluded the first part of this hearing."

The U.S. marshal guarding the bench area raised his wrist to his face and said something as he walked toward Whitmore and escorted him out. A second marshal came out from the entrance the judge had originally entered from and took up the post the first marshal had vacated. Whitmore was clearly not happy about the unfolding events, but he knew better than to argue with a federal marshal acting upon the direct orders of a federal judge. Thus, he begrudgingly followed the marshal out the door.

"Now that the court room is clear, Mr. Hanson, please explain to me why I should order the Rogers County Sheriff's Office to release their entire investigative file in this matter to you?"

Steve stood, gathered his notes, and approached the podium.

"Your Honor, when I was appointed to this case, everyone asked me how it felt to represent a murderer. I usually answered with some sort of holier-than-thou constitutional argument. Then, I met Scottie Pinkerton—a man who is not a murderer. No, not a murderer. He is merely a man who was wrongfully convicted of capital murder."

Steve went on to explain, in detail, the evidence he had discovered which pointed to Scottie's innocence. He showed the court the picture of the door and other facts that shed doubt upon the conviction. He cited other cases where questions of factual innocence of the defendant had led the respective judge in each case to grant extraordinary relief. Lastly, Steve detailed the threat made against himself. He argued it was proof that his digging around had garnered the attention of the real killer, the real killer who was still roaming free while Scottie Pinkerton sat on death row awaiting his execution.

Ms. Bass went next. She spoke clearly and authoritatively. "The evidence supporting the conviction of Scottie Pinkerton is mountainous, Your Honor. Moreover, a jury of his peers has already convicted Scottie. At this level of the appellate process, it is not appropriate to retry the case. The only true issue before this court is whether or not Scottie received a constitutionally fair trial. The police file can shed no light on that subject. To have the Rogers County Sheriff's Office turn over the file is a waste of their time and this court's time. Lastly, we have no true idea where this threat came from. For all we know, it may have even been created by Mr. Hanson himself to lend credibility to his arguments."

"Ms. Bass," Judge Henry interrupted as he scowled down at

her. "I assume you just misspoke. I know you aren't accusing a fellow member of the bar of fabricating evidence. I happen to have known Mr. Hanson for over two years when he clerked for me, and I have always known him to be a man of character. Unless you have evidence to support such a serious allegation, I would suggest you move on."

"Sorry, Your Honor," Ms. Bass stumbled through the rest of her argument. "I am merely saying this information can do nothing to support any constitutional arguments Mr. Hanson may make at this level. The information in those files may have been useful at the trial level, but now they are not. I respectfully request the court deny the defendant's motion." She sat down hurriedly.

"Thank you, counselors," Judge Henry said. "Let me begin by saying that I, to some degree, agree with Ms. Bass. I can usually only grant habeas corpus relief if the petitioner proves a constitutional violation occurred at the trial level. However, I can also grant relief if the petitioner can prove they are factually innocent of the crime charged. Although the second instance is very rare, it is still allowed under the law. Thus, in this case, if Mr. Hanson can find evidence proving Scottie Pinkerton did not murder his wife, I would then have to grant him relief and order he receive a new trial. At that point, it would be up to the Rogers County district attorney to decide if he wanted to proceed with another trial, knowing the new evidence, or drop the charges entirely.

"In twenty-plus years of sitting on this bench, I have never once granted a habeas petition based upon the factual innocence of a petitioner. As I said before, it is a rare circumstance indeed, but just because something rarely happens does not mean the possibility should not be considered by this court." Judge Henry frowned. "I would like to add that I was originally inclined not to grant this motion, but when Mr. Hanson received what can only be considered a serious death threat, it caused me great concern. It makes me wonder if this may be the one rare instance where actual innocence will be the reason I may grant Scottie the total relief he has requested. I believe the greatest injustice our government could commit would be the execution of an innocent person. Accordingly, in an abundance of caution not to potentially participate in such a tremendous atrocity, I am ruling in favor of Scottie on this motion. I want to see what else Mr. Hanson and Mr. Thomas can discover."

Steve knew not to overtly celebrate his victory in the courtroom, but he could not help from allowing a small smile to break across his face.

"Ms. Bass, please inform the Rogers County Sheriff's Office they need to make their entire investigative file available to Mr. Hanson at a time convenient to both parties within the next ten days. Mr. Hanson, you will be allowed to go to their office and make copies of anything you deem useful. You will not be able to leave the building with anything other than the copies you make. Additionally, since this is a bit unorthodox, Mr. Hanson, I will not allow any additional time or expense on your budget. Anything you do in this regard will be pro bono. The federal government will not pay for you to expend time reinvestigating a case that is officially closed. Do both of you understand?"

Both attorneys stood and said, "Yes, Your Honor."

"This hearing is hereby adjourned." Judge Henry struck his gavel and returned through the door he had entered.

Ms. Bass quickly gathered her belongings and stood to leave.

She gave Steve a look that penetrated his soul as she stormed out of the courtroom.

"Does opposing counsel always love you so much?" Booger asked as he and Steve walked out together.

"Yeah. I'm even more popular with the Rogers County District Attorney's Office, a relationship which will only get better after they hear about this ruling," Steve said sarcastically.

The two men left the courtroom and decided to walk to Kai Vietnamese for lunch. On the way, Steve's phone buzzed. He looked at it and saw that he had received a new Snapchat. He showed the notification to Booger.

Booger put his hand on Steve's and said, "Don't open it. Call Emily. See if she is available."

Steve called Emily. She said she could drop what she was doing and told him to come over immediately. The two men left the courthouse and drove straight to her office.

CHAPTER 29

As soon as they arrived, Emily took Steve's phone and connected it to her computer to similarly make a mirror image containing the recent Snapchat message. Emily sat at her desk, and the two men hovered over her shoulders, watching her computer screen intently. Once the transfer was complete, she opened the message.

A picture of Steve appeared on the screen. It was a duplicate of one of the photos he used on his website. After a few seconds, a gunshot could be heard, and a hole appeared in the middle of his head. Blood oozed out of the bullet wound as the words "Stop Digging or Die" appeared in red, one letter at a time, across the screen.

They all looked at each other.

"Well, no doubt about this one being a death threat," Emily said, attempting to bring levity to the situation. She began to search the file's metadata. Soon, she was on the cell tower website. The message originated from downtown Tulsa, and the specific tower was on a building directly across the street from the federal courthouse.

"Whitmore was downtown less than thirty minutes before I got this message," Steve said. "The judge threw him out of the courtroom before the hearing began. It looks like we've got our man. It was Ashley Pinkerton's brother!"

Emily and Booger looked at each other with the knowing smiles of two people that had done their fair share of investigative work. Their shared expressions clearly showed what each of them was thinking. He's smart, but a bit naïve.

Steve recognized the look immediately and said, "Or… maybe it was someone who was not foolish enough to be seen by us before sending me a death threat twenty-some minutes later from the same part of town."

"Maybe. However, in your defense," Emily said, "whoever's doing this doesn't know we are able to track the location of where the messages are being sent from. Thus, Whitmore actually is my number one suspect. But it is still conceivable that someone else was downtown, and that this other person sent the message. Everyone interested in this case likely knew you had a hearing set for today. Anyone could have been down there in hopes of finding out the ruling as soon as you were done."

"That's right," Booger said. "We haven't exactly matched James Marshall's discovery of gold in California, but we do have ourselves one helluva good suspect."

"Listen," Emily said, "I know I am not an official part of this investigation. I assume there is a lot of information you are not sharing with me. But can I be your official computer forensics investigator? This whole situation has certainly piqued my interest, and my investigative mind has been doing backflips trying to figure out what the hell is going on here. I don't know if you call it OCD or what, but whenever a problem or riddle gets in my head, I can't get it out until I find the solution. In this case, the threats you have received, and my wonderment as to where they came from, have officially locked into my mind. So, I will help you voluntarily. But if you agree to let me participate, then you have to show me everything you have—everything about the case you are working on. It's the only way I can get a full grasp on what is happening here."

"That would be awesome," Steve said. "Let me check my appointment order to see what the rules are regarding volunteer experts and investigators. If it is okay with the federal judiciary, then it is more than okay with me. I would love to have you on our team. But until I figure that out, you are definitely a part of the team investigating these threats." He paused to take out his wallet. "Here's a dollar. I am officially hiring you to help me find out who is threatening me. Let's focus on that for now. Once I get the court's approval, I will be able to show you the entire file. Then, you will know everything, including any privileged information."

Emily smiled as she pocketed the dollar. "Perfect. What I'm thinking is that we come up with a way to lure whoever is sending these threats out into the open. Since he or she doesn't know what I am capable of doing, I think we can trick them."

Booger raised an eyebrow. "By we, I assume you in fact mean you?"

"Yes," Emily said. "And I have an idea on how we are going to do it."

"It's all you," Booger said with a sheepish smile. He raised his arms in an "I'm out of this" fashion, stepping back from Emily's workstation and sitting down off to the side.

For the next hour or so, Steve and Booger sat and watched Emily doing who-knows-what on her computer. Steve noticed she brandished Hermoine's wand on more than one occasion as she sat staring into nothing. Finally, Emily's head arose from her desk in a manner that made Steve think he saw a light bulb flick on above her.

"I think I've got it," she said confidently. "All we need now is some cheese to lure out your little mouse."

"Okay," Steve said. "What is the plan?"

Emily opened one of the many windows on her screen. "This is the Roach company website. I have hacked their system and can track usage of the number from cell tower to cell tower using the other website. It shows here, on this monitor." Her computer was actually connected to four different monitors on her L-shaped desk. She opened two windows, each on their own monitor so they were larger and easier to see.

"Now, all we need is for our mouse to start using the phone. For simplicity's sake, let's assume it is Whitmore. Every time he uses the phone to get on the application, make a call, check the internet, whatever, the phone will connect to the nearest tower. We can track his movements as long as the phone is being used regularly. Although we could just wait for him to use it, my guess is that he is only using this phone to send you threats. So, we may have to wait a long time if we go that route—"

"I could send him a Snapchat message back," Steve interrupted.

"Yes," replied Emily. "That is exactly what I was about to say. I have no doubt he will check the first time we send a message. But we also need to come up with something that will get him engaged in a Snapchat conversation. That way, we will be able to keep a continuous monitor on his location. I can watch from here as you two follow the signals. When you find him, we will send another message. If you can witness him using the phone to review that message, then we've got him."

Booger nodded. "I like the plan, but we must remember that we are dealing with a very angry person here. We need to use that against him to get him engaged in the communication."

"What should I say in the first message, then?" asked Steve.

"He is trying to bully you with threats," Booger said. "The best way to get a bully's attention is to challenge his power. I suggest you say something along the lines of how he doesn't scare you, and you aren't going to quit. That will surely get him going."

"How about I simply write back 'I'm not stopping'?" Steve said.

"I like it. Also, add a picture of a backhoe digging a large hole," Emily added. "It is simple, direct, and in clear defiance of the last threat. I think it will work."

Steve sent the message, and they all waited. A few seconds later, a ping appeared on the Roach website. The phone was being used. Emily quickly decoded the IP address and looked up the location on the cell tower website.

"Downtown Claremore," she said.

Then, Steve's phone buzzed. He had received another message back. It said, "That would be dumb. I said Quit or Die!"

They had their suspect on the hook. Now they just needed to keep him engaged long enough to see him or her use the phone in their presence. Then, they would know the identity of the perpetrator—and possibly the killer.

The two men got into Steve's car and hightailed it to Claremore. With any luck, they'd get there before the phone, and its owner, moved locations again.

CHAPTER 30

Once in Claremore, Steve called Emily to let her know they had arrived. He sent another Snapchat message, and shortly after, Emily called him back.

"The phone is still using the same tower as last time. So, whoever this is hasn't moved in the thirty minutes it took you to get there. Let's wait ten minutes and try again."

Ten minutes later, Steve sent another message. When it was retrieved, the small flashing dot showed the phone was once again accessing the same tower.

"In the last ten minutes, I have been looking at the cell tower map more closely," Emily said. "There are more towers located downtown than there are out in the countryside. Because the towers are positioned more densely, I can reduce the possible location of the phone to a much smaller area. Additionally, since we have now sent three messages and the phone used the same tower every time, I am fairly certain our suspect has not moved locations in the last hour. He or she must be stationary somewhere near one specific tower—the tower on the corner of Cherokee Avenue and Will Rogers Boulevard. Drive around in the intersection and see if you can find a place someone might stay at for a given period of time on a Tuesday afternoon."

When they got to the corner, Steve and Booger saw exactly what each had already assumed they were looking for—Whitmore's truck. It was parked outside the Sidewinder Bar at the exact intersection of Cherokee and Will Rogers. They pulled up next to Whitmore's truck and called Emily from the car's Bluetooth speakerphone.

"I have Booger on speaker so we can both hear you," Steve said. "We found Whitmore's truck sitting outside of a bar at the exact intersection of the cell tower location."

"Well, isn't that a coincidence." The giddy sarcasm was apparent in Emily's voice as she continued, "I think I found something else pointing to Whitmore, but I want you and Booger to look at it to confirm my thoughts. I am sending you each an email with a PDF file attached. As discussed earlier, we know Whitmore was at the courthouse, but we agreed it was possible someone else was there whom we don't know about. While you were driving to Claremore, I called a friend of mine who grew up in Rogers County. He told me that the most popular bank in town is the Will Rogers Bank."

"How does that help us?" Steve asked.

"Just keep listening," Emily said curtly. "After talking to my friend, I couldn't just sit here waiting on you two to get to Claremore. So, I decided to hack into the bank's computer system. The accounts themselves were highly protected. It would have taken me hours, maybe days, to crack the security protocols, but some of their less-important information was not as well protected. Surprisingly, the loan request files were fairly easy to break into; I guess they felt they have to protect actual customer accounts more than possible customer information. I digress. Anyway, I found a loan application Whitmore submitted for a new truck a few years ago, probably the one he is driving now. Although I am no handwriting expert, when I compared his loan application with the Roach phone application we previously obtained, it looks to me like the same person filled out both applications."

"Interesting," said Booger.

"Very. The email I sent should be delivered to your phones by now. I sent one of you a copy of the bank loan application and the other a copy of the Roach phone application. Open the files, hold your phones up next to each other, and tell me what you think."

Steve and Booger got out their phones and each opened the document he had received from Emily. They compared the files as she had directed.

"Wow," Steve said. "That sure looks like the same handwriting to me."

"Yes, it seems both applications were filled out by the same individual," Booger said, "We still have one problem though. We need to get proof beyond what you have found so far, Emily. If we had to turn over these documents to the police and the federal court, I don't think they would appreciate knowing how you procured it. I'm pretty sure neither the phone company nor the bank gave you permission to search their databases for application forms they likely claim to keep confidential."

"I agree. I really don't want to end up in a federal prison," Emily said matter-of-factly. "Anyone have any ideas?"

"I do," said Steve. "Listen up…"

After hearing his plan, everyone agreed it would work. Booger and Steve got out of the car and walked into the bar.

The Sidewinder was dark inside despite it being late afternoon with only a speckle of clouds in the sky. The large plate glass windows facing the street were heavily tinted, leaving only the dim bar lights and the occasional streak of sunlight breaking through tears in the tinting to illuminate the room. Two pool tables were stationed near the entrance. The bar ran along the wall to the left. They saw Whitmore at the far end drinking with three other men. Steve and Booger planned to discreetly settle into a corner booth near the front.

However, when Steve opened the door to walk inside, a beam of sunlight busted through the entrance. Since there was no one else in the place, the bartender was standing directly in front of Whitmore's crew when the light hit her eyes. She had long brown hair and a white tank top bearing the words "Jefferson Airplane" that showed off her natural assets. The shirt hung loosely so that her pink laced bra could be seen from all angles. She looked up and yelled, "I'll be down to get your order in a minute boys. I'm the only one here, so give me a little leeway, please!"

"So much for being discreet," Booger mumbled to Steve as he smiled and waved to the bartender. Still, they stuck to their plan and found a corner of the bar to sit down.

Steve noticed all four men had their cell phones placed in front of them on the bar.

Booger leaned in and said, "Send him the next message. If it is Whitmore, he won't be able to resist the temptation."

Steve sent the message they had prepared in the car. This one was a copy of the famous picture of Muhammad Ali standing over Joe Frazier. Along the bottom of the screen, Steve had included the words: "I'm over in the corner. If you have something to say to me, bring it on."

A few seconds later, Whitmore reached into his back pocket and pulled out a second phone. He nonchalantly checked it without his friends even realizing he was watching a Snapchat message. His head shot up and turned immediately toward the corner where Steve and Booger sat.

Whitmore backed up off his bar stool so quickly that he nearly fell down. The mix of emotions boiling within him, coupled with the copious amount of alcohol he had clearly consumed since lunch, almost brought him to the floor. Luckily, one of his buddies caught him. Whitmore recovered and headed toward their corner, undeterred by the embarrassment burning on his own face.

"Where are you going?" one of Whitmore's friends asked as he marched away from the bar.

Whitmore shouted, "Don't worry about it!" without stopping. Despite Whitmore's order, all three of his buddies got up and started following him. They could tell something was brewing.

When Whitmore neared them, he asked gruffly, "What the hell are you two doing here?"

Steve sat calmly at the table, looked up, and answered, "Just trying to catch a criminal. We know you are the person sending me death threats. You know that is a crime, right? But I guess committing a petty crime like sending threatening videos is nothing compared to murdering your sister?"

Just as Steve finished his question, Whitmore sent a clenched fist across the side of Steve's face. The blow sent the young attorney falling back against the booth seat. Whitmore moved as if he was going to start pummeling Steve right there at the table. Booger stood to help protect Steve from the assault.

Suddenly, a hand grabbed Whitmore from behind and threw him backward and across the bar. When Whitmore regained his feet, he stormed toward Deputy Blackburn, who was now standing between him and Steve.

As Whitmore closed in again, Deputy Blackburn put one hand on his sidearm and his other hand palm-out toward Whitmore. "Freeze, Brent. You know you don't want me to have to arrest you today."

Whitmore's buddies were near enough to assist. They grabbed Whitmore and held him back. One said, "Sorry, Andy, we've got him." The three men dragged their drunk friend back to the end of the bar where they had been sitting earlier. A few moments later, Whitmore calmed down. Soon, the four men were giving each other high fives and laughing as they talked about what a great shot Whitmore had landed on Steve.

Steve stood up, thanked Deputy Blackburn, and said, "Lucky you were nearby, Deputy."

"I was across the street, finishing up a traffic stop, when I saw you two park and walk into this bar. I also noticed Whitmore's truck sitting in the lot. I know he isn't happy about you guys reinvestigating his sister's murder. I guess my instincts told me to come check on you. Good thing, or else you and the old man here would have been in for an ass beating from that crew."

Deputy Blackburn nodded toward Whitmore and his three friends and said, "It looked like your partner here was about to step in to save you. The cowboy code among these guys is to always let two guys fight it out one-on-one. The posse only jumps in if someone from the other gang jumps in first. If the old man here had stepped in, that would have been invitation enough for all of them to start pounding away on the both of you."

"Thanks, Deputy," Booger said. "We wouldn't want that."

"Do you want to press charges against him for assault?"

"No," said Steve. "But I may want to press charges for threatening my life and for murdering Ashley Pinkerton."

Steve explained everything about the death threats. Trying not to get Emily in trouble, he told Deputy Blackburn that they happened to be in town, already working on the case, when they saw Whitmore's truck parked in front of the Sidewinder. They had recognized the truck from when they went out to Whitmore's house, the first day they met Deputy Blackburn. Steve explained how they sent a message to the person threatening them to see if Whitmore would check his phone. He further explained how they watched Whitmore get the message from a second phone, before immediately coming over and punching Steve.

"Well, aren't you two just a modern-day Sherlock Holmes and Dr. Watson?" Deputy Blackburn said wryly. "Just because he may have sent you some threats doesn't mean he killed his sister. I told you the scumbag who did that is sitting on death row. However, I will talk to Whitmore about this stuff and see what he says. I am not ready to arrest him just yet. Remember, as far as he is concerned, you two are trying to help the man who killed his sister—which means you two aren't exactly at the top of his Christmas card list, if you know what I'm saying?"

"Yeah," Steve said with a nod. "Plus, I don't want him arrested just yet, anyway. We need more evidence against him, which I am hoping we can find in your file."

"You two have been awful busy today, huh?" Deputy Blackburn asked, all humor gone from his tone. "The district attorney called me earlier and said I have to show you our investigative file. I've never had to do that before. And to be honest, I am not exactly thrilled about you two trying to make me look bad. What are you hoping to find?"

"At this point, something that points to that man down there." Steve nodded toward the man seated at the other end of the bar, who was still gloating with his friends. "Would it be possible to meet sometime on Thursday?" Steve asked. "Neither of us are available tomorrow, and I would like to get this done as soon as possible. Especially with that nut out on the loose. I honestly think he might kill me if I give him enough time."

"Thursday is fine," Deputy Blackburn replied curtly. "My life is pretty routine. Like I told you last time, I work Monday to Thursday, 6:00 a.m. to 4:00 p.m. And don't worry about Whitmore. He likes to throw punches after a few drinks, but I don't think he is capable of murder. He was always a bit of a wuss back during high school football."

"Well, I'm not sure how that proves he is not capable of murder," Steve said. "Anyway, can we meet you earlier in the day this time? It will probably take us a while to go through all of your files and make our copies."

"Although I come in at six, the office doesn't open until eight. I would like one of the support staff there, watching you to make sure you don't take anything you aren't supposed to take. I have a motto—never trust a defense attorney." His eyes narrowed at them both.

"We will be there at eight," Steve said. "Thank you."

Steve and Booger left the bar. As they got into Steve's car for the drive back to Tulsa, Booger looked at Steve over the roof of the vehicle and said, "Remember the first day we met? You promised me I wouldn't get into any trouble or harm. Now look at you, with that bloody napkin up your nose."

Steve grinned sheepishly. "Okay. Maybe I was wrong on that one. But at least you didn't get hit."

"Not this time. And only because that cop magically appeared."

"Did that seem weird at all to you, that he was suddenly there?" Steve asked as they pulled away from the bar.

Booger snorted. "Only a lot. Especially since he said himself that he gets off at four every day, and it is well past five now." That was all the investigator said, leaving them both to ponder all that had occurred in the last seven hours.

During the drive home, Booger glanced at Steve and said, "Looks like he got a pretty good lick on you."

"Yeah, it's throbbing a bit. By the way, although I am the one that got punched, I would say you were definitely in the path of danger." Steve handed Booger his wallet. "I guess I lost our bet, and I always pay off my bets."

Booger took his one-dollar winnings, laughed, and said, "Looking good, Randolph."

Steve replied, "Feeling good, Mortimer." They both laughed.

Next, they called Emily to let her know what happened at the bar. After the two men returned to Tulsa, they decided to call it an early night to ensure they would be properly rested for the drive to McAlester and their meeting with Scottie the next morning.

CHAPTER 31

When Steve woke up the next morning, a man sporting a black eye greeted him in the bathroom mirror. After he examined the damage, Steve got dressed and drove across town to pick up Booger. From there, they planned to drive to McAlester to meet Scottie.

"Good morning, Rocky," Booger said as he got into the car.

"Ha. Very funny."

"I've been thinking more about what happened yesterday," Booger said. "Two things are inexplicably bothering me. First is how quickly Deputy Blackburn showed up when Whitmore attacked you. Second is the fact that he should have been off work before we even thought about going into that bar. If I was a gambling man, I'd bet anything Deputy Blackburn saw us come into town and followed us."

"Yeah," Steve said, "that bugged me too as I tried to sleep last night. It was incredible timing. I'm not sure what we do with the information, but it's definitely something we need to keep in the hopper."

They arrived at the Oklahoma State Penitentiary shortly before their scheduled meeting at 9:30 a.m. After going through the usual routine with security and meeting Deputy Warden Gilcrease, they found themselves once again in the small visitation room contained in H-Unit. They sat waiting on Scottie to join them from his cell.

When Scottie walked in, he immediately noticed Steve's black eye.

"Holy shit. What happened to you?" Scottie asked.

"Your ex-brother-in-law. Apparently, he is not very happy about us snooping around and investigating this case."

"Apparently not," Scottie said. "He can be a real asshole sometimes. You okay?"

"Yeah, I'm fine. First black eye since I duked it out with Robbie McDaniel on the fifth-grade playground, but I think I will live. Now, let's talk about keeping you alive longer than the State of Oklahoma has planned."

Steve went on to explain everything that had been happening on the case up to this point.

"I can't believe Whitmore is threatening your life," Scottie said. "More importantly, I can't believe you get to go through the police file. That is incredible. First, thank you so much for believing me and actually working on my case. That worthless piece-of-shit Hixon and the lawyer they appointed me for my state appeal just went through the motions, assuming I did it. I truly appreciate you working for me," he said smiling. "So, what do you hope to find in the police file?"

"The first thing we are looking for is any evidence pointing to Whitmore as the possible assailant," Steve explained. "If there is anything the police dismissed or overlooked during their investigation because it pointed at him, instead of you, we might be in business. If we can couple any original evidence with the proof we have with these threats, I think we will have an excellent shot at getting you a new trial."

"A new trial?" Scottie repeated, stunned. "I don't want a new trial. I want out of here"

"Well, first we have to get you a new trial," Steve said, "Then we can worry about getting you out of here by winning that one."

"Oh. Ok. How are we going to get me a new trial?"

"We would get there under an 'ineffective assistance of counsel' claim. The job Hixon did at trial was very poor but probably not enough to get a new trial under the strict standards set forth by the Supreme Court for constitutionally ineffective assistance of counsel. However, an attorney is not just supposed to do his job in-court proficiently. He or she is also constitutionally required to properly investigate and prepare for trial out-of-court. In Wiggins v. Smith, the Supreme Court spelled out the standards for effectiveness of trial counsel in regard to investigation. One of the primary jobs of the defense attorney is to investigate any mitigating or exculpatory evidence. If we can show there was evidence pointing to a different suspect, and if we can prove Hixon did nothing to even investigate those people, we may have enough to get you a new trial."

"Wow..." A tear filled with hope and joy began to form in the corner of Scottie's left eye. "You really think I might get out of here alive?"

Steve nodded in affirmation. "Yes, I do. Now, I'm not guaranteeing anything, but I think we have a very good chance. The second thing we want to see is if Deputy Blackburn is telling the truth about originally seeing the picture of the bedroom door intact and dismissing it as irrelevant. If he lied to us about that, then we have to try and figure out why."

"I see," Scottie said. "But it sounds like we have the killer. Whitmore is threatening you. He must be the one. You just have to prove it."

"It definitely looks that way," Steve said cautiously.

Scottie gestured wildly as his voice rose in vindication. "It has to be him! That's why he is threatening you. I told you I didn't kill Ashley! I told you it was him!"

"Calm down," Booger said. "Right now, we have four suspects:

you, Whitmore, Walters, and the X factor."

"Wait, what's the X factor?" Scottie asked.

"That's either for someone we are missing or the slim possibility that some totally random person happened to show up and kill her right after you left. Until somebody confesses or we find a video showing who did it, we aren't going to eliminate any possibilities. One reason you are sitting here is because the police got tunnel vision in their investigation. They only looked at evidence that pointed to you and dismissed any evidence that pointed to someone else. That's not how I do my job," Booger said. "I keep all options open until I have all the evidence. Otherwise, you don't go down the paths that may end up leading you to the true culprit."

"I'm still on the list?" Scottie asked. "I thought you believed me?"

"We do believe you," Steve answered, "but like Booger just said, you have to be a suspect until we find more evidence against someone else. It is our hope the police file will eliminate someone from the list, maybe even a couple of people, hopefully you. We hope there is something showing Whitmore was there that morning. A statement showing someone else was in the house that morning will give us a stronger case."

Scottie looked down and said, "I see." He sat with his head down in silence for a few seconds before saying, "Well... there is one thing I have been keeping from you. I'm not sure if you will discover it from the file or not, but I want to tell you now so you will hopefully continue to trust me."

Steve looked at Booger, who gave him a knowing nod as if to say, Here we go. The final truth, revealed.

"After all we have done for you, you still haven't told us everything?" Steve said.

"No, I haven't. I feel really bad about it, too," Scottie said earnestly. "I was honestly just trying to protect Heather."

"Heather? She helped get you here with her testimony," Steve said. "Is this the last thing you have kept from us?"

"Yes, I promise. This is it. I have told you everything else," Scottie assured them.

"Before you begin," Booger said, "I want you to look us both in the eyes and tell us this will be the last time you have something to come clean about. No more untold stories."

Scottie looked Booger squarely in the eyes and said, "I promise you. This is the last thing I have been keeping from you both. Scout's honor." He raised two fingers and held his hand out in front of him like a boy scout. He then did the same to Steve.

"Were you ever even a Boy Scout?" Booger asked.

"No," Scottie admitted. "I was a Cub Scout once, and it is just something I have said ever since when I am being 100 percent honest."

"Okay, continue," Booger said. He gave Steve a look that showed he was finally satisfied that this would be Scottie's final confession.

"On the morning of the murder, I told you that I met Heather at the hotel when I was supposed to be golfing. Remember?"

Steve and Booger nodded as they stared at Scottie.

"Well, what I didn't tell you is that she went to my house after we finished in the hotel room—"

"What?!" Steve exclaimed. "You knew she went over there? When she told us that, we assumed you didn't know about it."

Booger said nothing, but the look on his face clearly conveyed the displeasure he felt inside.

"I know, I know... I didn't think it was important because she left before I even got home," Scottie said.

"She was in your house the morning of the murder, and you didn't think it was important?" Steve sat still while his voice rose in frustration. "Why in the hell did she go over there?"

"Heather and I agreed that she should go see if Ashley knew who my mistress was. We knew Ashley had discovered that I had one, but we didn't know if she knew it was Heather. So, Heather left before me and went to the house. The plan was for Heather to go there in the role of Ashley's best friend, to see why she had seemed so upset lately. She knew Ashley would tell her I was having an affair because they had been friends long enough that Heather could get Ashley to spill all her secrets."

Steve began taking notes as Scottie continued.

"Heather got to the house, talked to Ashley, and texted me that Ashley had no idea she was the other woman. That is when Heather left, and I went home. The only reason I never told you this before is because I didn't see how it mattered. But now that you are going to see the police file, I think she gave a statement to Deputy Blackburn during his investigation. She didn't tell him anything about our affair, of course. She just told him she had gone over to see her friend that morning after her workout. I wanted to tell you before you saw it for yourself. I don't want you to stop believing me because of this one piece of meaningless information."

"Thanks for telling us. But for the record, nothing is meaningless," Steve said firmly. "Are you positive there is nothing else you consider unimportant that happened that morning?"

Scottie stared at the wall for a second and then said, "Heather and I also decided that morning to end our affair. She was feeling guilty about cheating on her husband, and I was feeling guilty, too. We both decided it should end. We figured, as long as Ashley didn't know Heather was the one, I could just make up someone to be the other girl. Then we could all go back to living our lives as we had before Heather and I hooked up. Heather agreed that was the best plan."

"What were you going to do if Ashley did know it was Heather?" Booger asked.

"We didn't actually get that far. We just hoped she wouldn't know, and then we could both go on with our lives."

"Thank you for telling us everything," Steve said as he jotted things down on his legal pad.

"Are you sure Heather wasn't upset about ending the affair?" Booger pressed. "That seems like something that might set her off."

"Yes, I am sure. Hell, it was her idea. She brought it up in the first place. I just agreed. We both had been thinking about ending it for a while. There were times I actually threw up in the hotel toilet from the guilt I felt in my stomach after we finished having sex. Heather often said she felt the same way."

"But you still kept doing it?" Steve asked.

"Yeah..." Scottie lowered his head in shame.

Steve reached up and hit the intercom button to signal the guards their meeting was over. Soon, Steve and Booger were headed out of the prison, back through all of the sliding walls of metal bars.

On the drive home, Booger asked, "What do you think about our boy's confession?"

"You mean about Walters?"

"Yes," Booger said. "I find it very interesting. I even think maybe she killed Ashley. Regardless, I think it's time we confront her about the affair."

After a few moments of silence, Steve said, "I agree we need to confront her, but, for the record, I don't think it was her. I think there is still something we aren't considering. If she sets up Scottie to go to death row, how does that help her? She doesn't get to end up with him. Even if she were a killer, she would want someone else to take the fall, so she ends up with Scottie. Remember, at trial, she was a key witness against him. It just doesn't add up to me."

At an intersection, Steve pulled his phone out of his pocket and called Walters. He told her they had a few follow-up questions and asked if she would be available the next morning. Walters said she could meet them at her house at eight thirty, after she got home from dropping her kids off at school.

Then, Steve called Deputy Blackburn and let him know they wouldn't be at the sheriff's office until sometime between nine and nine thirty the next morning.

CHAPTER 32

Walters opened the door, wearing tight black yoga pants with a red Lululemon top that accentuated her muscular arms and full chest. Her blonde hair was pulled up in a ponytail and she almost seemed to prance as she moved.

"Please come in. Can I get either of you a cup of coffee?" Walters asked as she led them inside.

"Yes, please. Just black would be great," said Steve.

"No, thank you, ma'am," said Booger.

They sat on the same couch as last time, and Walters soon joined them with Steve's coffee. Walters had fixed herself a drink as well; her glass was filled with some type of dark-green juice.

After a few pleasantries, Walters said, "I am not sure what you came here to ask me about today, but when you left last time, you asked me to tell you if anything came to mind that you might find interesting. After you called yesterday, I began thinking about it, and I remembered something. I am not sure if it will help you, but I thought you might like to know."

"Please," Steve said, "anything could be helpful."

"Well, there was one time in high school when I think Ashley cheated on Scottie. It was during our junior year. Scottie and Ashley were not getting along so well. They may have even broken up at some point; I'm not sure." Walters settled back in her seat. "Anyway, Ashley disappeared on several weekends during a two- or three-month stretch. I remember it drove Scottie crazy because she wouldn't tell him where she was going. She would just leave on Friday, after school, and come back late Sunday."

"Her parents let her disappear all weekend without knowing

where she was?" Steve asked.

"No. She told her parents she was visiting Tracy Phillips down at OU. Claremore is such a small school; you knew everyone in every grade. Tracy was a senior when we were sophomores, and we knew her freshman year as well. We were all on the cheer team together."

Steve followed up, "Her parents didn't tell Scottie?"

"No. She asked them not to. She told them she was thinking about breaking up with him and didn't want him just showing up out of the blue. She knew he was possessive and jealous enough to do that if he knew where she was. Her parents were never big fans of Scottie. So, they kept her secret from him."

"Is that where she went?" Booger asked.

"Well, I am pretty sure she went to Norman, but I don't know if she stayed with Tracy. I remember Tracy came to the funeral. We spoke a little afterward, and I mentioned something about that year Ashley went and visited her at college. She said Ashley never came and stayed with her. I was so upset about Ashley's death that I didn't press Tracy on it. I hadn't honestly even thought about it again until yesterday."

"Is there anything else out of the ordinary you can remember?" Steve asked.

"No. That was the only thing that has popped into my head. It just made me wonder who she was actually visiting on all those trips to Norman."

Booger gave Steve a nod, and Steve quickly moved the conversation to Scottie and the affair.

"I think I have told you that we have met with Scottie on a few occasions, and there is one thing he told us that we didn't want to bring up in front of your husband," Steve began tactfully.

Walters's face remained steadily blissful.

She would make a great poker player, Steve thought. "We know you and Scottie were having an affair at the time Ashley was killed. He told us all about it."

The words broke her instantly. Tears immediately began to flow out of her eyes. "I am so ashamed of what I did. Please don't tell anyone. Jim and I are now in a much better place. We are happy. Please don't ruin that for me." She reached for the tissues on the side table.

"We don't plan on telling anyone. We just need you to answer some questions for us," Steve said reassuringly. "When was the last time you saw Ashley alive?"

"That morning. The morning he killed her. I was at their house. Steve and I had decided to end the affair. I went to see if Ashley knew I was the other girl. Once I found out she didn't know it was me, I left. I texted Scottie and told him what I had found out as I was pulling out of their driveway. That was it. Next thing I know, I am getting a phone call telling me that Ashley is dead, and they think Scottie killed her."

"What exactly did she tell you that morning?" Booger asked.

"She told me she knew Scottie was having an affair, but she didn't know who the other woman was. That was about it. She was crying a lot. I tried to comfort her, but it felt kind of wrong knowing I was actually the one causing her pain. So, I left as fast as I could."

"Are you sure she didn't say anything else?" Steve asked.

"Like what? It seems you are expecting me to say something in particular," Walters said intuitively.

Steve clarified, "Did she say anything about her plan to get Scottie in trouble?"

"No. I mean, she was devastated. Hurt. Mad. Like I said, she was crying a lot. But no, she didn't say anything about getting him into any kind of trouble. What do you mean plan?"

"After you left, did you go back to their house that morning?" Booger asked.

"No... I didn't go back." Her tears stopped as she slowly discerned the meaning behind Booger's question. "Wait, you think I....no, I didn't go back and kill her, if that is what you are getting at."

Walters stood abruptly and motioned at them. Steve and Booger followed her silent instruction and stood as well.

"Listen, I know I'm not perfect," she said as she shepherded them to the door. "I made a huge mistake cheating on my husband and doing it with my best friend's husband makes it even worse, but I could never kill someone. The Bible says 'thou shalt not kill,' and I walk with the Lord. I don't appreciate you coming into my home and insinuating that I am capable of murder, let alone that I am the person who killed my best friend."

As Walters opened the front door, she said, "Not that you two deserve this, but on the second Saturday of every month, for the last nine years, I have worked the church bake sale at the First Baptist Church of Claremore. When I left Ashley that morning, I went straight to the bake sale, which starts at 10:00 a.m. Anyone who goes to the church can tell you that. When it happened, there were two other ladies working with me—Eloise Blackburn and Florabelle Martin. "

"Eloise Blackburn," Steve said. "Any relation to the deputy?"

"Yes. Eloise was his grandmother," Walters said.

"Can you give us a way to contact them, so we can confirm your story?" Steve said.

"Eloise passed away six years ago, but I think I know where Ms. Martin is living." Walters left them standing by the opened front door and walked back to the kitchen. From there, she spoke loud enough for them to hear her say, "I have a church directory in a drawer back here, I am pretty sure she is still listed in it. Ah, here it is."

She returned shortly with a piece of paper containing an address: Restful Meadows Assisted Living Center, 1547 Blue Starr Drive.

"She suffers from Alzheimer's, and she has been living at Restful Meadows for a while now. You can go talk to her, but I'm not sure what she will remember." As she handed Steve the paper, she simultaneously ushered the two men completely out of her house. She paused in the entryway, holding the door, as they stood on the front porch.

"Look. I may not have been the best friend to Ashley. I know that. But I didn't kill her. The more you guys stir this up, the bigger the chance that whole deal with me and Scottie will get discovered. I don't want that to happen. Please, just stay away from my home, and let me get on with my life. Like I said, Jim and I are doing great now. We have two wonderful kids, and we are happy. Please don't ruin that by bringing up ghosts." Walters shut the door without giving them a chance to respond.

Steve looked at the slip of paper in his hand. "Do you want to go check this alibi now or after we review the file?"

Booger shrugged. "It's only 8:53. Let's make a quick stop at the nursing home, then go to the sheriff's office. I don't think visiting with Ms. Martin will take long."

Steve and Booger pulled into the parking lot of the Restful Meadows Assisted Living Center a few minutes later. The front entrance had two doors, with handles in the middle, that swung outward; they were wide enough that a medical gurney could easily fit between them. Steve reached for the door on the right. It was locked. So was the door on the left. Then, he noticed the intercom and keypad on the left side of the portico.

Steve pushed the intercom button and said they were there to say hi to an old friend, Ms. Florabelle Martin. The door buzzed, and they walked in. They were now in an entryway with a second set of double doors in front of them. It reminded Steve of the two-door system at the state prison. Except, rather than gray metal bars, these doors were designed like the front of a French country estate. When the door behind them closed, a second buzzer went off, and they passed through into the foyer. They signed the guest registry and asked where they could find Martin.

"How do you know Miss Flora?" asked the nurse on-duty at the front desk.

"We used to go to church together at First Baptist," Steve said easily. "I always loved getting her bake sale items every month. She was one hell of a cook."

"Yes. I remember she made the best apple pie I have ever tasted," the nurse said with a smile. "She is sitting on the couch in the TV room over there, wearing the red sweat pants and the gray shirt." Steve looked around the room, his eyes first went to Martin and then to the other patients sitting and staring at the television in silence. One was mistakenly looking at a wall, but he seemed to be enjoying his show just as much as the others enjoyed theirs.

Steve and Booger walked over to Martin. She was in her late

eighties, with several strands of gray hair upon her balding head. Her face was thin and pale. She looked like she was wasting away one day at a time.

"Hello, Miss Flora. How are you today?" Steve asked.

She gave him a giant smile. "Hello, Peter. How are you? You sweet young thing." She reached up and softly touched his cheeks as she said, "You are such a handsome young man."

"Thank you. I'm good. I've just been thinking about all the bake sales you used to do for the church. Do you remember those days?"

"Oh, yes. I loved baking. I wish they would let me bake something in here every once in a while."

"Me, too. Your apple pie is still the best I have ever eaten." Steve played along, hoping this would help him get the information he needed. Besides, she seemed happy to have "Peter" visiting her; he saw no reason to take this little bit of joy away from such a kind, fragile woman.

"Do you remember that young woman who used to help with the bake sales? I can't remember her name," Steve gently prompted.

"Heather Walters. Never forgot that girl. She was such a treat to be around. Young, athletic, smart, and she had the most beautiful blonde hair."

"Yeah. That's her. Do you—"

Martin interrupted Steve as she stared blankly to her left. As if she were reading a teleprompter, she continued, "One thing about her I will never forget. She was the most organized person I ever met. Always had everything in its place. In all the years I worked with her, she was never once late to any sale, any meeting, or any service of any kind. I wish I was as organized as her."

Steve glanced at Booger upon hearing this information. Booger nodded back.

Martin then seemed to gather her wits for a second. "I'm sorry. You were about to ask me something?"

"Never mind. It wasn't important. We need to go now. It was good seeing you."

"Good seeing you, too, Peter. Please tell your mother I said hello."

As they got up from the couch, Booger whispered to Steve, "Ask her if she remembers the day Ashley was murdered."

"Miss Flora, one last thing. Do you remember the day Heather's friend Ashley Pinkerton was killed?"

"Of course, I do. What an awful, awful thing that was. That shook the nerve of everyone in town down to their core. To think, something like that could happen right here in Rogers County. I remember Heather was especially upset when she found out. As best I can recall, she had brought banana cream cupcakes to the bake sale that morning. I was eating one of the cupcakes when she got the phone call. She immediately broke down into tears. It was just plain horrible. Only word to describe it. Horrible." She shook her head slowly as she spoke. It was the first time her spirits seemed low since they had arrived.

"Was Heather on time that day?" Booger asked.

"Yes, like I said. She was always on time, everywhere. She always arrived at 9:50 for the bake sales. Always ten minutes early to everything. I'm sure she was there at 9:50 that day as well." Her mood improved as her mind shifted from Ashley's murder back to the bake sale.

"It was good seeing you again, Miss Flora," Steve said. "We have to go now. Have a good day."

Martin put her arms out to hug him goodbye. Steve bent down

and gave her a hug. She kissed him on the forehead and said, "Would you like to buy a cupcake, young man? We have banana cream and red velvet this month."

Steve smiled back at her. "No, thank you."

After they walked out of the building, Steve said, "Well, she certainly didn't seem to know who I was, but she seemed pretty clear about Walters and her timeliness."

"Yeah," Booger replied. "I have been around a few Alzheimer's patients over the years; it runs in my family. They tend to have some lucid moments, at least in the middle stages. She is clearly still in the middle stages because toward the end they usually can't even form a sentence. Don't even use real words half the time they try to speak, just say a lot of gibberish. Some doctors call it 'word soup.'"

"She was very clear in her speech and seemed certain of her memory," Steve said.

Booger nodded. "Right. Now, let's get to the sheriff's office and look at that file."

CHAPTER 33

When they arrived at the sheriff's department, Steve and Booger checked in with the receptionist in the lobby. A few minutes later, Deputy Blackburn came out and directed them to a large conference room near the back of the building. There were several boxes on the table and a copy machine in the corner. A young deputy was sitting at the table, not actually paying attention to anything except his cell phone. When he noticed they had already walked in, he stood up quickly. In a rushed attempt to put his phone away, he dropped it onto the tile floor. His face reddened as the sound rattled through the room.

"We moved this machine in here this morning to make things easier on you," Deputy Blackburn said, "and to make sure you aren't leaving this room with anything except your copies. Like I said before, I don't trust you damn defense attorneys, and I don't want you taking anything with you or planting something in my files. This here is Deputy Parker. He drew the short straw this morning. So, he will be sitting outside the door watching every move you make until you are finished."

The officers searched Steve and Booger. "Every time you come or go, Deputy Parker is going to search you," Deputy Blackburn said. "Like I said, I don't want you taking something and then claiming we lost it or hid it from you. Good day." With that, Deputy Blackburn turned and walked out the door with Parker following just behind him. Parker sat in a chair in the hallway. He could see them through the plate glass door and windows, although he seemed more interested in his phone than watching them.

Steve and Booger stared at each other and then at all the boxes stacked on the table.

"I'll start at this end. You start down there," Steve said.

"Okay. I think we should copy everything that looks remotely interesting. Never know what might matter once we dig into this stuff further," Booger said.

Steve walked to the far end of the table and opened a box; at the same time, the door to the hallway opened again. Deputy Blackburn stuck his head in.

"One more thing," Deputy Blackburn said. "I spoke to Whitmore about your threats. He confessed he was the one who sent them. He said to tell you he is very sorry and that you guys coming around just brought back tons of emotions he hadn't felt in years about his sister's death. He got freaked out and thought you might stop if he threatened you. He wants the whole thing to be over." Deputy Blackburn continued after shooting a look at Steve, "He needs closure, and the final piece for him will be when your client is executed. I explained to him that his threatening you probably made you search more. He promised me he would stop. I honestly believe he will. I think he just still misses his sister."

"Bullshit," Steve replied. "The reason he threatened us is because he is the real killer. You need to go arrest him immediately."

"He ain't the killer. That scumbag you represent is. How many times do I have to tell you to get it through your thick skull?" Deputy Blackburn scowled. "Look in those files, and you will see there is no way he killed his sister. He was over at his parents' house that morning. So, unless his parents are in on your grand conspiracy too, it wasn't him."

Steve and Booger looked at each other in astonishment. Neither had said it yet, but both had secretly determined Whitmore was their man.

"Sorry to burst your bubble, gentlemen, but you represent the asshole who killed Ashley Pinkerton. No matter how hard you look for someone else, it is always going to keep coming back to him. Regarding Whitmore, it is my duty as an officer of the law to arrest him on those threats if you want me to do it. Say the word and I will go get him right now, but I would rather let him be. The man did lose his sister."

"Don't arrest him yet," Steve said. "I want to see all of this evidence first."

"Okay," Deputy Blackburn said. He pulled his head back out of the door and left.

After about an hour, Steve found a file labeled "Eloise Blackburn." Inside was one sheet of legal paper containing some handwritten notes. Based on all of the other documents he had looked at that day, Steve could tell the writing was Deputy Blackburn's. The notes stated Blackburn's grandmother had called him to let him know that he shouldn't waste time looking into Heather Walters as a suspect. Heather was with her at the church bake sale when the murder occurred. On the top of the page, Deputy Blackburn had written: August 11, 2008, 8:17 a.m.

"Looks like both of Walters' alibi witnesses have the same story," Steve said, handing the file folder over to Booger so he could see the statement for himself.

"Yep. Cross her off the list."

Steve made a copy of the file, and they both continued their search. A little while later, Steve received an email from the federal court clerk's office. It stated that Emily was approved to assist as an additional investigator on the case. The court did not approve funding but did approve her helping in a pro bono capacity.

Steve called her to let her know the good news. "I just received an email from the federal court. You have been approved to work with us as long as you are willing to do it free of charge."

"That's great," Emily said. "Of course, I will. I am hooked on this case and can't wait to find out all the details."

"When can you get started?"

"I can start now. Everything I'm working on here can wait until next week. Do you want me to come to Claremore and help you guys there?" Emily already knew they were in Claremore today as she and Steve had been spending quite a bit of time together in the evenings lately.

Steve looked at the yet-untouched boxes crowding the table. "Sure, there is a ton of stuff to go through here, and we only have today to accomplish the task. Also, if it's not too demeaning, would you mind bringing us lunch? That would save us some valuable time."

"As long as I get to do some real work, I don't mind being your lunch girl, just this once," Emily said teasingly. "Text me your orders, and I will go get sandwiches. I need to tie up a few loose ends here before I bail for a couple of days, but I'll be there as quick as I can. I can't wait to see you. Bye."

Emily arrived a little over an hour later. They all greeted each other, and she handed out the deli-style sandwiches Steve and Booger had asked her to bring. The trio sat down at the table to eat.

"Have you discovered anything interesting yet?" Emily asked.

"Only one thing," Steve said. "It looks like Walters has a clear alibi. Two different witnesses place her at the Claremore Baptist Church helping with a bake sale at the time of the murder."

"That's good news, right? One less person on the list."

"Good and bad," Steve said. "If we cross too many people off of the list, all we will be left with is Scottie."

As everyone finished with their lunch, Emily said, "Time to get cracking, boys. Didn't you say we have to be out of here by five? That gives us a little over four hours to finish up. My gut tells me we will find something in all these boxes that will help us. We just have to work for our reward."

"I sure hope so," Steve said with a new-found energy as he moved toward the box he was digging through before their lunch break began.

"What can I do to help?" Emily asked.

"Just pick a box on this end of the table. When we got here, we moved everything to this side. As we finish a box, we move it to the far end, so we know it has been examined."

"Got it. Good plan. I guess you boys aren't as dumb as you look," Emily said, grinning.

Soon, they were all going through the boxes of information one page at a time. Each person would pull a sheet out, read its entirety for even the smallest clue, then place that sheet down and retrieve the next one from the box. If they found something they thought was even remotely helpful, they made a copy and labeled the document with a post-it note for easy future reference. The cycle continued for what seemed like days until, finally, Emily exclaimed, "I found something!"

Steve looked up to see she was holding a file in her hand.

"It is the sworn statement of Brent Whitmore. He says he was at his parents' house the morning of the murder," Emily explained. "It further states that he and his parents were on the back porch when they saw the police lights pull into Ashley and Scottie's driveway.

He says he had ridden his four-wheeler up to visit them, so when he saw the lights, he immediately drove across the acreage to see what was going on at Ashley's house."

"That would explain why he showed up so quickly," Steve said, "and it would explain why Deputy Blackburn is so sure he isn't the one who killed Ashley."

"It is at least a good story," Booger said. "Is there a statement from either of his parents backing up his alibi?"

"Not that I saw," Emily said.

"We need to keep looking. That story seems almost too convenient for me," Booger said. "If we don't find a confirming statement from at least one of the parents, then I am still not sold. If Whitmore was the murderer, he would be smart enough to make up an alibi that explains why he showed up so quickly but also puts him far enough away at the time of the murder that it exonerates him."

As 3:00 p.m. neared, the contents of nearly all of the boxes had been examined. Yet, they still hadn't found anything else that looked material to their task.

"Emily, since it looks like we have plenty of time to finish here, why don't you go to my house and start looking through my file," Steve said. "You have a lot to catch up on to be up to speed with us on this case. The file is spread out in my dining room. On a yellow pad is an outline I prepared of the trial testimony. I would suggest you start there."

Emily held out her hand. "Okay. Can I have your key?"

"I don't carry a key to my house. I know it's kind of weird, but I saw this movie once called Sex, Lies, and Videotape. James Spader played the main character in it. He had a theory that the more keys you carry around with you, the more baggage you have in your life. I thought that kind of made sense on some eccentric, karmic level, so I try to have as few keys as possible on my key ring. I get into my house using the garage door opener and I leave the door inside from there unlocked." Noticing the look he was getting from the other two, Steve quickly said, "I do keep a key outside for situations like this, I leave it under a small Oklahoma Sooners yard gnome in a flower bed in my backyard. The gate to the right of the garage is unlocked. The gnome is to the left of the back door. Go through the gate, find the key, and then use it to get in the house. Once you get in, please put the key back in its place."

"There are several layers to you, Mr. Hanson," Emily said. "I can't wait to unravel them all. Too bad we are coworkers now. You know I have a rule against dating coworkers. Right?" She winked at him and left.

It took Steve and Booger a couple more hours to finish going through the remaining boxes. After Emily had left, they found one more item of interest, which Steve carefully took a picture of. He looked forward to showing it to her when they met up at his house later.

CHAPTER 34

When Steve and Booger pulled up to Steve's house, Emily was waiting on the front porch, smoking. She remained seated and put out her cigarette when she saw them pull up.

"How are my new partners doing?" Emily asked.

"Worn out," Steve replied. "Hard to imagine how exhausting it can be sitting in one place, reading through pages and pages of investigation material. It's not like we ran a marathon or something."

"Yeah, too bad you didn't have an outline to assist you. I was able to expedite the process here by using your notes and only looking at the information that was germane to our mission. I feel like I'm caught up with everything you know. All I need is for you to tell me exactly what Scottie has told you, and I will be completely in the circle. Did you guys find anything else of interest in the investigative file?"

"Kind of," Steve said. "We found a piece of notebook paper where Deputy Blackburn noted the inconsistency of the door being intact and the 911 call claiming Scottie broke it."

"So, he didn't lie when he told you guys, he already considered that information?"

"I'm not sure if I would go that far just yet," Steve said. "The paper the note was on seemed new compared to all the other hand-written notes in the files. I took a picture of it since we could only leave with copies. Let's go inside, and I'll show you what I mean."

They sat down at the table in the dining room, which Steve had turned into his war room for the case. All of the files he originally obtained were in there, along with the notes and pictures he and Booger had taken during their investigation. Emily had organized everything during her review of the material. The boxes containing pleadings and other materials that wouldn't help with their investigation were moved to the living room. The items she had deemed pertinent to their work were placed neatly in specific piles all around the table.

Steve pulled out his phone and showed Emily the picture he had taken of Deputy Blackburn's notes. The picture showed two pieces of paper side-by-side on a table. The handwriting on both appeared to be from the same person, and each note was written on paper pulled from a yellow legal pad with perforations at the top. Even from just the picture, Emily could tell the paper looked different; one appeared faded and old while the other looked fresh and new.

"The notes about the door not being broken sure look new to me," Emily said. "You should attach that picture to a motion and ask that both originals be placed into evidence with the court."

Steve nodded. "I agree. I will get to work on that after we finish up tonight."

"At this point, I think we should make a list of what we know and don't know," Booger said. "I think that will help us decide on a direction moving forward."

"Good idea," Emily said. "I would even take it a step further and suggest we make a separate list of what we know for each suspect—a sort of pros and cons list for them. Except instead of pros and cons, we divide the list into evidence pointing to guilt versus evidence pointing to innocence."

Steve reached for a legal pad and tore out four pieces of paper. At the top of each sheet, he wrote the names of their suspects: Scottie Pinkerton, Heather Walters, Brent Whitmore, and X factor.

"Based on the note that appears to have been recently added to the police file," Booger said, "I think we need to add one more suspect. Deputy Blackburn was the last person to see Ashley alive, and now he is tampering with the police file. He could just be trying to cover his ass in regards to the investigation itself, or he could be trying to cover the fact he is the killer."

"Okay," Steve said and tore out a fifth sheet. "Ackerman did warn us that he is one of the bad cops; plus, we know he may have killed that black teenager a few months ago without cause." He wrote Blackburn's name on the fifth sheet. "Now, who do we want to look at first?"

"I say we start simple and work toward the more complex," Booger said.

"Okay," Steve said. "Who would that be?"

"To me, the easiest suspect to dismiss is the X factor, or unknown assailant. If it turns out that it was some random person who killed Ashley, there is basically no chance we will figure it out seven years later, and I think the chances of that are slim to none anyway. As much as I hate to dismiss a subject without evidence, I think we shouldn't waste any more time considering the unknown assailant theory."

"I agree," said Steve. "Even if that is what happened, I don't think the judge would grant Scottie a new trial based on our suspicion that some unknown person committed the crime. For us to succeed, we will have to find some hard evidence to present to the court that we know who killed Ashley—and that it wasn't Scottie."

"So, we all agree the unknown assailant theory is unlikely. And short of the discovery of new information, can we set that aside for the moment?" Emily said.

"Yes, but we must still keep our eyes open for all possibilities. Just in case," Booger said.

"Then, the next easiest elimination is Walters," said Emily.

"True," said Steve. "Although she has the motive, and possibly the means, she has two alibi witnesses, both of whom are unrelated to her." He set aside the Walters and X factor sheets.

"Next," said Emily.

Steve held up the next sheet. "Deputy Blackburn," he said. "He was the last person to see her alive. So, we know he had the means. Blackburn investigated the case, and he could have easily corrupted the evidence and made it point toward Scottie, keeping himself off the hook. Additionally, we have what appears to be forged evidence documenting that he considered the inconsistency of the kicked-in door during his original investigation. A perfect example of covering his tracks."

Booger responded negatively to this assumption, "But he had no motive. As a person who has worked in the criminal justice arena for my whole life, I truly believe most law enforcement are good, honest people trying to give back to society with integrity. However, as a black man in America, I also know certain police officers are capable of performing horrendous acts. Moreover, it appears Deputy Blackburn himself killed an unarmed black man without cause a few months ago, and as you said earlier, Ackerman already warned us he is a no-good, piece-of-shit cop. But I simply can't wrap my head around the theory he decided to randomly kill a young white woman just because he thought he could get away with it. We have to find a motive before we can bring this allegation to light."

Booger started a new list on a sixth sheet of paper, which he labeled and underlined "Items to investigate." He placed "find a motive for Deputy Blackburn" directly under the heading.

"That leaves us with just Whitmore," Steve said.

"Don't forget about your client, Scottie Pinkerton," Emily interrupted. "After reading everything, I think he did it. Maybe you two defense-oriented souls are just a little too deep into this conspiracy theory to see the truth. The only evidence on your side is a picture of an undamaged door and a feeling in your gut. On the other hand, the evidence against him is immense." She listed the facts off frankly. "The 911 call, the DNA, the fact he showered before they arrested him, the scratches on his face, the bloody shoe prints. I could go on and on."

"She has a point," Booger said. "Although I trust my gut immensely, I have to concede there is a possibility it is wrong this time."

"I agree it looks bad, but we can't give up," Steve said. "I swore an oath to represent this man to the best of my ability and to work as hard as I could on his behalf. Until we uncover every stone and investigate every path of evidence, I am not willing to quit on him." He gestured at the sheet in front of him. "Look at Whitmore. We know he sent me those threats; he even admitted it to Deputy Blackburn. We know he lived near enough to ride his four-wheeler over to Scottie's house in a short amount of time. We know he was on the scene shortly after the crime happened, and in every cop movie or TV show, they say the perpetrator always returns to the scene of the crime. We also know he had the motive. He stands to inherit twice as much money now that Ashley isn't around."

"Yes," Emily interjected, "but his statement says he was at his parents' house that morning."

"True," Booger said. "But after reviewing the file, the thing I found interesting was not what we did find, but what we didn't find. There was no statement from the parents supporting his alibi. It appears Deputy Blackburn just trusted Whitmore when he said he was at his parents' house. A good investigator would have followed up with the parents to confirm the story. You never remove a suspect from consideration just because he or she gives you an alibi. You wait until you obtain corroboration from an independent source that the alibi is true. I think the first thing on our list is to talk to Mr. and Mrs. Whitmore. Let's pay them a visit tomorrow to see what they remember happening the morning their daughter was murdered."

"Sounds good. I'm free," Emily said.

"I have a court appearance in the morning and some other matters to take care of at the office," Steve said, "Let's meet here around 2:00 p.m., and we can all drive out to the ranch together."

CHAPTER 35

The main entrance to the Flying W Ranch had a wrought iron arch over the entryway, held up by two similarly constructed posts on each side of the road. A six-foot-tall wooden fence was connected to the outside of the posts, which then ran off in each direction away from the entrance and around the residential area of the property. The words "Flying W Ranch" were welded across the center of the arch. The "W" in the middle-had wings coming out from each side, giving the impression the letter could fly away at any moment if it so chose.

As they passed under the gateway, the trio saw the main house sitting atop the hill in the distance. The driveway was paved asphalt that ran from the gravel road of the county line all the way up to the house—almost a mile in length. The house itself looked large, even from a mile away. It must have been at least six thousand square feet and overlooked the valley below, where Steve assumed all of their cattle were kept. To the right of the house was a barn and stable.

As they rounded the circle drive in front of the house, Steve noticed three ranch hands heading toward them from the barn. He was beginning to regret their decision to surprise the Whitmores.

The large cowboy leading the group stopped right beside Steve's car. "Can we help you?"

"My name is Steve Hanson. With me are Harold Thomas and Dr. Emily Babbage. We would like to talk to Mr. and Mrs. Whitmore, please."

"You guys are the ones snooping around town and bringing back bad memories, aren't you?" As the man spoke, two more men came from around the back of the barn and joined the phalanx of ranch hands headed Steve's way.

"I suppose that is us. But look, we don't want any trouble." Steve raised his arms in a placating fashion. "Like I said, we just want to talk to the Whitmores."

The lead hand crossed his thick arms. "Well, Mr. Whitmore passed away a couple of years ago, and I don't think my ma'am would like to be bothered right now."

As he said this, an elderly voice came from the direction of the front door. "Walter, calm down. These nice young people are just doing their jobs." A kindly-looking old woman stepped onto the front porch and waved. "You three don't mind him. Come on inside."

"Sorry, ma'am," said the lead hand as he tipped his hat in her direction. Suddenly, all the men turned and sauntered back to their respective jobs.

As the three would-be intruders walked toward Mrs. Whitmore, she asked, "Can I get you some tea or coffee? Or something else to drink?"

"An iced tea would be great," Steve said and the other two agreed as well.

Steve, Booger, and Emily introduced themselves before following Mrs. Whitmore through the house and out to the back patio. She showed them to some seats and excused herself to get the drinks for everyone.

As Steve sat on the porch, he admired the land laid out before him. At the far corners of the property, he could see the houses the Whitmores built for their two children. Steve was amazed at how far and wide the property spread. He had never realized how much area ten thousand acres actually encompassed. It was immense. He was surprised that he smelt nothing onerous despite the fact tens of thousands of head of cattle were on the property.

Soon, Mrs. Whitmore returned and handed everyone a glass of tea. She sat down with them and asked, "How can I help you folks?"

"We just have a few questions for you," Steve said. "We won't be here long, and we truly appreciate your willingness to help."

Mrs. Whitmore nodded somberly.

"First, I would like to say that we are all very sorry for your loss. I don't have children of my own, but I imagine there could be nothing worse than losing one before your own passing."

"Thank you," Mrs. Whitmore said.

"We are also sorry to hear about your husband," Steve said.

"Thank you for that as well. I truly appreciate your manners, young man. So many young people today are in such a hurry to do this or do that, they forget how to be respectful. I find it refreshing." Mrs. Whitmore looked at each of them in turn. "That said, I would appreciate it if you would stop dilly-dallying. Ask me whatever it is you came out here to ask me. Talking about Ashley's passing still upsets me to this day. I would like to get this over with as quickly as possible... I am sure you understand."

"Yes, ma'am. Of course," Steve said. "Let me add I am sorry we have to put you through this."

"Young man, you have a job to do. I get it. I respect it. Ask away."

"We would like to know what you were doing on the morning Ashley was taken from you."

"Oh. That is a morning I will never forget." Mrs. Whitmore became teary-eyed and paused for a second. "Brent had driven his four-wheeler over to have breakfast and give me my birthday present. My birthday is August 11. We were out here on the back porch celebrating when the sheriff's patrol car pulled up to Ashley's house down there."

"You saw the police car arrive at her house?" Steve asked.

"Yes. I know it's pretty far off over there, but you can see it." She pointed at the house in the distance. "The emergency lights on the patrol car were on, so we could see it clearly. As soon as we saw the red and blue lights, Brent got on his four-wheeler and drove straight down to see what was happening. As a matter of fact, I happen to have a video of the whole thing."

She went inside and returned with her smart phone in hand.

"Brent gave me a new phone for my birthday, the first phone I'd ever had with video-recording capabilities. He was showing me how to take a video when the car pulled into Ashley's house.

She handed it to Steve. "I still have the recording. You can watch it."

Booger and Emily watched over Steve's shoulder as he played the video. Sure enough, everything was exactly as Mrs. Whitmore had described it. Whitmore and his parents were on the same back porch, making a video, when Mrs. Whitmore said to look down at Ashley's house; there was a police car. Brent Whitmore had been holding the camera at the time, and he panned in that direction. You could hear the concern in all their voices. While they talked, the red and blue lights of Deputy Blackburn's patrol car could be seen pulling into the driveway. The video ended at that point.

After a brief silence, Steve handed the phone back to Mrs. Whitmore. She sniffled and removed her hand from her teary eyes and accepted it back.

Steve put his arm on her shoulder and said "Thank you for the tea and your time, Mrs. Whitmore. Once again, we are very sorry for both of your losses."

Booger and Emily said their goodbyes as well and the three disheartened investigators left the house.

Once inside his car again, Steve sighed. "If I hadn't seen it with my own two eyes, I wouldn't believe it. I was positive Whitmore was our man. He had the motive and the means. The fact he was threatening me just seemed to confirm it."

"You're right," Emily said. "I thought the same thing. But there is no doubting that video. Whitmore definitely did not kill his sister."

"Not unless he can be in two places at once," added Booger, dejectedly.

When they returned to Steve's house, the first thing Steve did was crumple up Whitmore's page and throw it in the trash. Now they were down to two suspects: Deputy Blackburn and Scottie. One who appeared to have no reason to kill Ashley and the other whom they desperately wanted to believe did not kill Ashley.

The trio spent the next several hours going back through all of the evidence. They needed to find something that could give them a reason why Deputy Blackburn would kill Ashley Pinkerton, a person he was connected to in only two ways: One, they went to high school together for a year. Two, she was the victim of a standard domestic violence call for him.

Finally, after finding nothing of consequence, Booger said, "It's late. We have had one helluva week, and this old man is beat. I'm out of here. I say we take tomorrow off and let things simmer in our minds a day or two. I have a lot of work to catch up on at the shop anyway. It is funny how doing bodywork clears my brain.

Probably has something to do with all the chemicals in the air. Hopefully something helpful pops in my old noggin while I'm at it tomorrow."

After Booger left, Steve and Emily spread out all the case files and copies of the police investigative documents on the kitchen table.

"Booger is right; there has to be something we are missing," Steve said as they both stood over the various documents. They each started circling the table as if searching for the next piece in a jigsaw puzzle.

On one pass, their hands brushed against each other as they stared down at the table. A spark ran through their bodies. Emily put her arms around Steve and pulled him in toward her. They kissed, softly at first, then more passionately.

Steve pulled away briefly, grinning. "I thought you didn't hook up with coworkers."

Emily kept her arms around Steve. "I don't, but the more I've thought about it, we aren't in actuality coworkers. I'm not getting paid. So, this is more of a volunteer position than a real job, and I don't have any rules about dating a fellow charity worker." She smirked. "Plus, every time I touch you, a spark of energy runs straight to my pussy. I have never had that happen before with any man in my life. I need to know how electric our physical connection will be. Not to mention the fact I am stressed and tense from everything that has happened this week. I need a release." Her hands slid from his shoulders up to the back of his head. "Now shut up and give me what I need."

Emily grabbed Steve by his thick, curly hair and pulled his lips to hers. Their hands roamed feverishly over each other's bodies as their make out session began to resemble two teenagers discovering the joys of foreplay for the first time. Emily knelt down, slowly kissing a trail down to his crotch and unfastening his belt and pants. As she took him in her mouth, Steve leaned his bare ass against the table, feeling both the cold, polished wood behind him and the moist heat of Emily's mouth. His knees shook as he found his own release.

"Now, it is my turn," she said with a devilish smile.

She quickly stripped off her jeans and panties before pushing some papers to the side so she could fully sit on the table. She used both hands to grab Steve by the head and nudged it down her body. He started by lightly kissing her inner thighs. He teased her at first, alternating between her thighs without quite touching her hottest part. After a minute or so of his teasing, Emily tangled her fingers deeply into Steve's hair and, more firmly this time, guided his tongue where she needed it to be. Emily came almost instantly and again shortly thereafter.

The excitement of Emily's climaxes aroused Steve once again. As soon as he felt fully recharged, he slowly kissed up her belly as he removed her shirt and bra. He removed his shirt as well. They were both now completely naked.

He entered her quickly at first, then slowly as the reality of this dream settled into his head. Their lovemaking lasted for hours as they worked their way through the house, eventually stumbling onto his bed. Finally, their night of passion ended as they crashed into each other, their legs and arms pretzeled, as they drifted into a peaceful slumber.

CHAPTER 36

Steve woke first the next morning. He went to the kitchen with plans to make breakfast for Emily. He always enjoyed cooking breakfast on weekend mornings, either before or after he went to the gym, and he had everything necessary to make a traditional American breakfast—pancakes, eggs, bacon, toast, and coffee for both. However, before he could begin cooking, he needed caffeine. He placed a pod in the coffeemaker and hit the start button. As he waited for it to brew, he stared happily at the documents and photos that were now strewn across his dining room table and floor.

Last night had been magical, like none he had ever experienced before. There was definitely something special about Emily, a connection he didn't completely understand, but one he looked forward to learning more about. He couldn't stop himself from grinning goofily as he thought, She may be the one. As he daydreamed about Emily walking down the aisle toward him, his eyes wandered over to something on the floor that immediately pulled him back to the present.

Two pictures were lying next to each other amidst the mess of papers they had thrown off the table during their romp last night. Seeing the pictures sit side by side, Steve wondered, How did we not see this before? The answer to the question—what was Deputy Blackburn's motive to kill Ashley Pinkerton?—lay before him. He snatched up the photos and ran into the bedroom. He quickly woke Emily with a shake and put the pictures in front of her.

"What do you see?" he asked.

Emily rubbed her eyes and reached toward the nightstand. An instinctive move, Steve realized with some amusement, probably for her glasses. She must keep them on her own bedside table. This morning, obviously, they weren't there. They had come off somewhere else in his house, long before either of them laid their heads down to sleep. "I need my glasses," she said.

Steve ran hurriedly throughout the house, looking for them. He found the glasses in the living room and brought them to her.

Emily put her glasses on and stared at the pair of pictures for one second, two at the most. Her jaw dropped.

"He's Gabriel's father!" Emily said. She held in her left hand the picture of Deputy Blackburn taken by Booger when the two men had met him at the park a few weeks ago. In her right hand was the picture of Gabriel taken the same morning at Whitmore's house. The deputy and the young boy both had the exact same facial expression, the same eyes, the same jaw line. The resemblance was uncanny. Gabriel was Deputy Blackburn's son.

"How is this possible? And how did we not notice this before?" Emily asked, her blue eyes still wide with shock.

"Do you remember when Walters told Booger and I that Ashley was very secretive about going to Norman almost every weekend of her junior year? She thought Ashley was seeing someone at the University of Oklahoma, but she never told her the details. She always kept it hidden from Walters."

Emily nodded. "Yes. I remember reading that in your notes."

Steve continued, "Well, when we visited Deputy Blackburn at his office, he had pictures from when he played football at OU. He was two years older than Ashley, Scottie, and Walters. He would have been a freshman at OU during Ashley's junior year of high school, the year she was gone all the time. Here is my theory," Steve said, holding up the photos. "I think that when she broke things off with Scottie, she decided to go hook up with this older football star. She must have gone up there a few times to test the waters. Then, for whatever reason, she ends it with Deputy Blackburn. Maybe she found out he had other girls at college, or maybe he ended it with her. Who knows? It doesn't exactly matter either way. After the fling with Deputy Blackburn doesn't work out, she goes back to dating Scottie. A year later, she gets pregnant with Scottie's baby and marries him.

"After Deputy Blackburn graduates from college, he comes back to Claremore to work as a sheriff's deputy. Ashley and Scottie are in an unhappy marriage, and she decides to give it another shot with the deputy. Then, after she gets pregnant, I would guess she told Deputy Blackburn that she was staying with Scottie even though Scottie wasn't Gabriel's father. Deputy Blackburn must have been upset that someone else was going to be playing dad to his own son. So, when the call came in of domestic violence at the Scotties' house, he got there faster than he said he did, killed her, called in the murder, and set Scottie up for the death penalty all in one smooth action."

"Makes sense," Emily said.

"As for why we didn't notice sooner," Steve said while looking at the photos, "I think people just assume certain things all the time. People see what they want to see. Or they don't see what seems illogical or impossible. Since no one knew about Ashley and Deputy Blackburn's relationship, no one would ever guess that the deputy is Gabriel's father. Even if a person briefly thought the two looked similar, it would be easily dismissed and forgotten based only on facts they knew. Beyond that, for all we know everybody in town thinks Deputy Blackburn is the dad, but they wouldn't share that with an outsider like us and Scottie hasn't seen him since he was a little baby.

"It's all finally clear," Emily said. "I guess your client really didn't do it. But how do we prove this?"

"I will ask the court to order a DNA test. If the test shows Deputy Blackburn is Gabriel's father, then that should be enough to save Scottie. At minimum, I think we can get Scottie a new trial based on the fact that the lead investigator in his case was having an affair with his wife, who also happens to be the victim. If I can't show that situation is an example of a constitutionally prejudicial investigation, then I might as well give up my license and start delivering pizzas again." Steve grinned. "Best case, we convince the district attorney's office Deputy Blackburn is the one who killed Ashley. Then, they could drop the charges on Scottie and file against Deputy Blackburn. Scottie would be released almost immediately."

It didn't take long for Booger to pick up Steve's call.

"We found something you have to see."

"Can't you just tell me what it is? I'm knee-deep in bodywork here."

"No. This is something you have to see with your own eyes. Kind of like the handwriting examples earlier this week. We want to see if you see what we see without us putting any preconceived thoughts in your head."

"All right. Give me some time, and I'll be on my way. See you soon."

While they waited, Steve found Emily an Avett Brothers concert T-shirt and pair of athletic shorts for her to wear. After she dressed, she walked into the bathroom while he was brushing his teeth.

"I know you are extremely excited about what you discovered, but before we get lost in the moment, I want you to know that I had an amazing time last night." She put her arms around him and lightly kissed him on the cheek, avoiding the mint-flavored foam on his lips. "I look forward to spending a lot more time with you, Mr. Hanson."

She reached down and pinched his butt before walking out of the bathroom to wait in the living room for Booger to arrive.

The first thing the investigator noticed when he walked through the front door was Emily's attire. "You two finally took the leap. Glad to see it. Hopefully, there won't be any more of that sexual tension floating around you guys."

"Very funny," Steve said.

"LOL," Emily spelled out dryly.

After Steve handed him the photographs, Booger stood there in the living room, dumbfounded, as he stared at the two pictures in his hands.

Finally, he shook his head. "I can't believe I never noticed this before. Looks like it's time for me to hang up my trench coat and magnifying glass. I never would have missed something so obvious ten years ago."

"No. You need to keep doing what you're doing. We never would have gotten this far without you," Steve said.

Other than the instances where Steve and Emily engaged in their new favorite hobby together, Steve spent the rest of the weekend writing what he hoped would be the penultimate motion in the Scottie case. The motion requested the court order a DNA test comparing the likely paternity of Deputy Andrew Blackburn to Gabriel. In the motion, Steve included all of the evidence they had gathered and found case law supporting his position. He believed it was the most eloquent and persuasive piece of legal writing he had created in his budding legal career.

He filed the motion electronically and waited for a response from the court.

CHAPTER 37

By Thursday, after such a long wait with no response, Steve was beginning to think his motion wasn't quite the grand legal treatise he had originally imagined. But, in the middle of the afternoon, he finally received an email from the court clerk. Judge Henry entered an order giving the state fifteen days to respond to Steve's motion and set a hearing for a week after the due date. Normally, a party had thirty days to respond to any motion filed by the opposing party, and the original party would have fifteen days to file a rebuttal brief. Afterward, both parties often had to wait months for oral arguments, or, occasionally, a judge would enter a ruling based solely on the briefs. However, in this instance, Judge Henry stated in his order that, due to the overwhelming possibility an "extreme travesty of justice may have occurred wherein an individual who could be a prime suspect was the lead investigator on a death row inmate's case," he was shortening the normal time frames. The judge made it clear he was concerned about hearing what may or may not have occurred in the underlying state court case.

Steve would still have to wait several weeks to get a final answer, but he knew his brief had made an impression on the judge. Not once in the two years he had worked at the court, nor in the time since he had been in private practice, had Steve ever heard of a judge shortening the time for opposing counsel to respond to a party's motion—not for any reason, ever.

Steve and Emily went to dinner that night, just like they had every night for the past week.

During the course of their meal, Emily said, "I must ask you something. How do you represent rapists and murderers? I wouldn't be able to sleep at night if I helped those types of people." She paused. "I mean, the only reason I am helping Scottie is because I don't think he did it, but you have to know that most of the people you represent are guilty."

"Well, I haven't represented anyone charged with rape yet. So, I'm not sure if I will feel differently when that happens, but my answer for how can I represent a person charged with murder is simple. I know this is going to sound pretentious, but I truly don't mean it that way. I honestly mean it from my heart."

Emily smiled. "I think we are past that. Go ahead."

"I believe the American legal system created by our constitution is the best in the world. The cornerstone of the system is the adversarial process. In every case, an attorney for each side presents their case to a jury comprised of twelve citizens. Then, that jury determines a just result. I further believe that, in order to derive the full benefits of the system, everyone, rich or poor, must get competent legal counsel when they are accused of a crime. The state almost always has competent counsel, and the defendant should have something equal. I am willing to spend my life's work trying to be that someone equal.

"I think this rule is even more important when the government is not just trying to put you in prison but actually trying to end your life. Even if there were twenty eyewitnesses and DNA evidence showing a certain individual committed the crime charged, that person still deserves a competent attorney at all stages of the legal process. Look at O.J. Simpson. However you feel about that case, the fact he had money to pay for a great defense is not what got his acquittal. It is what made it a fair fight, but it was not the deciding factor. What got his acquittal were all the errors made by the investigators and prosecutors in the case. If the police, district attorney, and defense lawyers all do their job, most of the time, the guilty will be convicted, and the innocent will be acquitted. Our system is set up to work that way, and it usually does.

"The problem is when the defendant can't afford competent counsel and the one appointed doesn't do a good job for him. Then, innocent people go to jail, or guilty people go for twenty years when maybe five is all they deserved. This leads to overcrowding of prisons, which leads to states like ours spending more money on prisons than schools..." Steve noticed Emily's eyes were beginning to roll back into her head.

"I'm sorry. I need to get off my soapbox," he said sheepishly. "I can sometimes lose it a little when I start talking about this stuff."

"It's okay. I find it interesting." She reached across the table to touch his arm playfully. "I was just messing with ya."

Steve laughed. "Anyway, let me just say one last thing, and then we can move on to something more interesting. No matter the evidence, wouldn't you agree that everyone accused of a crime in the United States of America still deserves a fair trial?"

"Yes... a fair trial and then string 'em up," Emily said with a devilish smile upon her face. She straightened her gaze to look Steve in the eyes. "Does that mean you are against the death penalty? Or do you just think they deserve a fair trial, and as long as they get that, it's okay if the jury gives them death?"

Steve shook his head. "I have always been against it. In my heart and soul, I believe it is an archaic punishment. However, it is the law right now, and I respect that aspect of it."

"Why do you say that?"

"The long answer would take all night, and I think I have already bored you once with my long-winded answers."

"No, I want to hear it. I kind of like your long windedness," she said with a teasing smile. "Just don't go too long."

"Okay. I will give you my best Twitter-esque answer. I can't promise it will be less than 140 characters, but I will make it short."

"Okay. Go."

"In this day and age, I believe there has to be a better way to get people to quit killing other people. Number one, it costs more money to execute someone than to incarcerate them for life. Number two, all of the studies on the subject show the risk of death penalty is not a deterrent. The murder rate per capita is actually higher in states that have the death penalty than the rate of states that don't. I could go on up through about number forty-seven, but I think those first two make the point."

"You honestly don't think it deters people from killing?" Emily asked. "I know I would never kill someone, knowing the penalty exists."

"Well, I don't think you would kill anyone even if there was no punishment for doing it."

"True," she conceded.

"But I also think you would probably never commit any crime, knowing you could go to prison. That is deterrent enough for you."

"Actually, I spent some time in prison for some dumb stuff I did when I was younger."

"What?" Steve said, genuinely surprised. "I never would have guessed that about you."

"Just kidding, I got you," she smirked.

"You did," Steve said as they shared a laugh.

"In all seriousness, you are right about me. I hardly ever even drive above the speed limit. Nonetheless, some people out in the world do have it in them to kill, and they don't care about going to jail or prison. But I bet they do care about their own life," Emily countered.

"I believe everyone cares about their own life to some degree. That said, I think that when the state condones killing someone as long as you have a good reason, then all an individual needs is a good reason. It's a sort of subconscious acquiescence to murder."

Emily raised an eyebrow. "How so?"

"In capital punishment's case, the state says it has a good reason to kill you because you killed another person. Right? You kill someone, done; you deserve to die. However, for some people in our society, it may be that you have ten dollars, and they want your ten dollars so they can eat. To them, killing you for ten dollars is a good enough reason if all they need is a 'good reason' for killing to be okay."

"So, you're saying some people just need an excuse?"

"Not an excuse but a reason—a justifiable reason. In their mind, killing is acceptable as long as it's justified in a society that supports capital punishment. On the other hand, if the government says killing is wrong on all accounts, that no one should ever kill for any reason other than war, then that creates a different perception of killing in the general public. Those people now live in a country where killing is wrong, no matter what, and that belief permeates their conscious. I believe that makes them less likely to commit any type of murder at some point later in their life."

"Okay. That makes some sense, but you are looking at the people who did commit murder knowing there is a death penalty."

Emily hesitated before continuing, "What about all the murders that never happen because of the death penalty? When I was a little girl, my house was broken into while my whole family was home. It was two men, and they put guns to our heads and tied us up in the living room. They stole all of our valuables but ended up leaving us tied up there. My mom, dad, younger brother, and I were all terrified. Luckily, when we didn't answer our phones, my grandparents came over and untied us that night."

Steve placed his hand over Emily's in a comforting gesture.

"It was the worst experience of my life. It is why I decided to have a career helping the police. I was always good with computers. So, now I use that expertise to help send people to prison."

"I'm so sorry that happened to you."

"Don't apologize. It was a long time ago, I'm okay now. Nonetheless, I honestly believe the reason they didn't kill us is because they knew that they would be sentenced to death if they were caught; if they left us alive and happened to get caught, all they would get is prison time. Not to mention, if they had killed just one of my family members, I would have wanted them dead. I probably would have even tried to do it myself."

"First, let me again say I am so sorry that happened to you. On your other point, I would also want to kill someone who killed a person I loved. But that is exactly why we shouldn't have the death penalty. The government should take emotion out of the equation. Like I said, if killing is wrong, then killing is wrong—no matter who you are killing. I would argue those people who broke into your home didn't kill you because they were thieves, not because they were scared of the death penalty. To begin with, they didn't have it in them to kill. I do believe some people have murder in their blood and some don't, but by giving those that do the chance to find 'justification' in a country that already makes its own exceptions using the death penalty, we create more murder than we would otherwise."

"All right, you make a good argument. Maybe I will rethink my position and get back to you on that. What are you, a lawyer or something?" Emily smiled and leaned back comfortably in her chair. "Enough of this deep talk, Mr. Liberal Defense Attorney. I can't believe we have to wait another week to hear what the state is going to say in their response brief. In the meantime, let's get back to your place and have some fun."

CHAPTER 38

The date for the state's response brief was finally here. Steve must have checked his email a million times before his phone finally buzzed with an email notification from the Court Clerk of the U.S. District Court for the Northern District of Oklahoma at exactly 4:52 p.m.. The state had filed its response brief.

He opened the email and began to read. When he finished, he honestly believed there was no chance Judge Henry would grant his motion. Assistant Attorney General Julie Bass had done an excellent job attacking Steve's position on various legal grounds. In reality, Steve was requesting that the court order an officer of the law and a motherless child to submit to DNA testing based on nothing more than his own unfounded allegations. It truly was an outlandish request to make or expect to be granted. Bass made salient arguments with supporting case law that made Steve question his own sanity for even filing the motion in the first place.

Steve slumped over in his chair and rested his head on his desk. He had failed Scottie Pinkerton. The corners of his eyes stung with tears. Because of this failure, he would have to sit and watch his client, an innocent man, get strapped to a gurney. State officials would inject Scottie Pinkerton with a deadly cocktail which would cause him to pass from this earth before Steve's eyes.

As Steve sat there, his forehead planted squarely on his desk, a single thought snuck into his dejected mind. It was a memory of a conversation he once had with Ackerman.

It was from six months ago, shortly after Steve went into private practice. A young woman who had been charged with misdemeanor drug possession had hired Steve to represent her. After reviewing the police report, he had filed a motion to exclude all of the state's evidence based on what he considered to be an unconstitutional search. When he read the state's response, he had felt like they were right, and he had no chance of winning his motion.

He had gone to Ackerman seeking guidance on what to do when the state was right, and you were wrong. They sat on the front porch, having a Scotch and watching the sunset, and later Ackerman gave a fatherly laugh when Steve finished sharing what had upset him so much.

"Steve, every time you write a brief, you should ask a fellow attorney to read it before you file it. If he or she doesn't think you have a clear winner of an argument, then you aren't done writing that brief. Likewise, if you ever read the opposing counsel's response and don't initially think you are on the losing side, then that lawyer should find a new profession. Drink that Scotch, lick your wounds, and let the opposing counsel's arguments sink in overnight. Tomorrow, get up and go figure out what is wrong with their position. Write your rebuttal and win this damn motion at the hearing. Your client is counting on you."

Remembering the words of his mentor, Steve picked his head up off his desk and called Emily. "I just read the state's brief in our case. This isn't going to be the slam dunk we thought it would be. The assistant attorney general made some great arguments against us. Tomorrow, I plan to figure out how I'm going to beat them, but tonight I just want to wallow in my own misery. Can you meet me for a drink at Empire?"

"Sounds good. I have a few things to finish up here before I head over."

Next, Steve called Booger. The investigator couldn't make it for drinks, but he said he would be over at Steve's place first thing in the morning to help organize their thoughts for the upcoming oral argument. Finally, Steve printed the state's response, put it in his briefcase to be looked at again tomorrow, and left the office to meet Emily at The Empire Bar.

Steve was waiting at the same table where he and Emily first had drinks together a few months earlier; it was now "their" table. The pair had been there several times in the last few weeks, so she knew right where to go when she arrived. Steve saw her as soon as she walked out to the patio. He was already drinking a Guinness, and a cold Hoegaarden was placed in front of the empty chair beside him.

"Aw, you already ordered me a drink. Such the gentleman," Emily said with a luminous smile.

Steve smiled back at her and stood up to pull out her chair. Emily leaned in and gave him a kiss on the cheek before she took her seat.

"Do you want to tell me about the state's brief?" Emily asked.

"Not really," Steve said, almost pouting. "The long and short of it is that Bass did an excellent job arguing the legal reasons why the court should not grant our request for DNA evidence. Now, I honestly feel like our chances of getting the court to order a DNA test are low, and, if we don't get that test, any shot at getting Scottie a new trial lands in the pond. That means I've failed Scottie."

"You say that way too often. You need to stay positive."

"I know. It's just that the thought is always lingering in the back of my mind. That thought alone is what drives me to work harder every day for him; it's what will drive me to work my butt off this weekend. I have to come up with counterarguments and find law to support those arguments. It is the only way we can still win this thing." Steve stopped himself from thinking about it any further.

"But tonight, I want to forget all of that and just escape to my happy place. I want to forget about the state's arguments and the possibilities that may come from it. Instead, let's talk about you," Steve said with a smile. "Please tell me more about the beautiful Dr. Emily Babbage and her wonderful life."

"What do you want to know? I feel like I have told you almost everything in the last three weeks. Other than being apart for work, we have been together nonstop. I actually can't believe I haven't gotten sick of you yet," Emily said teasingly.

"I know. It's weird how our time apart always seems to go by in a flash. Yet, when we are together time slows down, and it feels like no other person or thing exists in this world. It is just you and me and the joy I feel in my soul."

He reached over, and as their hands touched, he said, "I think I might have fallen in love with you." It was the first time either of them had made reference to the L-word.

"You might have?" Emily asked as she pulled her hand away and mockingly turned her back to him.

"Okay, okay." Steve grabbed her shoulders and turned her back around so he could look directly into her eyes. "I am falling in love with you."

"That's nice," she said as she ducked her head quickly away, her dark hair concealing her face. A second later, Emily slowly looked up at Steve again. "I might be falling in love with you, too." She leaned in and gave him a long kiss.

They merged into each other's arms, holding the embrace for what they both felt in that moment was an instant and an eternity.

CHAPTER 39

Steve and Emily were lying naked in his bed when they awoke to the sound of the doorbell ringing.

"That must be Booger," Steve said. "He said he would be here first thing in the morning. I forgot how early that usually is." It was already 8:23 a.m. They overslept.

Last night, they had stayed out late drinking and simply enjoying each other's company. At some point, Steve had even forgotten about the state's response to his motion.

Steve went into the bathroom. "Can you go let him in? I need to take a whiz."

Emily nodded sleepily as she dressed and walked out of the bedroom to open the front door. As Steve finished washing his hands, he heard it—the soft whisp of a gunshot muffled by a silencer. He had never actually heard the sound before in person. Yet, somehow, he understood exactly what it was and it tore his heart into pieces. He knew what had happened even before he rounded the corner. His greatest fear hit him hard in the gut like being dumped by the person you thought you would be with forever."

There was Emily. Lying motionless and slumped against a wall, a dark red liquid oozed from the middle of her head. Time stopped.

Steve thought about all the crime scene photos he had seen over the years. How the bodies always looked like they'd been placed into position like a scene from a movie rather than real life. This, however, felt much different. It was real. The camera does not do justice to the nature of a murder scene, he thought. There was no doubt that Emily was dead. He could see it in her lifeless blue eyes. He wanted to cry, but his survival instincts kicked into high gear. Steve whirled around to see who had fired the shot.

There she stood—Heather Walters—dressed in her usual Saturday morning workout attire, with a Glock pistol in her hand. Smoke trailed off the end of the silencer. Steve stood staring, mouth open with nothing to say.

"It's amazing how much she looks like my little sister," Walters said almost gleefully. She raised the gun from pointing at Emily's body and aimed it at Steve.

"You know, my mother always loved my sister more. I was only her stepdaughter, less important than my little sister. My mother never let me forget that. My sister was her only biological child. My sister was loved. After my father died, she would put me in my sister's closet. As long as I was good and didn't fight her, I could bring Boopie into the closet with me. I could hear them playing and having fun somewhere else in the house while I sat in the closet all day long. She usually kept me in the dark. But on good days, she left the light on for me and gave me a Bible. I found the Lord in that closet. He helped me survive all those years. And because of my great faith, the Lord allowed me to speak to my biological mom. The day before I met Ashley was the first day Boopie told me to start listening to my mom. I have talked to her regularly ever since. She speaks directly to God in heaven and tells me his plan. Last night, she promised me a special prize if I came here this morning and got rid of you. I never realized it would be such an amazing gift. The Lord provides to those who service him. That is what my mom always says." Walters smiled with the utmost contentment as she rambled, staring blankly at Steve.

He could say nothing. He just continued to look at her in horrified awe.

"Oh, I'm not crazy," she said, smirking. "I know she isn't in actuality my sister. I could never kill my own sister. The Lord would not approve of that. So, he gave her to me." With the pistol still aimed at Steve, Walters turned her smile toward the body slumped against the wall. "It is uncanny how much she looks like her though... The feeling I had as I watched her fall dead to the ground was the most joy I have ever felt in my life. Killing Ashley felt good too because I was doing the Lord's work then, but this time he gave me such a wonderful gift." When she focused again on Steve, she was beaming. "I have wanted nothing more than to kill my sister my whole life. Today, I got to experience that sensation."

Steve noticed someone else walking up the driveway and finally mustered the ability to talk. "Why did you kill Ashley?"

"I'm surprised you haven't figured this all out yet, Mr. Smart Attorney Man. She had a baby with a man who was not her husband. A few weeks before I saved her from herself, she confessed to me all about her affair with Deputy Blackburn..."

Booger made eye contact with Steve, whose eyes darted from Walters to Emily to the back door and back to Walters. Thankfully, Walters was too involved in her story to notice the exchange that had transpired.

"You see, she always told me everything. A few days before that fateful Saturday morning, she informed me she was going to keep that extracurricular activity secret and raise Gabriel with Scottie. When I told my mother, she let me know that the Lord does not condone such actions..."

Steve hoped Booger remembered the key Steve kept under the gnome in his backyard. If Booger found the key, he could enter through the other door and circle through the back hallway and guest bedroom to come up right behind where Walters was standing.

"I was asked to fix the situation. Ashley needed to atone for her sin, and Scottie deserved to be punished in his mortal form before we could be together." She pointed the gun toward Steve's head. "Now, I must kill you, and Scottie will be with me forever. I didn't understand it all at first, but now I see this was a test of my faith. I stayed true even after Scottie was sent to death row. I knew, one day, the Lord's plan would unfold, as long as I maintained my devotion to Him."

"Wait. If you kill me, you will surely end up in prison. How could that help you be with him?"

"No. That won't happen. My mom has explained the Lord's plan to me. It is, in fact, quite simple." Walters held the gun up to her face and looked at it.

"This gun belongs to one Deputy Andrew Blackburn. I took it from his bedroom this morning. You men are so easy to seduce when a woman has a body and face like mine. His downfall began a few months ago, right after you first started stirring things up again. That was when I made the deputy my new Saturday morning workout partner. His biggest problem was his ego. He began telling me about all his guns a few weeks ago. When he showed me this one with the silencer attached, the Lord's plan became clear to me. The deputy's second biggest problem was that he always fell into a deep sleep right after I was done pleasuring him. This morning I told him that his punishment for doing such a bad job keeping you from meddling in the case was that all he got was my hand, nothing else. After he was dead, I left the dirty tissue on the nightstand and rubbed some of the lotion I had used into his hand. They will think he took care of himself right before he took care of himself. You know what I mean." She laughed out loud at her play on words.

Walters smiled as if thinking blissfully about a baby sleeping, then continued, "I was able to use his own hand to blow his brains out all over his bedroom. Then I came up here to finish you off. After I complete this task, I will place the gun back in his cold dead hand. Once it all comes out that he is Gabriel's father, everyone will figure out that he is the one who killed Ashley. After that, it will be easy for the police to determine he killed you because you were about to catch him. Unfortunately, he had to kill your girlfriend too. The guilt from killing an innocent bystander got to him on the drive home, and he ended his own life with the same gun used to kill both of you. I hope it makes you feel somewhat happy that your death will be the last thing I do before I get what I truly deserve."

"And what is that?" Steve asked.

"Scottie Pinkerton's love, of course." Walters spoke like a little girl who had finally convinced her parents to get a puppy. "Like I said, your investigation will lead them to see that Deputy Blackburn is Gabriel's father. They will find you and your friend's bodies here. Then, they find his body at his home in Claremore. It won't take much for them to determine the same gun was used in both cases. They will conclude that he is a killer, that he killed you two, and he must have killed Ashley that day long ago as well. Then, they will have no choice but to release Scottie. I will leave Jim, and Scottie and I will be together forever. I must admit, there were days when I didn't originally understand why the Lord wanted Scottie to be punished rather than to be with me. But now I see it was all just a test—a test to prove my faith and love in Him. Oh, God is so good." She bit her bottom lip as she finished her sentence.

Steve could tell from the self-satisfied look on Walters's face that she was done bragging about her pending accomplishments and ready to achieve them. At the same time, he saw Booger sneaking up behind her. If only she had ranted just a few more seconds before pulling the trigger, Steve might have survived this. Then, it happened.

Booger stepped on a plank in the old wooden floors of the hallway that let out a creak that was just one decibel too high.

She turned, saw Booger, and fired her gun immediately. The investigator fell back as the bullet caught him off balance in his upper chest. Steve was moving before she had even fully turned around. He lunged across the room and tackled her, knocking the gun away as they fell.

He was now on top of her, yet not fully in control of his position. She was able to regain control of herself on the floor while Steve still lay loosely over her, struggling without a solid foundation. He heard bells ringing; she'd elbowed him hard in the side of his head. While he was stunned, Walters smacked him twice more with an elbow to the jaw in rapid succession. Steve fell off of her and slumped to one side. Seizing the opportunity, Walters clamped her hands around Steve's neck.

"Stop, young lady!" Booger stood nearby, pointing the deputy's gun directly at Walters' head. She froze and looked up at him.

The expression on her face showed she knew the fight was over. Her body loosened. She crumpled to the ground, broken. Her head lowered between her arms on the floor. She began to sob.

Steve regained his senses and grabbed her wrists, pulling them behind her back. In the distance, he could hear police sirens approaching. He looked up exhaustedly at Booger.

"Thanks."

"No problem," Booger said. "I phoned 911 earlier in the back-yard. The real heroes should be here any minute. They can take that psychological mess away with them..." As the rush of adren-aline left Booger's body, the reality that he had been shot slowly overcame his nervous system. He fell back against a wall and slid down to a sitting position. The gun rested loosely in his fingers.

Shortly after, two squad cars and an ambulance arrived on the scene. An officer from the Tulsa Police Department placed Wal-ters in custody on one count of first-degree murder along with many other charges. He walked her to his patrol car and left for the county jail.

The emergency medical personnel tended to Booger in the living room. Luckily, the bullet had gone straight through his body, missing all of his vital organs. As the paramedic on site finished patching up the holes in the front and back of his right shoulder, Booger looked across the room and sighed, visibly sad.

"I'm honestly going to miss that girl," he said to Steve, who also turned to look across the room at Emily's body.

The sight of her hit Steve for a second time. With everything that'd happened in the past few minutes, he had pushed it from his brain, but now the thoughts came flooding in like a tsunami hitting a small island hut. Emily is dead. A psychopath shot her in the head in my living room. If I hadn't gotten her involved in this case, she would still be alive. Was it worth saving Scottie's life in exchange for hers?

Steve fell to his knees beside Booger and leaned in for consolation as he began to cry. Booger put his arm around him and cried, too.

CHAPTER 40

Steve greeted Emily's parents at the front of the church as he went in to attend the funeral; this was most assuredly not the way Steve had imagined he would meet them. The services were nice, and the cathedral was packed with friends and family. Steve met a number of her classmates from high school, college, and graduate school. Several employees of the district attorney's office and law enforcement she had worked with over the years attended. Emily was clearly loved and respected by people from all stages of her life, and she was someone who would be deeply missed by her community.

Afterward, Booger and Steve went to The Empire Bar. They ordered two Hoegaardens. Outside, the clouds were dark, a light rain fell from them. But the two partners chose to sit at the patio table Emily and Steve had always shared. Each man sat holding his umbrella in an attempt to ensure neither their suits nor their beers got wet.

"I really thought she was the one," Steve said, wondering if he had just lost his one true love. A tear formed in the corner of his left eye. Since Emily's death, Steve had had trouble sleeping and eating. There was an empty space inside him he hadn't felt since the third grade.

"Yeah, she was a great girl. You two genuinely seemed to hit it off."

They quietly drank their beers in the rain for a bit until the door connecting the patio and bar opened. Adam, the twenty-something bartender who had waited on them almost every time they ordered drinks, waved hurriedly at them. "Steve. You need to come see this."

Steve and Booger quickly walked inside. On the television overlooking the bar was a local reporter standing in front of the Tulsa County jail.

"This is Sandy Shores, reporting live from David L. Moss Criminal Justice Center. My sources have informed me that Heather Walters, a.k.a. 'The Murdering Mistress,' just hung herself in her cell. As I am sure you remember, Ms. Walters was facing murder charges in two counties, including a charge for the murder of Rogers County Deputy Sheriff Andrew Blackburn. She was also likely to be charged with the 2008 murder of Ashley Pinkerton, whose husband is still sitting on death row and awaiting the completion of the county's reopened investigation. Reports surfaced this morning that her diary was found during a search of her residence after she was arrested. Jailers say that after she saw reports of the diary on the morning news, Walters returned to her cell. Shortly after, another inmate informed the staff she had hung herself with a tied-up bedsheet."

"Well, so much for getting a confession from her on Scottie's murder," Steve said.

"Don't jump the gun, young man. I bet there is something in that diary that implicates her," Booger speculated. "Probably the reason she went ahead and ended the suspense."

"I bet you are right. It makes me wonder what exactly she wrote in that diary." Just as Steve said this, his work phone rang in his pocket. It was Ian Battel, Rogers County's assistant district attorney.

"I am calling to let you know that we plan on dismissing all charges against Scottie Pinkerton," Battel said. "I just finished reading Ms. Walters' diary, and I believe Scottie had no involvement in his wife's murder. I will submit the appropriate paperwork to the federal court and the Oklahoma Department of Corrections this afternoon. I suspect he should be released tomorrow."

"Wow, that is great news. Today may be both the best and worst day of my life," Steve said humorlessly. "I just finished burying a dear friend this morning."

"Yes. I have heard you and Dr. Babbage became quite close. I am very sorry for your loss." There was a brief pause on the other end of the line. "Since you lost a loved one in this matter, and since you have saved me from being the catalyst to executing an innocent man, I am willing to bend the rules for you a little bit. I think you would find Ms. Walters' diary very interesting. If you can make it to my office this afternoon, I will let you read it. I would ask that you give me your word, as an officer of the court, that you don't let anyone else know you have read it or the contents in it. I'm doing this only for your own peace of mind."

"Can I share this with my investigator?" Steve asked. "Without his assistance, I never would have uncovered the truth in this matter, and I wouldn't be alive today."

"Yeah. I know Booger. I even worked against him on many cases. I trust him; he can come, too."

"We are on our way now. See you in about thirty minutes."

CHAPTER 41

When they arrived at the Rogers County District Attorney's Office, Battel met them at the door. He led them to a small conference room in the back. On the table was what appeared to be an ancient book. The cover was leather and the pages were clearly handmade papyrus sheets. The writing was done in calligraphy. Next to the book was a small stuffed elephant with tattered edges.

"We have been telling the media it's a diary, but it is actually something slightly different," Battel said. "It appears to be written as a new book for the Bible. She titled it The Book of Heather."

"When she attacked me, she mentioned the Lord spoke to her through her mother and she mentioned someone named Boopie." Steve said inquisitively.

"Boopie was her stuffed elephant, the thing you see there. Her mother died during childbirth, and the stuffed animal was the only thing Heather ever owned that her mother bought for her. Apparently, her mother had purchased it while she was pregnant. We found the doll hidden in the closet with this book when we searched Walters' home. When she was eight years old, the severe trauma she had endured finally caused her psychological break; it was then that Boopie told her to start listening to the other voices in her head. Her mother was one of those voices. Over time, her mother began giving her instructions on things that God wanted her to do. That is why she killed Ashley Pinkerton."

"So, she admits to the killing in here?" Steve asked.

"Yes. She goes into great detail about how she planned the murder. It is honestly quite chilling how intricate her plan was. Of course, according to her, all of it came as an order from God, told by the stuffed elephant."

"How intricate?" Booger asked.

"I don't know if your client told you this, but Walters was having an affair with him when this all occurred. She was also sleeping with Deputy Blackburn at the time, whom, as you two figured out, was Gabriel's father. This was the reason Walters believed that Ashley needed to be killed. Her sin was punishable by death."

"What about the two affairs she herself was having?" Steve pointed out. "God didn't want to punish her?"

"We are dealing with a sociopath here," Booger said. "What they think doesn't always add up logically to those of us in the real world.

"Originally, the plan was for Deputy Blackburn to be convicted of the murder, and she was supposed to end up with your client. She started sleeping with Deputy Blackburn to learn his work schedule. She even talked him into changing his hours to include Saturday mornings so that he would be on duty when the 911 call came in. During the two weeks before the murder, she came up with excuses not to see him. Then, that morning, she told him to meet her at the Will Rogers Downs Racino because she wanted to give him a special gift in his patrol car as an apology for not getting together in so long. She also paid some homeless drunkard two hundred dollars to raise a ruckus and get the sheriff called so he would have an official reason to be that close to the Scotties' home, not just to meet her."

"How did she manage that?" Steve asked.

"According to her diary, she had met the homeless man several months before, and she regularly brought him food. She gave him a hundred dollars the Thursday before and told him to be at the casino Saturday morning at 9:00 a.m. He was to act belligerent and get the sheriff's office called. Once the deputy arrived, she told him to calm down so as to avoid arrest and leave peacefully around 9:45 a.m. She promised him another hundred dollars if he performed well. This put Deputy Blackburn in his patrol car five minutes from the Scottie residence when the 911 call was made."

Booger shook his head. "I guess that means she is the one who talked Ashley into making the call and setting Scottie up."

"Exactly. She talked Ashley into making the 911 call and told Scottie that if anything weird happened, like a 911 call, he was to leave immediately and go back to the hotel. It's all there in the diary."

"It sounds like she was a puppet master over all these people," Steve said.

"You have to remember," Booger said, "none of these people realized she was delusional. It is very easy to talk people into doing things when they trust you. Look at Charlie Manson or Jim Jones. Most importantly, she wasn't getting Ashley or Scottie to kill themselves or others, just to do things that seemed somewhat reasonable."

"True." Battel said. "The most interesting thing is that her original plan was for both Deputy Blackburn and your client to look equally guilty so that neither could be convicted. She set Scottie up with the 911 call, the scratches, etc. She even took a pair of his tennis shoes and put them on before she killed Ashley and purposefully left bloody shoe prints in the house. For Deputy Blackburn, she was going to make an anonymous call the following Monday telling them he was Gabriel's father and to search his home, where they would find the bloody knife. Since he was the last person to see her alive and the knife would be found in his possession, she figured he would be convicted of the murder despite the evidence she planted against Scottie. Unfortunately, Walters accidentally left the knife at the house in her rush to get out. I assume Ashley fought her harder than she expected, and it took Walters longer to kill Ashley than she had planned. She had set an alarm on her phone, and when it went off, she dropped the knife in her haste and ran out the front door. Once in the driveway, she quickly changed shoes and then ran around back and through the field to where she had hidden her car."

"She set an alarm?" Steve asked.

"Yes. Like I said, she had everything planned meticulously. She knew how long it would take Deputy Blackburn to get to the residence from the Racino. So, as soon as the call was made, she set an alarm on her phone and put it in her pocket to ensure she would not be seen by Deputy Blackburn when he pulled up to the house."

"Okay. Start from the beginning. You have given us a lot of different information," Booger said. "Now, put it all together and give us the timeline of how the murder occurred."

"Walters went to the Scottie residence around nine o'clock that morning. At the same time, the homeless man was causing a commotion at the Racino to get the sheriff's office called. When Walters got to the house, she talked to Ashley about the affair your client was having and convinced her to set him up for a weekend in jail. While in the house, she excused herself to the restroom, grabbing the tennis shoes and unlocking the back door without Ashley noticing. Then, she left the house and texted your client, telling him it was okay to go home. While he was driving over from the hotel, she took her car around the field and parked. From there, she walked back to the house. She put the tennis shoes on and waited outside the back door while everything went down between Ashley and your client. When the 911 call was made, Walters set an alarm on her phone for four minutes and thirty seconds. As soon as your client left, she went inside and attacked Ashley with the butcher knife. When the alarm went off, she dropped the knife by accident, walked out the front door wearing the bloody tennis shoes, and changed shoes in the driveway. That was why the bloody footprints ended in the driveway. It was obvious from the blood splatter the shoes were placed into the secure Walmart bag in the driveway. We always assumed Mr. Pinkerton did that right before he left, since we never found any of Ashely's blood in the car."

"Yeah, I wondered about that too," Steve said.

"Since she left the knife, she decided not to mention Deputy Blackburn and Gabriel's relationship?" Booger asked.

"Correct," Battel said. "God told her that, because of her mistake, she wasn't going to get to be with your client yet. She was now supposed to help get him convicted."

"What about her two alibi witnesses?" Steve asked. "Eloise Blackburn and Florabelle Martin. Deputy Blackburn's investigative notes said his grandmother told him Walters was at the bake sale when the murder happened, and Martin backed that up when we talked to her a few weeks ago."

"Once again, Walters used her charm to get what she needed. Eloise Blackburn was her friend from the bake sales, and she told Eloise a story about her husband making her late that morning, convincing her to call her grandson and tell him Walters was at the bake sale before ten, even though she didn't get there until almost ten thirty. Eloise was just trying to be a good friend because she never imagined Walters was the real killer. Apparently, she thought she was helping both Walters and her grandson by lying about the timing because then, he wouldn't waste time investigating Walters and Walters' fight with her husband wouldn't become public knowledge. Plus, he was having liaisons with Walters at the time. So, Walters herself also convinced him to focus his investigation only on Scottie. How she got Martin to be an alibi witness is even more interesting. She began visiting Martin every Saturday morning when you started snooping around the case a few months ago. She would go see her at ten o'clock on the dot every Saturday. She would talk to Martin about how she was always on time and how she was incredibly organized. Walters basically planted the thoughts in that poor old woman's head. When anyone talked to Martin about Walters, she would talk about nothing but her timeliness."

"Wow," Steve said, "the detail of her planning almost reminds me of the Kevin Spacey character in that movie, Seven."

"That's not all. She was even the one who got Brent Whitmore to send you those threats. She tried to seduce him, but I guess he actually loves his wife and didn't fall prey to her advances. However, she was able to persuade him it would be a good idea to send you those threats. She even tricked him into getting the burner phone long ago with some sob story about domestic abuse. She held on to it this whole time waiting to use it when you got appointed because she had learned the federal court always appoints a new attorney to death penalty cases. After you got appointed, she convinced him to start sending the threats in hopes you wouldn't do anything to keep Mr. Pinkerton from getting the sentence Brent truly thought he deserved."

Steve turned to Booger and said, "You see, someone in this deal is good. Whitmore didn't cheat on his wife."

"I told you once, and I'll tell you again," Booger said with a sigh. "Ain't no one in this world's truly innocent. You realize you are referring to the man who sent you death threats as the one good person in this whole mess?"

"Oh, yeah. I guess there is that little fact," Steve said sheepishly before he looked back at Battel and asked, "Why did she decide to kill Deputy Blackburn and me in the end?"

"According to The Book of Heather, God told her that she and your client had suffered enough for her mistake of leaving the knife at the scene of the crime. He said she needed to kill you both to set your client free; that was the only way she and Scottie could be together. Once again, God gave her a meticulous plan to follow. Several weeks before everything went down at your house, she had Deputy Blackburn show her his gun collection. You know, most police officers have pretty extensive collections. When he showed it to her, she noticed one gun in particular had a silencer attached. On the morning she attempted to kill you, she went to his house and gave him 'oral pleasure,' as they say. From previous experience, she knew he would fall into a deep sleep after completion. Once he was asleep, she got the gun and ended his life in a way that made it look like suicide. That psycho even made it appear he had masturbated right before he shot himself."

"Doesn't she know the time of death would have been off?" Steve asked.

"Actually, the time of death is a best estimate within a window of an hour or two," Booger replied. "They can't narrow it down to an exact minute. So, as long as she killed you within an hour of the time she killed him, and neither body was discovered for a while, the timing would be close enough for no one to ask questions. Once again, people fill in the blanks with what seems most likely. A murder-suicide, considering everything else going on, would have been the most likely conclusion. It's an example of the Occam's razor principle being used to determine the wrong answer."

"Well, now we know how she did it, does this diary tell us why?" asked Steve.

"Like I said earlier, Walters' mother died giving birth to her. As she grew older, her stepmother regularly told Walters that her mother's death was her own fault, and she eventually felt a tormented sense of responsibility for it. Her father, Henry, worked at the fishing reel factory just outside of town. He was a machinist on the assembly line. Walters was supposed to be the first of many children for the Robertsons; instead, Henry became a single father in just one day. When Walters was three, her father married a woman named Debbie Parker, whom he'd met at the First Baptist Church of Claremore. They had one child together, Mary, a year after their marriage. Shortly thereafter, Debbie legally adopted Walters. Unfortunately, a drunk driver killed Walters' father in an automobile accident two years later as he drove home from work one night."

"She lost both of her parents before the age of seven?" Steve asked.

"Yes," Battel said. "Moreover, Debbie was what one might call an evil stepmother. She always felt jealous of Walters because her mother was Henry's true love, and Debbie knew it. Once Henry was gone, Debbie stopped pretending to like Walters. She would lock Walters in a closet all day long while she played with Mary, her biological daughter. Sometimes, she would bring Walters a pet and tell her she was in charge of it. When it did something wrong, Walters would be punished. She would even use the pets themselves as punishment. On several occasions, she would beat the dog in front of Walters because she didn't clean the house properly or got a bad grade in school."

Booger frowned. "Sounds like that lady deserves the death penalty, if anyone does from this whole mess."

"True," Battel said. "And the only things Debbie let Walters take into the closet were a Bible and Boopie, her stuffed elephant. I had a clinical psychologist review the diary and, according to him, around the age of twelve, after six years of spending hours alone in the closet any time she was at home, Walters started showing signs of disassociation to the point of having a psychotic break, which led to her believing her dead mother was speaking to her. Her mom said she was in heaven with God and that He had a plan for her. Boopie told Walters to listen to her mother, and that as long as she followed her mom's instructions, she would eventually find true happiness."

"Can we charge Debbie with three counts of murder?" asked Steve seriously. "It sounds like she is truly the one to blame for all of this."

"Unfortunately, no," Battel said. "It is too late to even charge her with child abuse; the statute ran out on that several years ago."

Steve and Booger spent the next few hours reading through The Book of Heather. They were shocked at how deep Walters' anti-social behavior went and surprised at the detail contained in the account of her life story. Each section was numbered like a passage in the Bible. "Heather 4:15" was the story of the first time Boopie told Walters to start listening to her mother's voice because her mother was relaying information straight from God. "Heather 10:26" described how Walters felt when she stabbed Ashley the first time. The accounts went on and on, up until her plan for killing Deputy Blackburn and Steve.

At 4:50 p.m., Battel walked back into the room.

"It's almost five, so we are going to have to shut this down. I'm sorry, I know you haven't had enough time to read everything, but I hope I answered enough questions to help you sleep at night."

"Yes," Steve said. "Thank you very much for sharing. I know you didn't have to, and it was beyond the call of duty to let us in here."

"You're welcome. It is the least I could do, considering what you've been through and all that you've done to bring justice to this case. By the way, I just got a call from Deputy Warden Gilcrease at Big Mac. They are releasing your client at 10:00 a.m. tomorrow."

They both thanked the assistant district attorney before they left.

CHAPTER 42

Booger and Steve spent most of the drive to McAlester talking about the surprising news that Donald Trump would be the presidential nominee for the Republican Party. When they arrived at the prison, they were equally surprised to see Brent Whitmore waiting outside the main entrance to the facility. As they approached Whitmore, he walked over with an outstretched hand.

"I would like to humbly apologize for threatening you. I was wrong, and I am very, very sorry."

Steve grabbed his hand and said, "Apology accepted. You have been through a lot in the last few years. But can I ask why you are here?"

"Scottie is my brother. I owe him an apology too, and a man makes his apologies in-person. I am going to drive him back to Claremore and help him try to get his life back together. Since he's not the one who killed Ashley, I must try to do everything she would have done for him."

Soon, the front doors to the prison opened and out walked Scottie Pinkerton. As he strode into the morning sunlight, he raised a hand over his eyes and squinted up at the sky. The sun was shining and there were just enough white clouds to make the blue sky appear even more vibrant. The corners of his lips turned upward as he took a long, slow breath.

Steve arrived at work Monday morning with a copy of the Sunday Tulsa World under his arm. The headline read, "Local Attorney Saves Innocent Man." He planned on taking the front page to be framed later that afternoon. On his desk, he saw that he had received a letter from Frank Ackerman over the weekend.

He opened it to read:

Dear Steve,

Congrats on all your hard work. You saved the life of a fellow man, and there aren't too many attorneys who can say they have done that in the course of their work. Welcome to the club. I am proud to call you my peer.

Fiat justitia, et pereat mundus,

Frank Ackerman

As Steve finished reading the letter, he smiled proudly to himself. He placed the letter on top of the newspaper, now having two items to frame that afternoon.

The buzzer on his office phone sounded, and Carol chimed in, "Hey, Frontpage, there is a Mr. Wright on line three. He says his daughter's boyfriend was killed a few months ago and she fell apart after it. She got into drugs and now has charges against her. She saw your name in the paper and remembered meeting you once, so he wants to hire you to help her out. Her name is Alex Wright."

EPILOGUE

August 9, 2008

As I lay here in my living room floor. I am in awe of the mechanism of the human anatomy. The first time the knife pierced my chest was a pain more intense than I thought possible, but now, after 38 more cuts, slices and stabs, I feel nothing. I am at peace. As I take my last breath, my biggest fear is not my life passing. My biggest fear is that my husband will be wrongfully convicted of my murder thereby leaving my son to grow up parentless.

. . . . . .

For Bubba and Sterling,
my brothers on the inside.